D0044010

CALGARY PUBLIC LIBRARY
SEPTEMBER 2015

ALEXANDRA GRIGORESCU

CAUCHEMAR

ecw press

for my parents

CHAPTER
ONE

Hannah waited exactly seven minutes before touching Mae's cold body.

Earlier that morning, Hannah had watched from the doorway as Mae massaged olive oil into the frayed ends of her hair, so heavily flecked with white. She'd watched the woman's arthritic hands gingerly stopper the bottle of olive oil.

Mae had noticed her looking and cocked an eyebrow. "The sun's getting on," she'd chastised, "and you've done nothing yet with your day. Go bother Doug for some mint and limes and I'll fix us something sweet."

Hannah had taken her time. She'd let spectacled Doug clasp his chest theatrically at the sight of her, and she'd smiled as he slid the too-ripe limes and a glossy, glazed Satsuma orange tart into a paper bag. She'd felt Doug's fatherly eyes on her back as she walked away from the shoddy fruit and vegetable stand he'd built in front of his house. Then, unable to the resist the potent mix of pastry and fresh citrus, Hannah had waded down through long grass to the water and eaten slowly on a sun-warmed rock. All those minutes, and Hannah hadn't felt it happen.

By the time Hannah walked through the front door, Mae was coughing.

"What's wrong?" Hannah cried, kicking off her shoes as she dropped the bag of limes. She rushed to help the woman into her chair.

Mae struggled to speak as she gripped Hannah's hands between hers. Her eyes were wide and her throat worked furiously. "I'm sorry," she wheezed. "I tried."

"For what?"

"Listen, girl," Mae began urgently, then was silenced by another convulsive fit of coughing. Her face was flushed, her eyes bloodshot. "I want you to go." The coughs turned her voice ragged.

"Go where?" Hannah asked, as she thumped Mae's back.

Throughout Hannah's life, Mae was always trying to keep her home, keep her close, but now she practically hissed, "Run."

"I'll get you some water," Hannah said, and hurried into the kitchen.

Something sharp pricked her foot and she noticed a broken glass, roughly swept into a corner of the room. As she ran the faucet, a shiver danced down her spine. A candle was lit in the windowsill, and the wick was almost spent.

"Mae?" she called out, setting down the glass of water.

Silence.

"Mae," she said, more quietly, and inched into the living room. Mae was slumped in the chair, her hands limp on either side of the armrests. Hannah hurried toward her. "Come on, Mae," she urged, shaking Mae's shoulders. The woman's head rolled back and forth with each movement. Hannah settled Mae's head back against the chair and ran her hand in front of Mae's face, as if polishing a mirror. There was no breath. She held her palm to Mae's chest and felt a horrible stillness.

Sensation drained from Hannah's body as she retreated to the couch. Her hands trembled in her lap as she tried to calm her breath. She felt paralyzed, not knowing what to do and unable to guess. So she sat.

Hannah watched time trickle around the carved wooden face of the living room clock, already knowing that Mae was dead, but relishing the moments when another possibility still seemed to exist. In waiting, all things were possible. She fixed her attention on the slants of noon sun that stretched themselves toward Mae's feet. The arches of her feet faced each other, fallen open like two dark halves of a cracked nut. "Mae?" she pleaded again, weakly.

Ten minutes would have been too much. Ten minutes would have been a long time to live with, later.

Hannah rose unsteadily from the couch and carefully put her pale palm over Mae's neck, covering all the veins still and tight as clothespins. There was no pulse, but she thought she felt something bunched just above her clavicle. She slipped one arm under Mae's neck and hugged her tightly for a second, then began to sob as Mae's head sagged when released.

Through her tears, Hannah noticed the line of copper Mae always wore around her wrist. She ran her finger over the nine small knots along its length. There was no clasp. "For protection," Mae had told her when Hannah asked about it as a small child. She'd been drawn to the flash of burnished orange.

"Protection from what?"

"There are plenty of hungry spirits aching to take a bite."

Hannah had snorted, holding up her own bony arm. "A bite of who?"

Mae hadn't answered.

Carefully, Hannah rolled the bracelet off Mae's wrist and onto her own. Tears fell down her face faster than she could wipe them. She couldn't stop touching Mae as if life could be lent that way. Finally, she stood, realizing she would need to call someone. She turned to go, then stopped to spread the hem of Mae's apron, patterned with big, alert sunflowers, down over her knees.

In the kitchen, Hannah dialed the police and felt her heartbeat quicken. What would she say? She placed her hand over the receiver's mouthpiece, as if she could read instructions in its Braille. But some instinct took over, answering the questions posed by the police operator. She spiraled the phone cable around a finger and sniffled. "Natural causes, I think."

"You're all alone up there now, child?" the operator asked, her voice gentle, and Hannah was startled by the words. All alone. She heard a man's voice, raised in shock, in the background.

Captain Gabour came on the line. "I'm sorry, Hannah.

She was a fine woman, your mother," he said, his voice garbled. Calls into town were always hollow and distorted, as if they were whispered down a pipeline and carried through echoes. Hannah imagined Keith Gabour at the other end, his face pitted by a beaten bout of prostate cancer. "I'll get someone to you as soon as we can."

Hannah scratched under the table to draw Graydon's attention. The cat was pawing at Mae's ear, and Hannah fought a wave of nausea.

"Do you need anything, sweetheart? Food or supplies?"

Hannah looked around the kitchen, at Mae's racks of spices, at the hanging basil plant that swayed lightly in the breeze by the window. Her new reality wasn't sinking in. Something in her resisted the corrosive realization that Mae wouldn't be coming back.

"I'll come in with the officers to make arrangements," Hannah heard herself say. "Thank you, Keith."

Hannah hung up the phone and listened to the heavy silence. She walked into the living room and carefully covered Mae's body with the patterned afghan that had been her favorite. The outline of her face through the thin wool was a stranger's, and Hannah stared so long at it that she almost convinced herself that the blanket rose above the slump of her mouth.

"Come on, kitten." She nudged the cat, coated in matted gray fur and close to his last breath, with her toe. Hannah slammed the screen door on her way outside, and slumped down on the back porch stairs, her jacket loose over her shoulders. She drew her knees to her chest as Graydon purred curlicues around her feet.

It would be a long wait, she knew, so she closed her

eyes. Almost immediately, her ears picked out a rhythm in the pulsing hum of the water. It seemed to massage her limbs into a dumb listlessness. The sun was harsh overhead despite the early December chill, and sweat trickled down her spine, reminding her of Mae's tickling fingers. The only family she'd ever known, gone.

Hannah didn't move until the boat's horn scythed the quiet.

"Coming in," a man yelled. James Robichaud, a dark-haired man, several years older than her, who had once pinned her arm against a chain-link fence during a street festival in town. "I know who your mother is," he'd hissed, cherubic cheeks flushed. "Your real mother."

"I do, too," she'd answered, maneuvering her keys between two fingers in her pockets with her free hand. "And I know what she can do."

A trembling fear in his lip, slight as a plucked string, and her bruised elbow had been dropped. He'd left her alone since, and over the years, his expression had turned from hostility to something akin to curiosity.

Now he stood above her with two men flanking him, a trooper insignia pinned to his shirt. He was nimbus-lit in afternoon sun. "She's inside," Hannah said. "I haven't moved her."

James cleared his throat, and gestured to the two men in medical response uniforms. They carried a stretcher with them. "How'd it happen?"

"She's sixty-eight. Too young, but something gave out, I guess."

James tongued a cigarette out of a crumpled box, then jabbed the pack down at her. She pulled one out and tucked it behind her ear. "I'm sorry, Hannah," he said, and she detected real remorse. "The Captain said she'd had trouble with her heart for years," James added, and Hannah remembered seeing Captain Gabour in their living room, dressed in a deep blue cotton suit jacket and holding a planter of irises like they were his beating heart. His eyes misty as he regarded Mae.

Hannah imagined that she could hear the sounds of a stiff body being positioned in the body bag, and she shivered under the meek sun.

"He said you'd be coming back to town with us. I think we'll have some questions. You know, completely routine stuff," James said.

Hannah looked up at him, cringing. "I don't really like the water, so try to take it smooth." But James's gaze was focused on the house behind her. She read barely schooled fascination on his face. Hannah turned away as Mae's body was wheeled past.

Hannah felt her stomach heave. "I just need to use the bathroom." She barely made it, then collapsed over the toilet. Only sourness dribbled out. Graydon pushed the door open and sprang up onto the edge of the tub, casually licking a paw.

Dizziness swept over her as she stood and washed out her mouth. It was tempting to lie down on the cool tiles. Her body felt leaden, and some small part of her still expected Mae to barrel in, a cool peppermint-scented washcloth in hand.

One of the men knocked on the door. "Everything alright in there?"

"Just a minute," Hannah called. In the mirror, her

wan reflection stared back at her. Her fear made her look younger than her twenty years, as though she was some baby bird cast out of the nest and made to fly.

Hannah wondered if she'd had the same uncomprehending expression as Mae choked before her, and if Mae had recognized that she'd be no help. Something Mae had said tried to surface in her memory of that moment, but Hannah could only remember her own dumb hands, frozen in her lap.

The first time Hannah became aware that Mae would one day die, flu-ridden, feverish Mae had stripped off her dress without closing the door and Hannah had seen loose skin and gouged muscle, always there but expertly tucked beneath collared shirts and thick fabrics.

"Lord, I'm dying," Mae had moaned as she fell into bed.

Hannah had carefully placed the cup of steaming lemon tea on the bedside table. "Shall we bury you in a St. Louis Cemetery? Next to that old voodoo queen, Marie Laveau?" Hannah teased.

Mae's mouth had tightened. "Don't you dare, child. Just heat me up and scatter me somewhere nice, away from the swamp. Pick some sunny spot that I'd like to haunt." Hannah felt sick to think that she'd laughed at that. She fingered the knotted copper around her wrist.

Outside, James was crouching on the dock, a fresh cigarette dangling in his hand. "Ready?" he asked. The men dropped their playing cards when they saw her, and one of them moved behind the boat's steering wheel. Graydon edged back from the dock, hissing at the water.

The boat wobbled as Hannah stepped in, and she immediately curled up on the ledge, tightening her red jacket around her body. The lowered stretcher lay a few feet away from her, and she was grateful at least that Mae was shapeless inside the zippered body bag.

Hannah tried to focus on a nick in the wood. As a child, she'd always drifted off to sleep by looking into the darkest corners of her room and imagining what might be crouching there. Beyond the edge of the boat, bald cypress trees formed a lattice. Their knees, directly above their roots, had always unsettled her. They looked like too-big onion bulbs rising from the water.

At first, the water was murky and clogged with tree roots, but soon they broke into a river and the sky was reflected on its glassy surface. Broken tree trunks lined the riverbed like ossified sentries.

One of the men settled in beside her with his cap over his face. Soon, the only sounds were his snoring and the whirring of the motor, and above them, somewhere, a faint warbling.

James's firm hand on her shoulder startled her awake. The freckled skin of his nose was splotched with windburn, and she wondered if her own cheeks were peeling already. "Sleeping in a boat if you've got seasickness is a bad idea, but you looked like you needed it," he said.

Hannah rubbed her eyes. Mae's body was already gone. She took his offered hand to dismount from the boat and murmured a weary "thanks." Even the solid ground felt moveable beneath her feet.

"We'll take you back home when you're ready," James said. "I guess you'll stay in town tonight."

Hannah started. The blessed fogginess began to retreat in a hurry, and thoughts galloped in its place. Where was home? "Not sure yet. I guess so. I haven't really thought about it."

"That was your mother's—that was Christobelle's house?" James asked, and Hannah had the sense that he was speaking carefully.

"What does it matter?" She sighed as she looked over her shoulder, at the long channel of placid water behind her, dotted with light green moss. "I haven't seen her in a long time."

Hannah could count on one hand the number of times she'd spoken to her biological mother.

On her ninth birthday, a grim-eyed Mae had packed Hannah's chubby form into a sundress, then nodded tight-lipped at a strange man who'd helped them aboard a boat and steered through the shaded waters. Once they'd reached their destination, Mae averted her eyes and said, "Off with you," shoving her gently onto dry land. Mae had settled back into the boat, tightening the shawl across her shoulders.

Her mother had been waiting for her, her hair shorn, a light dusting of stubble like a rose-colored halo around her head. A tall man, thin as a reed, stood beside her.

Christobelle had cocked her head and inspected her daughter. Hannah had the sense that she'd never been seen so thoroughly. Her past, her future, and the meager secrets of her present, all bared.

"Hello, child," Christobelle said in a low voice, and Hannah flinched. Christobelle stretched out a hand imperiously. Hannah hesitated, unsure whether she was meant to kiss it, then presented a tight, resentful fist in return.

"Your hands are so warm," Christobelle murmured. Hers felt cold and pocked as a stone. "I forget sometimes."

Hannah pulled back her hand and glared pointedly at the man. He licked his white-flecked lips.

"That's Samuel," her mother said. "Not your father, child." One long finger hooked under her chin, pulling her head up sharply. "He's a partner of a different sort."

Samuel and Hannah stared at each other, the man's impassive expression betraying nothing. Below the brim of his hat, his cheekbones jutted like stone bluffs.

"What about you, child?" Christobelle had asked, her cold hand tracing Hannah's jaw.

"What about me?"

Christobelle smiled, revealing ground-down nubs of teeth that didn't quite meet. "Tell me, Hannah, do you ever see things that others don't?" Christobelle's eyes had reminded her of reptiles watching from the verdant dark. Hungry.

Hannah had muttered "no," but in her room, as she tried to fall asleep, she would see the doorknob turn back and forth slowly, although there were no shadows in the clear light under the door. She glimpsed things out of the corner of her eyes, men and women standing still and slack-jawed in the grocery store or out on the street. But when she whipped her head around, they'd be gone.

Walking through town one evening, she'd watched a fire hydrant expand into a hunched figure, but a blink brought it back. Living in the swamp, it was the sort of thing that might be called "having a second sight," but Hannah knew that elsewhere it would just mean "crazy."

"Hannah?" James's voice brought her back.

Hannah added, "She's as much a stranger to me as she is to you. I haven't seen her in at least a decade."

James weighed her words, and nodded. "Well, that's okay. Mae's already with the, uh, coroner. We can get you started on funeral arrangements."

"I want to see her," Hannah said suddenly, a desperate edge to her voice. "One more time."

He cleared his throat. "If you think you're ready, we can go take a look."

She nodded, then walked ahead, absentmindedly running her hand over the candy veneer of a red truck. A churning returned to her stomach, fear and desire grappling. It was the feeling she got whenever she came into town. The promise of other people her age telling secrets, and kissing under slitted moons. But it was a promise never made to her. It'd been years since she'd stood on a playground, listening to taunts of "Red Rover!" in the distance. Years and years since she'd been shoved against lockers, and struggled as a lit cigarette hissed to embers against her skin, strong arms holding her in place. All because of her mother.

The coroner had a quick gum-chewing jaw. James introduced them, and she immediately forgot his name. "Looks like a massive stroke," he told her, fidgeting. He had the panicked eyes of someone unaccustomed to conversation. "Natural, by my estimation," he added to James, whose hand hovered politely near his face, never quite clasping his nose shut.

"Are you sure?" James asked, and Hannah looked at him in surprise.

The coroner folded down the white sheet. He tapped two fingers steadily down Mae's stomach. "There's something here," he said, massaging a slightly swollen area on her belly.

Hannah stepped forward and touched Mae's stomach. It felt like a bad bruise, gathering momentum to grow beneath the skin.

"And here," the coroner added, his gloved hands roughly moving Hannah's to another bloated area. When his fingers brushed the copper bracelet that now wound around her wrist, he flinched as if scalded. Hannah had spent so long with Mae's superstitions that she'd forgotten about other people's.

"Could be there was a small tumor metastasizing. Living out where you do, you don't exactly come in for regular check-ups. We could know for sure if you wanted her opened up."

Hannah blinked back tears as she nodded slightly, and James made a small, chastising sound. The coroner simply said, "Sorry," in the flat voice of someone who didn't know or care what he was apologizing for.

It wasn't the words that upset Hannah, but the way this man touched Mae, as if testing a melon at the market. Still, Mae's stomach held Hannah's eye. Unbidden, an image of a bird's nest camouflaged in the moss came to her mind.

"We'll just take a quick poke around," the coroner said, as Hannah nodded. "You'll be wanting a cemetery burial?"

Mae's toes peeked from under the white sheet. Hannah

still struggled to understand that she was dead. "Who do I speak to about cremation?"

"That'd be Manny Ardoin and his wife. They run a little funeral home." Hannah blinked and then Mae was covered. "James can take you down." The coroner let out a long breath and gripped the steel table with both hands as he wheeled her into a corner. His work was done.

"I'll be right out," James said, and she felt his hand on the small of her back, acute as a bee sting. It propelled her down the hallway and back out into the afternoon sun.

The street was mostly empty. The trucks that shuffled in and out of parking spots could've been alligators, gliding through the water. The twang of a steel guitar floated out of a bar, and a curly haired girl in an oversized denim jacket winced under the weight of a laundry basket.

Hannah crossed the street to the corner store, and heard a bell ring as she stepped into the shop. She moved through the stacks, idly touching candy bars and bags of chips, before pulling open the cooler door in the back and holding a cold can of orange soda to the back of her neck.

The teenage boy behind the counter had a sweet smattering of pimples on either side of his nose. "I haven't seen you around before," he said.

"I live on the swamp," she answered, and placed the can onto the counter. "Or I did."

"You're moving into town?" His hopeful brown eyes plumbed the neckline of her buttoned jacket.

"My mother just died," she said, and her heart skipped a beat. It was the first time she'd spoken the words.

His face fell, and he pushed the can back across the counter. "Shit," he whispered. "I'm sorry. It's on the house."

"Get back, Rodney." An older man appeared out of a back room, and snapped his fingers. "Now."

The boy, Rodney, smiled hesitantly at Hannah. "I'm with a customer, Dad."

"She's no customer of ours. I said now, boy, or do you need me to pull you by your damn collar. And you," the man added, glaring at Hannah, "should leave now."

Hannah held up her empty hands. She'd never mastered the art of bracing herself against people's anger. "I'm just getting a soda," she said, trying to smile.

The man nodded stiffly. "You've got it."

Rodney rubbed his neck, his wide eyes moving back and forth between them.

Through the window she saw James, shielding his eyes against the sun as he searched the street for her. "Right. Thanks."

The bell rang on her way out and she heard Rodney say, "Take care."

James waved her over. "I can take you over to Manny's now if you want. Or are you hungry?"

"I couldn't eat," she said, honestly. She opened the can of soda and took a sip. The orange was too artificial, the sweetness unnatural. "I want to go home."

"Are you sure? There are just a few things that need to be taken care of. And besides, you're all alone out there. Shouldn't you stay here for a while?"

Hannah wondered whether he worried for her or his investigation, and shook her head. "Tell them to cremate her and send me the bill. If there's a will, just have them open it and call me with the details. I want to go."

"Hannah," James said softly, "it's just a few more hours."

"No," Hannah said firmly. Her shoulders hunched forward and she was aware of the people half-hidden on the streets. A pair of women huddled in the shade beneath an awning, their bespectacled eyes squinting at her. How many of them knew who she was? How many of them had entertained thoughts of harming her? "Please. Have someone take me back. They have the body. They can do the rest."

CHAPTER
TWO

The house was silent, sapped of the thousand noises, the openings and closings, the coughs and steps, that announced another human body. Sitting in the living room in her stiff black dress, Hannah felt gnawed by loneliness.

All the mourners were late. The cremator's wife had called early that morning to confirm the guests. "So, we'll send the bill to you, then?" Manny's wife asked, her rasped voice betraying years of chain-smoking.

"Yes, and thanks for doing this."

"Oh, we do all sorts of things, honey. Callum's the boat captain. He'll be ferrying in the mourners, and," she lowered her voice, "the urn with the remains. He's going to bring along some business cards as well. Just fan them out on a table there, if you don't mind."

The doorbell chime echoed through the house.

Hannah rose and took one flat look at her sharp-boned face in the mirror, pinching color into her cheeks. Her collarbone peeked out above the boat neckline of her dress. Her strawberry blonde braid made her look like a teenager, and her eyes were red-rimmed. Sighing, she opened the front door.

"Hannah, sweetie?" The large, huffing woman was a stranger. "My goodness, how you've grown!"

Hannah let herself be wrestled into the woman's perfumed neck, who sobbingly introduced herself as an old friend of Mae. "Here I am!" She brandished a photo frame off the mantel, her every sentence ending in an exclamation.

Some were like that. Old friends, coworkers, and admirers of Mae. James arrived in a gray dress shirt, his dark brown hair parted to the side, and offered her a neat bouquet of daisies. "I heard that lilies are the thing, but these have some cheer to them." Hannah fingered the papery edges of the blooms and smiled.

James touched her elbow. "I need to talk to you about something, but I'm not sure this is the place."

A tall man bore a platter of food into the house, which was suddenly thumping with footsteps and voices. Hannah raised her eyebrows at James, but he shook his head at her, mouthing the word "later."

"I've got some deviled eggs and cornbread salad," the tall man said. "There's nothing that'll go bad too quick, but you'll want to keep them cool. And little sandwiches, too. Do you have plates?"

Hannah gestured toward the kitchen. She spied a thin stack of business cards on the edge of a cellophane-wrapped platter, the words "funeral home" and "catering" nestled beneath the petals of a pixelated flower.

The last guest caught Hannah's eyes instantly. His white collared shirt, with sleeves rolled to the elbows, stood out like a beacon in the swarm of black. Fibrous was the word, Hannah decided, for his body. Sinews and muscles stood out on his arms as if his skin were inches thinner than most.

"Hi there," he said. His light blue eyes showed sympathy. "I know we're late. I had a bit of trouble finding the place."

"We don't get many visitors." Hannah stared down at her pointed black flats. There was no *we* anymore.

"Sorry," he said, and touched her hand lightly. "Could I trouble you for something to drink?"

"I made lemonade," she said, and led him into the kitchen. James grabbed the man's arm, and whispered something in his ear, but the man only shrugged and pulled out of James's grip. He took the tall glass from Hannah and emptied it. "Thanks," he said through puckered lips. "I like it sour. I'm Callum, by the way. My condolences."

"Hannah," she said, suddenly conscious that the kitchen was full of watchful faces. "We don't have much, but help yourself to whatever looks good." Hannah's eyes fell to the ceramic pot nestled in his armpit. Markings had been carved along the mouth of the urn.

Callum followed her gaze. "Sorry, this is yours."

Hannah wormed her hands under his arm and grasped the urn. A tremor went through her. Mae was inside the squat pot, reduced to ash. It didn't seem possible.

Martha, who lived in the next house over, put a long

arm around Hannah's shoulders. In her fifties, Martha was statuesque. The local men claimed she was the only lure needed to make her living as a fisher. Her motorboat returning to the next dock over was a noonday chime, fishing tack and hooks glinting like an hour hand. A long, elegant line of scar tissue ran down one cheek and she smelled, as always, of briny fish. "You should eat something, dear."

"I have."

Martha narrowed her eyes and slid her hand around Hannah's wrist. Her fingers latched. "Eat more, then."

Over Martha's shoulder, the locals were beginning to spin tales. Young Mae standing vigil all night during a storm, or making poultices out of herbs and greens. Mae's singing as she hung the laundry to dry.

Hannah swallowed hard and turned away. Every mention of Mae's name was an incantation, every story a failed resurrection. Then, as if she'd willed it, a hush fell over the room. James stepped forward, his hand reaching blindly for a holstered gun that wasn't there. Hannah watched mouths tighten and eyes narrow around her. She turned and blinked in surprise.

Christobelle stood just inside the back door, her eyes trained on Hannah. She was swaddled in a heavy wool sweater and thick cable-knit scarf, in stark contrast to the mourners in their dresses and light shawls. Hannah took a pointless step forward as if to push her out. The woman didn't belong in the house. *My house*, Hannah thought, with a ferocity that startled her.

"She's hiding," Mae had said of Christobelle. "She doesn't want to be tracked and she's got no last name I know of. Christobelle can make up whole rich histories for herself this way."

"What's her *real* history, then?"

Mae had snorted. "Who knows. She came from Alabama to have you, I know that much. Back then, she was just a young, frightened woman who needed help. Everything else—the church, the hoodoo—grew out of the powers she was just then discovering."

"What powers?" Hannah had asked, worming her foot into Mae's lap to be massaged. Mae's nails felt like cattail husks, tickling her toes.

"Some abilities invite people into your life, others push them out. Hers do the latter. It's been a lonely life, and loneliness, in great quantities, has a way of eclipsing one's God-given morals. If you ask me, I think she stayed here because she knows the people, knows how to needle and mold them. And, of course, to keep an eye on you."

When Hannah frowned, Mae had given her a hard look. "Child, the only connection you've got to that woman is that you came out of her. The rest is your own making."

When she'd first found out who her real mother was, Hannah hadn't slept for weeks, panicked that Christobelle would want her back. She'd told Mae about that side of her fear but kept quiet about her deeper worry—that someday, Mae might choose to give her up. But Mae had stayed, until death took her.

Conversation in the room had stilled, and the mourners busied themselves with folding their cocktail napkins and moving the stuffed eggs across their plates. Callum turned on the kitchen faucet in a gush, prompting a scatter of startled giggles, and he winked at Hannah.

Christobelle noted this exchange, then nodded her head toward the back door and glided out.

"Mae was an amazing nurse," a woman said as she drifted back from the bathroom, her hands clapping together as if in animated prayer. "I saw her heal injuries in less time than it would've taken someone to diagnose them." She fell quiet and covered her lipsticked mouth. "Are we having a moment of silence?"

"Excuse me," Hannah muttered as she squeezed past the sandwich-holding throng. She tucked the urn into a nook between the toaster and a rotating spice rack, patting it on her way out the door.

Christobelle waited by the water, tall and frail, her voluminous skirt heavy through the grass. She seemed to track the fog with her eyes as it crept over the bayou, alighting on the tips of ferns. It moved like a spirit, sly and slow, parting to either side of cypress trees. A lone heron, standing rigid on one slender leg, watched them from beneath his mantle of speckled feathers.

"Why did you come?" Hannah asked, rubbing her arms against the cold.

Christobelle turned, her joyless smile like a pasted cut-out. "I wasn't exactly invited. But yes, someone let it slip. Naughty of you to overlook me. You remember Samuel?" Christobelle gestured to the man, who rose out of the boat and moved unsteadily onto the dock. Although already quite skeletal when Hannah had first met him, he seemed almost mummified now. His skin had a sick, moist tint to it as he arrived at Christobelle's side, his arm winding around hers.

Hannah shrugged. "I didn't think Mae would want you here."

Christobelle's smile faded, and her face became eerily androgynous. The dappled sun played tricks with her lips, her eyes. She was man and woman all at once.

"Don't lie to me, child. You didn't want me here, although that wasn't your decision to make. Mae and I were close once. I did something for her, something she may have neglected to tell you about. She was *indebted* to me, and now she's passed." The word came out sibilant, snake-like. One hand suddenly shot straight to the side, all the tendons in her wrist tensed to vibration. "But not gone."

Hannah's mother closed her eyes and leaned her head back. Her lips parted and she sighed from some deep crevice inside herself.

Some glint of consciousness entered Samuel's eyes, and he imitated Christobelle. He let out a groan. Christobelle opened her eyes and calmly removed his hand from around her arm. "I've told you before, Samuel. Don't pretend," she chided him. "That's the surest way to block it. You have to accept it entirely. Its presence and absence, and the pain of both."

The man's mouth dropped open, and color rushed into his gaunt cheeks. He shoved his hands into his pockets.

Hannah watched this exchange, a choking anger rising in her. "Don't," she snapped. "Call on the dead in your own church. Do your song and dance. But not here, not for Mae."

"The dead are everywhere, child. No structure can contain them, or keep them out, forever. They are blessed by the patience that comes with existing outside of time."

Hannah's heartbeat pounded in her neck and thumbs. "Do me a favor and spare me the theatrics." She turned to leave.

"You'll stay here," Christobelle commanded. "Samuel, give us a moment."

Hannah remained frozen until Samuel disappeared around the edge of the house. Steeling herself, she turned back. "What do you want?" The woman gave off a musty smell. It was the scent of things chewing under the surface of water or brush.

Christobelle's head was cocked back unnaturally. "I came to pay my respects. After all, she protected you, didn't she?"

"She did, after you left me."

"Then she did as I asked, girl, but I was not as absent from your life as you'd like to think. And now there are certain dangers I can't control, some forces I can't guard you against. Some things have noses attuned to find you, no matter how deep in the trees you hide." Christobelle's gaze descended slowly, her eyes filmy and amphibian-like. She knit her fingers together over her stomach. "People will come into your life," she said, as though declaring that the earth was round. "You'll be tempted, but they'll make you vulnerable. You mustn't bend."

"You can see the future now, as well?"

"I know that you're out of my hands, child, and unprotected. There's a whole flurry of them circling you, hungrier than ever now that Mae's passed. You're a dandelion seed spinning in a storm."

Hannah's jaw locked, and she balled her hands into fists. "Don't think I don't know the parish's opinion of you. As long as we stick to our land, they've left us alone, and there's no reason to think they'll do differently now."

"There are many things to fear that aren't done by the hands of men," Christobelle said, bitterness in her voice.

Hannah rolled her eyes and turned again to face the house. The white exterior was broken by small windows, and the black roof shone like onyx. She spied the bright red feathers of a tanager as it traipsed over the shingles. Hannah could visualize the wood floors, the old eggshell-colored tiles in the kitchen, the walls that warmed with an apricot hue at noontime, and they were an antidote against her mother's disquieting words.

"That used to be my house. Our house." Christobelle sidled up to Hannah. "You were born here, twenty years ago. Right in there." She pointed to the large windows of Mae's bedroom. "Sixteen hours, and you took a full minute before you screamed. The longest minute of my life, which has been full of long minutes."

Hannah imagined being nursed by the bay window, mother and child encased in light. The thought of Christobelle tracing Hannah's just-born features with her lips was almost painful. "Mae never told me."

Christobelle sniffed. "I expect there's much Mae didn't tell you, but everything she did was in the hopes of keeping you safe. I believe she loved you. That was the important thing."

"I loved her," Hannah said simply, and felt no regret saying the words in the presence of this woman. They were nothing to each other. "Was my—" Hannah hesitated, and scanned the shadowed windows. Had there been laughter tinkling through the hallways? Had there been a man who'd lifted her clear off the floor and spun her around? "Was my father here as well?"

When Hannah glanced back, Christobelle's face was filled with raw ache.

"We were all here, at first. The three of us, although you were just a kicking in my belly then." Christobelle's gnarled hands, knuckles like the knotted roots of trees, covered her face for a brief moment. When they lowered, she was expressionless.

My father, Hannah thought. She wanted to ask how he'd died, but a stab of sympathy stopped her. She wondered whether there was a grave she could visit. But Mae had always avoided the question, and Hannah knew better than to ask now.

Christobelle straightened. "Come stay with us. After all, I am your family. Your only family."

Hannah laughed in surprise. There was a singular stillness on the property, as if all the creatures that shared it, the heron and the gators and the crickets, were rapt. "You couldn't fill an hour with the words we've said to each other, and still I've spent my whole life hiding from people who blame me for your actions and beliefs. So, no, I won't come with you. What kind of life would that be?"

"Better than what you'd have here, and safer. This house is not right for you. Loneliness has a way of changing you. Of infecting you."

"I've had practice." Hannah had trouble reconciling the unsettling tales she'd heard involving the woman standing beside her. Stories of men who'd left their houses for milk or a glass of rye and were next seen weeks later, looking as though they'd been ravaged by decades, and unwilling to speak of what had happened to them. Stories of men who never returned to their families.

"Not like this, child. Our people are," Christobelle looked up, searching the sky, "predisposed, you could say. We invite things in, sometimes without even knowing it."

"I am not your people," Hannah said, spitting out the last word.

"Care to gamble on that, child?"

Hannah examined her mother. "I've spent my whole life here, between these walls, between these trees. It's been as good a home as any. You said this was your house—is it still yours to give?"

"What?"

Hannah cleared her throat. "You gave this house to Mae while she cared for me. Do you want it back, now that she's gone? Or could I stay here?" It was all she had left of Mae. It was all she'd ever known. The silence would be painful at first, but the memories would keep her company. "Could it be mine?"

Christobelle watched her hawkishly, all signs of her earlier vulnerability wiped away. "It will be a different house now, child. The murk will seep. That life that Mae made for you—she took it with her when she went."

"I'll make my own, then," Hannah retorted.

Christobelle's eyes narrowed. "What makes you think that *your* gift is life? Have you ever considered that you were kept here not only for your protection but for theirs as well?" She swept her arm toward the house and the laughter that sounded from the kitchen.

The fog that lay low across the water had reached them. The cool touch of it made Hannah's body tighten. "I'm not like you."

"Maybe not." Christobelle was silent for a long moment. Her head moved languidly from side to side, swerving from the house to the muddy water and back again. She smiled at something she saw there. "So it is," she said softly. "The house is yours, child. Consider it a belated birthday present. We will wait and see what you make of it."

The memory of Mae's chocolate cake made Hannah ache. It seemed impossible that only a week had passed since it'd been set before her, bright with birthday candles. "Thank you," Hannah said, the words strange in her mouth. She didn't know whether to feel relief at the small victory of remaining in her childhood home or worry that now there was something owing.

Christobelle gestured to Samuel, who had returned and waited patiently by a nearby tree. "I should be going." Hannah recoiled slightly as Christobelle took her hand and kissed it lightly, her lips dry and feathery as lichen. "You rest now, and eat up. Then we can talk about income. You should know that the congregation is well connected."

Hannah shuffled uncomfortably. She hadn't even begun thinking of how she would support herself. Their needs had been few, but there'd always been food on the table. Hannah had never seen Mae's patients, who stepped tentatively into their house but left strengthened in some ineffable way, pay with money.

Christobelle seemed distracted. "How did she die?" she asked, as Samuel came to stand by her and offered his arm.

"Her heart gave out, they think." Hannah paused. "Why do you ask?"

"No matter," Christobelle said, looking askance at the house. "Keep safe, Hannah. Keep yourself closed, no matter how good it might feel to open. There are many who don't have your best interests at heart, and you don't know enough to spot them. Goodbye, child." Samuel inclined his head as he passed, and Hannah wondered if somewhere a family still awaited the man's return.

"Goodbye." Hannah watched her mother step gracefully into the small wooden boat tied to the dock.

As Hannah headed toward the back door of the house, an avian cry pierced the silence. She whirled around to scan the waters, but the ripples left by her mother's boat were already fading. The bayou was a cathedral, light washing over the ancient moss-coated roots, and she, slender and trembling, was the pulpit.

Doug opened the back door and raised his eyebrows in question. "Everything okay?"

"Thanks for coming," Hannah said, squeezing his arm.

"Of course. Anything you need. Mae was a saving grace after my little girl passed on. I wept at your kitchen table more times than I can remember, and Mae always knew which memory of Abigail would cheer my heart." He cleared his throat. "That Ellis girl dropped by, too," Doug said, fingering his beard. He didn't notice Hannah's smile fade. "Shame what happened there. She left the bayou so soon after, I never expected to see her again."

"It's nice that she came." Hannah tried to keep her voice normal, but found herself thinking of Sarah Anne's periwinkle blue eyes. Blonde curls so perfectly formed that Hannah always expected them to be plastic, each time she fit her finger into them.

Somehow she navigated the outstretched hands in the kitchen, all of Mae's mourners clamoring to share their grief with her, and headed out the front door. She scurried down the gravel path, looking left and right, until she saw the woman. Hannah recognized her from the back, although her hair was straightened, her curls ironed to a faded white-blonde.

"Sarah Anne," she called out.

The woman turned, a hesitant smile teasing at her mouth. Her body had lengthened, and her face, once sweet and round as peaches, was angular. "I wanted to give my condolences," Sarah Anne said. "I'm so sorry, Hannah. I know how much you loved her."

"Thank you. It was a shock." Her voice sounded strained to her own ears. "I didn't realize you were back in town." She wondered what it'd be like to hug Sarah Anne's adult body, even as she wanted to push up the scalloped sleeve of Sarah Anne's dress and see her right arm, the one she'd ruined that day, so many years ago. Hannah shook her head to clear her nose of the smell of charred flesh, pale hairs flashing like a comet's tail then dissolved. The guilt, which had felt overwhelming in the years after and then slowly dulled, felt fresh again.

"I've moved back for a bit." Sarah Anne pulled at the sleeve of her trench coat as though reading Hannah's thoughts. "My uncle has some business in the area, so he's renting a house. The real estate agent insisted it was a coup—I was expecting a hole in the wall, but the price got slashed. Someone died there apparently, but it doesn't really bother me. Look back far enough, and someone's died just about everywhere."

"How are you?" Hannah asked, the words a paltry substitution for all she wanted to ask.

Sarah Anne shrugged. "It's slow as ever around here, but I've managed to find a distraction or two. I'm just happy to see these fine Southern boys haven't changed a bit. Still dumb as posts but gorgeous as the risen sun."

Hannah laughed despite herself. "You haven't changed, either."

"Everything changes," Sarah Anne said, her voice faint.

Hannah searched her old friend's face and saw the evidence of her words. There was a heaviness there, as if she rarely smiled and only with effort. She wondered if it was the memory of that day, or the years since, that had eaten into her. "Come have some lemonade," she offered.

"Nothing reminds me of this place quite like the offer of drinks," Sarah Anne said. "Sweet tea, lemonade, or a stiff drink if you look like you've had a day." She kicked at something in the long grass, overturning the flattened body of a sparrow.

Hannah immediately bent down to touch the bird, but Sarah Anne held up a hand. "It's dead." Sarah Anne's dispassionate voice startled Hannah, and when she looked up, Hannah saw that her eyes were guarded, lashes like shutters. "I should go."

The tightness in Hannah's chest coiled and her breath caught. She had the sense that her one chance at making amends was slipping away.

"This is my address," Sarah Anne said and passed Hannah a folded piece of paper. "No telephone yet, but drop by anytime." Their fingers touched over the paper, and Hannah felt a static shock.

Hannah opened her mouth, wanting to atone for everything that had happened. But there were too many words, too many apologies.

"Take care of yourself," Sarah Anne said as she turned away, and Hannah heard the echo of her mother's earlier warning.

Sleep eluded Hannah for most of the night. The trill of laughter seemed to hide just beneath the wind chime's ring, and she could make out a deep moan as trees swayed laboriously outside her window. There were creaks on the stairs and at first, she thought it was Mae lighting candles and leaving food on white china plates as she'd been doing for years. It took just a few seconds for her to remember.

When sleep finally came, it pulled her down deep and hard. Hannah woke at dusk, after a long night of flailing in bed like a landed fish. She'd lost a whole day, but even when her eyes opened to fast-fading golden light, she remained in bed. There was nothing and no one to lift herself up for. She held the reins of time and it was horrible.

But yearning sounds came from her belly and drew her to the kitchen. She pulled out the heavy load of casseroles from the fridge. There was a bland-smelling lasagna, a mess of beef spaghetti, and a diluted gumbo with three crawfish curled meekly into commas.

She remembered Mae's blackened catfish, seared in

paprika, garlic, and thyme and slathered in butter, wine, and lemon.

"You sear it first," Mae had told her, lifting up the black iron skillet to waft the smoke. The kitchen turned hazy with it. "Go on, pick out the spices."

"Garlic," Hannah said, covering her mouth. Her eyes felt like they were leaking curry.

"That's easy. What else?"

"Thyme," Hannah said, coughing.

Mae smiled, unperturbed, and put down the skillet. She lifted a bouquet of crackling dried thyme and cupped her hands around it. "Smell that. Remember it. It's a generous herb, flavorful but not overpowering. It does a dish good. Put it in a tea and it'll cure a cough. The Greeks said it gave people courage."

Hannah looked up into Mae's dark eyes. "Is that why you're always putting it in everything?"

Mae pressed her warm lips against Hannah's forehead. "Don't read too much into it. It's just tasty." Then, "The Egyptians used it to embalm their dead" whispered against her skin.

"I'm gonna die if I don't get out of this kitchen," Hannah moaned.

"Now watch," Mae instructed. She dropped a chunk of fresh butter into the pan, then drizzled white wine over it. The sizzle filled the room. "Squeeze a lemon. Go on."

Hannah did as she was told, leaning in to smell the trickle of citrus.

"But take it off the heat quickly. You just want to warm it up a bit. Then pour it over your catfish. The sauce is like a balm over the wound."

"The wound?"

Mae held out the skillet, the catfish dark and pebbled as if it'd been tarred. "Look for yourself."

Hannah poured the warm salve over the fish, and it settled between the cracked black skin with a sigh.

"It's all about balance, child. Cooking's like a science. You have to temper the spice. That's why it's best to serve something cold with this dish." She brandished a colander brimming with vinegary vegetables. "Pickled root vegetables. Or a chilled gumbo. Are you listening?"

Hannah smacked her lips. The air tasted like black pepper. "Why do I have to learn all this stuff?"

Mae turned off the burners and the kitchen quieted. "This is how it's done, passing on knowledge. My momma taught me, decades ago, and now I'm teaching you. Someday I'll be gone and you'll have one of your own."

"One what?"

"A child."

All she had left were memories. Crouching in every cubby, latent in every scent. Hannah thought she could busy herself with them for years. "That must be how madness starts," she whispered. She was utterly alone, and yet she had the sense that there were eyes in the walls, watching her. Maybe the madness had started already.

She must have heard the sound minutes before she recognized it. It sounded like the slow thud of Mae digging preserves out of the back shed.

The shed was half-sunk into the ground and filled with shelves of aluminum cans, bottles of water, and canning jars full of pickled cabbage and cauliflower. Mae kept all the non-perishables there, behind a heavy wooden door.

Graydon slunk into the kitchen, his yellow flashlight eyes scanning her. The shed door slammed again and he let out a mewl. "Ignore it, little guy," Hannah said, reaching for him. "It's just some baby gator mucking about." Graydon's ears were pushed back on his head, nails peeking through the dirty gray fur of his paws. He shrank from her hand.

"Okay, okay," Hannah muttered and stood up. She peeked out the window, half-expecting to see some staggering drunk looking for beer. But beyond the tall bushes, the shed door winked like an eye, swinging back and forth on its own.

Graydon leapt onto the counter beside her and sunk into his haunches.

"I'm going," she groused, and pulled a long knife from the drawer. "Some guard cat you are."

Outside, the grass was arid and crackled underfoot. "Anyone there?" she called out.

The chirps of birds answered, and she looked down at herself. Her black funeral dress was askew from sleep, the long knife shook in her fist, and she was glad to be the only witness to her insanity.

Then she saw it, hunched down in the grass. It took her a moment to place the terrible ribbed back of it, white as a maggot. She drew a shuddering breath and gripped the knife harder.

How many times had she seen it skulking out of the corner of her eye, or half-submerged in the grassy swamp? Its back was singular, fracture lines like a roadmap across the carapace-like surface. She'd always attributed it to the lasting fragments of some recurring nightmare, something meaningful but harmless, and as a child, she'd always been able to burrow into Mae's skirts and rely on the scent of turmeric to right her.

But the sweat that drained down her back didn't feel like a dream, and there were no more skirts to hide behind.

Down in the grass, it released a wet, phlegmatic sound, and she saw its eye roll toward her. It had seen her. "Oh," she breathed, and backed away.

The phone began to ring inside the house and she focused on the sound, stepping backward. She clasped her hand around Mae's copper bracelet, the knots firm against her palm. "There's nothing there," she told herself. "You're still half-asleep." She willed herself to believe the words, and found that she was picturing Mae speaking them.

The shed door slammed shut with a splintering crash, and remained closed.

Her whole body trembled with the urge to run, but she forced herself to walk evenly until she was back in the kitchen, where she clutched the counter for balance. Graydon's eyes were still on the shed, his fur standing on end.

The phone began ringing again, and she fumbled with the receiver. "Hello?"

"Hi, Hannah? It's James Robichaud. How are you?" James's voice brought her back into herself.

She tried to swallow down the fear with each gulp of breath. "I'm alright, thanks. You?"

There was a pause. "Are you sure? You sound strange."

Hannah cleared her throat. "Yeah, everything's fine. I'm still a bit shaken up, I think."

"I'm sorry. How are you holding up?"

Hannah felt the silence like a presence, pressing against her, muffling her own urge to speak. She shook her head but answered, simply, "Fine."

"Listen, that thing I wanted to talk to you about? It's Mae."

"What about her?" Hannah glanced at the urn still squirreled away on a corner of the kitchen counter.

"We've received the results of the autopsy."

Hannah's hand closed into a fist. She'd forgotten that in the confused haze of that afternoon, she'd given consent. Her Mae, cut open like a fish at market. "And?"

"There was arteriosclerosis, and her heart was weakened. It could've easily been that. There were some small clots in her leg, too." James's voice changed. "But that mass wasn't a tumor. She might've choked, but she would've choked on feathers."

Hannah thought of the cat catching the canary. James's words sounded like the punch line to a joke. "I don't understand."

"Black feathers, looked to be hens', and quite a few of them. Dr. Kinney looked rightly spooked, and said it was like she'd swallowed them. They were far enough in her stomach that she would've either done it on purpose, or had it done to her."

Hannah shook so hard she almost dropped the receiver. "Jesus. What are you saying? That someone might've hurt her?"

"No, it's absurd. I mean . . ." He hesitated. "I don't know what it means, but did Mae rub anyone the wrong way? Some people in town think black hens' eggs are pretty powerful. You run them over your body to cleanse it of evil, or you can crack them open at one end and sprinkle in sulfur to—"

"James, that's ridiculous."

"Just covering my bases, that's all. There's no one you can think of? Or maybe Mae was working out a remedy? Some kind of tincture?"

Hannah traced the row of Xs carved deep along the lip of the urn. They looked as forbidding as barbed-wire fencing, and Hannah wondered who had ordered the design. She wanted to ask if the feathers had been removed, or if they were mingling with Mae's ashes. She stayed silent.

James's voice sounded wooden. "Right. I thought you should know. And while I have you on the line, I was wondering if you'd want to get out of the house for a bit? There's a band playing in town tonight, and, well, given Mae's death, I don't think it's the best idea for you to be by yourself right now."

Hannah braced herself before she looked out the window, but the shed door was closed. The long grass around it billowed harmlessly, and she held a shaking hand to her head. "I haven't even showered," she said, trailing off.

"Great. It'll take me a half hour at least to make it over."

"How . . ." Hannah sighed, running a hand through her hair. "How should I dress?"

"However you'd like. I'm sure you'll look good." James's voice was soft as cotton in her ear.

Hannah took a step back at the door of the bar.

"What's wrong?" James asked, leaning closer. He smelled like cedar wood, and she wasn't used to the scents of men.

"Are there always so many people? It's so loud." She laughed suddenly. "God, I sound ancient. I don't really get out much, in case you couldn't tell."

"We can always leave if you don't like it, but I think it might help for you to get out a bit. Be with other people."

"Other people," Hannah echoed. "Right. Because that's always gone over so well."

James rubbed the nape of his neck. "Look, I remember how it was for you, and how maybe I . . . contributed. But I was just a kid then, we both were. I'd like to make up for that. Truce?"

Hannah studied the serious set of his face and how he shifted his weight from foot to foot. She took his out-stretched hand.

Hannah found a seat on a barstool along the back and tried to make herself small. The walls were dark wood and peppered with mounted fish. A middle-aged woman, her auburn hair cut in a choppy bob, raised a glass to her from a nearby table. Hannah smiled tentatively, and looked down at herself. She'd found an old red dress of Mae's, slightly too big for her, and donned it like some exotic skin.

She'd tried on her own dresses, turning from side to side until she was dizzy, but they seemed childish, designed for a body she'd outgrown without noticing. Sweet Peter Pan collars and flower-printed cotton didn't go with whiskey and cigar smoke.

"What're you drinking?" James asked.

"Water. Last I checked I only just turned twenty."

James shook his head. "No, ma'am. With the week you've had, you've earned something harder. I insist."

"Are you always so footloose with the letter of the law?" James only smiled, so Hannah thought about it. "How about rye and ginger beer?"

"Coming right up."

Hannah pasted herself to the wall, studying the crowd. She was on the outskirts, as always, and watchful for the hate-filled glances she'd grown accustomed to in childhood. But there were none, and she felt herself relax a bit.

The dance floor was a living organism, animated hands like antennae. The women were sipping from short glasses, glancing around at whoever might be watching. Hannah could recognize the married men, their paunches and mugs of foamy beer, gathered together in huddles. She found herself wondering what they'd go home to later that night. Soft wives that smelled of lavender detergent, maybe, or avoiding their woes with some young girl like her.

Hannah coughed to clear her throat of the bar's perfumes just as the house lights went down, and four tall shapes took the stage. "This first one's called 'Been Tearing Me Open,'" the singer breathed into the microphone. He smiled and Hannah's heart somersaulted when she realized it was Callum. "It's for all the sad men out there tonight." Scattered claps rang out.

He closed his eyes and Hannah studied him as she moved up toward the stage. Some new feeling squeezed her. He was tall and bearded, with cracked sneakers on his feet. Skinny in his checkered shirt, but strong and sure-footed before the microphone. His face was expressionless, and there was only a slight wrinkle in his brow to betray that anything was stirring underneath. Then his guitar let loose an aching twang. His fingers alighted across frets as a vein began to pulse in his neck. As he played, his chin drew figure eights, outlining melodies.

The blues he played was dirty as week-old rainwater, streaming from his fingers, pooling in the whorls of her ears. In the small of her back. Sluggish bodies came alive around her, nodding at every chord he struck.

Behind Callum, the drummer's grin was ecstatic. When the drummer's eyes met Hannah, he lowered them humbly toward the silver of his set, consumed by the joy of rhythm.

Hannah felt herself moving forward through the crowd, taken by some new confidence. She wanted to be closer to Callum. She felt like someone new, someone unburdened by her mother's reputation.

"He's good, isn't he?" James handed her a glass.

Callum was backlit, but even so, when he opened his eyes, Hannah felt that they were resting on her. She was sure she'd never been studied quite so intently before. He had her pinioned.

The songs melted into each other, and Hannah drank quickly, grateful for the pleasant haziness that was taking over. James took each empty glass from her and replaced it with a fresh one. Soon, her head was spinning, and what she'd seen that afternoon was blurred.

She let herself entertain possibilities in the safety of a sweaty crowd. It was natural, she thought, to feel fragile after a death. Still, she couldn't shake the feeling that the creature in the grass had somehow been more *present* than it ever had before. More real.

But there were ways to explain it. An albino gator, maybe. She'd read somewhere that they existed, and it didn't seem such a stretch that years of crossbreeding had carried the mutation into the Louisianan swamp.

"God's garden is wide and varied," Mae used to say during Hannah's teenaged years, usually in response to the reports of violence and prostitution that trickled in from town. While she fished deep-fried oysters from her browned, bubbling pot of oil, Mae would tell Hannah about young doe-eyed boys whose hearts burst in the throes of ecstasy tablets. "And that's why I want you here, where you're safe."

Hannah was just beginning to bite at the bit, to yearn for the nightlife that frightened Mae. "So I'm not allowed in God's garden?"

Something had flitted across Mae's face and she'd turned away. "Making your own decisions might seem wonderful now, but when you're in the thick of it, you might feel differently. There'll be time enough for you to go wherever you want after I'm gone."

Callum's last note faded smoothly into silence, over-taken quickly by claps and cries for an encore, but he raised a slick hand toward the audience and hopped off-stage. "Band needs a beer, folks," the drummer whispered into the microphone. "Y'all stick around, though."

Hannah shrank back as Callum headed straight for her.

"You came. I asked James to bring you," he added, nod-ding at James. Callum accepted a beer and a chaste kiss from a lipsticked waitress. She ran her thumb across his cheek to wipe off the red mark.

"That was great, man," a heavily bearded man said, elbowing his way between them.

A delicate-featured woman with thick black curls clasped her arms around Callum's neck. "Totally great," she echoed.

"Hannah, these two are Tom and Leah. They're my whole fan club." A passing group of twenty-somethings raised their glasses toward him and Callum lowered his eyes.

"He's too humble, don't you think?" Tom said, bowing to Hannah with a flourish. "Nice to meet you."

Callum shared a private glance with Leah, so intimate that Hannah looked away. He undid Leah's hands and brushed his lips across her knuckles as she smiled.

"Nobody likes a show-off," Callum said, as the crowd lost interest in him and began to talk amongst themselves.

Tom rolled his eyes and tapped his beer bottle against Callum's. "Oh, fuck off." He thrust his chin toward James. "Fill me in on the goings-on, man. Let Callum and Hannah get a bit better acquainted." He winked at Hannah.

Hannah rolled her shoulders back. Leah still stood near Callum, mouthing the edge of her glass.

"How long have you lived by the water?" Callum asked Hannah. He leaned in close to her but gazed out at the crowd as they spoke.

"My whole life." His skin smelled like moss and cool night air, and his breath was sweet with rum. "Born and raised."

"So, are the stories true? Are y'all soothsayers, alligator hunters, and shut-ins?" Hannah smirked to hear the intonation of an old Cajun man. He was older than her. She could tell from the slightly tired look of his skin.

"Only if you're all chip-on-your-shoulder alcoholics."

Callum laughed. "Judging by my grandpa, sure. Me, I'm Irish in name only."

"Fancy that," Hannah muttered. She noticed his hands, large-knuckled around the bottle's neck.

Someone bumped her from behind, and Callum pulled her toward him, shooting a stern glance at the underage boy who retreated with arms raised. "Some of these people aren't my ideal audience," he murmured. "But you take what you can get, right?"

"I'll admit that I don't know much about music, but I thought you were amazing." She said it quietly, evenly, although inside her the sentiment boomed.

"Thank you, ma'am."

Leah was looking at them with a strange, rhapsodic intensity, pulling on her ropy strands.

"Why is she staring at us?" Hannah asked in a low voice. Immediately, she scanned the room for its exits. She felt like an intruder whose disguise was wearing off.

"Who?" Callum followed her eyes, and immediately took a step away from Hannah. "Oh, Leah. She's on E, habitually. It hasn't kicked in yet, or not enough for her. She's always a huge grump when she's sober."

"You want some?" Tom appeared behind them.

James snapped his fingers. "I'm off duty, but I'm not deaf."

"Brother, as I remember it, you might be a cop but you've never been a saint."

James took a step forward, but Leah, her pupils dilated

to a drowning black, grabbed his hand. "Come dance with me," she said, sweetly. James hesitated, glancing at Hannah.

"Go on," Hannah said. "I'm fine." She felt Callum's hand rest gently on her shoulder, felt the heat pulse through her chest. Hannah's skin was beginning to crawl. Every female set of eyes seemed to be on them, and every girl that walked by cast her a chilly, considering look. Callum was unconcerned, but Hannah had learned long ago that anonymity was safest.

"You and Leah," she began, and he shook his head, anticipating her question.

"Friends. Good friends, maybe, but if there's longing, it's not on my side."

Hannah chanced a glance at his steady eyes. She wondered if she knew enough to recognize sincerity.

"You should drink it neat." Callum gestured to her glass. "It's a waste of good rye, mixing it with that sweet shit."

"I like the spice of it." The music flooding through the speakers had a fast, thudding beat, and she felt her feet moving of their own accord.

"Drink it down quick," Callum urged, his breath warm on her neck. Leah had begun to dance with James, her hips moving like a gyroscope. Her body, outlined in colored fluorescent lights, was mesmerizing in motion. Hannah wondered where the girl had learned to sway like that.

She emptied her glass.

"Your hair is beautiful," Callum said. One finger traced her hairline so slowly she could feel each root flex at his touch. "Like the sky at dusk." His eyes lingered thoughtfully on her lips.

"Lines like that work, I guess," she whispered. She

realized that they were working, and that she wanted them to. His fingers slid like drops of water down her sides, grazing her hips.

"It's not a line." He drew his head away. "That's not what I'm bringing to the table."

She tasted acid in the back of her throat. "Excuse me," she croaked. She sensed him try to grab her arm as she fled toward the bathroom.

Hannah threw up until she was hoarse and spent, until the stench of it made burning tears pool in her eyes. A terrible pressure welled up in her cheeks and behind her eyes, and she felt close to bursting. She thought suddenly of hens' feathers packed into her throat, and could almost feel their tickle.

"Not a big drinker, then?" Callum's voice behind her, tinged in amusement, made a fresh wave of vomit crest in her.

"Hey, do you know that this is the women's restroom?" She dabbed at her face with toilet paper. Then she gave up and rested her forehead against the wall of the stall.

"At this time of night, people don't pay much attention to which restroom is which. There, now." He rubbed circles between her shoulder blades. "Poor pet."

"Is it over?"

He chuckled. "There's no way of knowing. You should enjoy this moment, though."

To her mortification, she began to sob. "Oh God, why did I even come here? I can't face a boat right now." The tiles beneath her knees were already rocking.

"I live five minutes away. You can clean yourself up there."

Hannah let herself be hoisted up against his shoulder. "I have to get home to Mae," she murmured, then stood up straight. Remembrance speared her.

"No. You don't." He kissed her forehead and his lips were full and cool. "Come on."

His apartment was the third floor of a walk-up. Hannah glimpsed a wooden balcony through glass doors in the back, its banister faintly lit by Christmas lights.

"Sit down. Put your legs up." Callum cleared a gray sofa of clothes.

There were framed black-and-white photographs on the walls and upright wine crates brimming with books. It wasn't quite what she'd expected.

Hannah glared at a chipped Tiffany lamp on the glazed coffee table and groaned. "Even the light hurts."

He threw a red silk scarf over the lamp and the living room became anatomical. "Better?" he asked.

Hannah nodded and lay down warily, aware that she barely knew this man and trying not to wonder if the scarf had once been wrapped around Leah's neck or her thin wrists. Trying not to wonder how often he found souvenirs between the cushions of his couch. Hannah let her eyes close for a moment, and she was instantly visited by the phantom sensation of Mae's palm on her forehead.

When she was startled out of sleep, her nausea had subsided and the sky was lightening outside. Through the lingering headache, she didn't recognize the room at first. The smell of aftershave and unwashed laundry was foreign.

Callum was sitting in a nearby armchair with his ankles crossed, sipping slowly from a glass. She noticed that he'd taken his shirt off. He turned his head toward her sleepily. "Feeling a bit better?"

Hannah's foot bumped the coffee table covered with sheets of music and brandy snifters as she sat up. She nodded. "Thanks for letting me stay here." A black knit blanket, flecked with crumbled chips, was spread over her legs. "I think I'm almost ready for the boat."

"It's five in the morning," he said, sounding amused. "All the boats are tied and docked."

"Still," she said, then trailed off. "I hate to ask, but you've got a boat, don't you?" Ribs showed through tanned muscles. "I'm missing my bed right now."

"I've had a few too many drinks." He shook his head. "Besides, certain animals prefer to ache on their own, but I'm a big believer in grieving in the company of others."

"It's not how I was raised. I don't think there's enough comfort in the world for what I'm feeling right now."

"This won't heal overnight, and you can't expect it to. It's going to take time, and you'll always miss her. But I promise that the sting of it, the feeling that you can't bear it, will fade. You just have to take it one step at a time, and the first of those is a bit more rest. Come on, I'll take the couch."

Hannah smoothed the red dress over her thighs. Looking around the apartment, at the photographs, the greeting cards, and the water-stained magazines, she realized she felt comfortable. At ease. She took a deep breath.

Callum sat down on the couch. "What is it?"

"I'm not tired anymore," she said, holding his gaze.

"It's really too bad," he said.

"What is?"

"That we met like we did. The things I would do, otherwise."

Hannah's breath sped up. The sense of being on the verge of something inevitable was almost pleasurable. "What would you do?" she asked in a small voice.

His face was an anchor, holding the spinning room in place. She saw desire in his dilated eyes, and unexpectedly, it made her feel powerful. "I'd like to say that I'd hold your hand, make you breakfast, pick up a handful of wildflowers," he said, smiling. "And truth is, I'd like that. But those are daytime things, and we can still rightly call this night."

"And what would you do, with this rightly called bit of night?"

"I'd lay you down," he said, his eyes suddenly serious. He leaned in over her and his tongue touched her like a butterfly's, tracing nectar along the inside of her arm toward her shoulders.

She'd so rarely allowed anyone to come this close to her, because she'd learned early that after the initial burst of pleasure came pain, and doubt, and regret.

She hesitated but didn't move away.

He slid down the straps of her dress. She moved instinctively to cover herself but he blocked her gently. His tongue flicked along her clavicle, down the subtle dip between her breasts.

"I think I'd let you," she said.

He pulled away to strip off his jeans, smiling, and she felt rudderless on the plush couch. He tugged at the bottom of her dress and she felt it slide down from beneath her. Inch by inch, her body was revealed, its hills and valleys. A terrain she hadn't had cause to examine for years was suddenly exposed. She sought his eyes for some sign of how she measured up, but they moved up and down her legs, her belly, and her shoulders like he was sating some thirst.

Slowly, he ran his hand over the pale peach cotton of her underwear. "Is this okay?" he breathed.

"I don't do this," she said. "I haven't done this in a very long time. But yes." She studied his body in the faint light. When she was seventeen, she'd had a brief flirtation with a boy from town. Toby, whose skin glistened in his parents' bed. His full lips and precious smile, his brown eyes peering expectantly up at her from between her thighs. That was before his parents had discovered them kissing in their boat. His mother's face had changed from confusion to anger to pure fury in seconds, and she'd chased Hannah down the street in bare feet. "You stay away from our boy!" she'd screamed. That was before Mae had discovered the condoms, and sat heavily, speechless, in a chair. Mae's arms crossed so tightly over her chest that her shoulders seemed to tremble with effort.

Hannah's legs wrapped loosely around Callum's waist. He pressed his thumb into her, and it felt firm and as sure as ringing a doorbell. Slowly, he pulled out his finger and licked it.

And then he moved into position and thrust, with a humming growl that elucidated every blues riff she'd ever heard. It rose to a fever pitch as she dug her short nails into his back. He answered by hoisting forward, his hand fitting against her neck. She let out a cry, suddenly panicked.

In that moment, she heard every nook and cranny of her windpipe. She thought again of feathers tangling in her trachea, and shadows began to stir at the edges of her sight, crowding in. Something flashed in the mirror, milk-white even in the room's red glow.

She tried to sit up, just as the creature disappeared behind the couch. "Callum," she breathed, and thought she saw a chalky claw stretch toward Callum's foot. How had it found her?

"Something's wrong," she tried to say as his fingers mapped the long cords of her neck, but a low vibrato started in her pelvis. He shoveled deeper, a steady spade. And then it happened. He struck ore, and they both wailed. An interminable note that made up for her many years of silence.

He stayed there, his arms trembling, gazing down into her eyes. With a tender smile, he licked her lips as she wheezed herself back to earth. Then he toppled to his side and nuzzled into her breasts, wrapping himself around her body. Beyond him, the room was empty.

"I'm going to hurt tomorrow," she said.

His wide eyes turned to her, sheepish. With hair matted in scrolls to his forehead, he looked impossibly young. He looked wholly himself. "I don't know what came over me. I got swept up in the moment, I guess."

She laughed, and pressed him against her shoulder. "Baby," she murmured. The dizziness had left her, but already she knew she would never again be painless.

CHAPTER
THREE

When she returned to her house several days later, she found a letter from a New Orleans estate lawyer who claimed to have been hired by Mae. He said there was a will.

Callum bundled her into his boat, her body sluggish with anti-nausea medication to weather the rocky trip, and by the time they arrived on the outskirts of New Orleans, Hannah's eyes were at half-mast.

They rented a car and Callum drove them down the highway into the city proper. Hannah noticed the blurry landscape in flashes: squat palm trees in the shade of construction cranes were overtaken by streetlights crowned in iron fleur-de-lis. White wooden crosses lined the road, fenced in by miniature American flags.

New windows sat inside weathered brick, and Hannah

craned her neck to peer inside homes as they drove past. She saw courtyards filled with lush plants, slow-moving streetcars, and above it all office towers glinting against the clouds. Hannah watched the parade of high-heeled women in fitted blazers heading home from work and caught a glimpse of a very different life.

The lawyer's office was down an alleyway near Frenchmen Street. Callum paused in front of the door as the energetic beat of a big band tune drifted down the street. "That's a beautiful sound," he said, smiling. "Joyful music on a Tuesday afternoon."

Hannah tugged the short hairs of his beard. "Let's go have a listen. The lawyer said his whole afternoon was open."

A dog barked from a balcony above them and was quieted in French.

"I tried it here, before. I tried hard and it didn't work, so why torture myself with it," Callum said. A measure of regret hung in his voice, and Hannah realized she wasn't yet privy to its cause. "You're just avoiding this. Go on. I'll wait out here," Callum said, and knocked on the thick wooden door. "Good luck, sweets."

The lawyer was a short man in a seersucker suit and white socks, his graying hair combed over an obvious bald spot. He explained the inheritance that run-in-the-stockings Mac had left for her.

"The contents of her bank accounts will pass to you. The house, she says, is not hers to give, but she is certain that its owner would grant it to you. She did make one note," he frowned as he rifled through the file. "Well, in any case, it was a short note. She urged you to sell the house and purchase elsewhere. Somewhere out of state. As for the house's contents, they are yours to do with as you please." He raised his eyebrows. "Is that satisfactory?"

Hannah nodded. She signed the papers in a daze and backed out of his office, declining offers of sweet tea as she went.

Callum was outside, perched on a fire hydrant. It was the magic hour before dusk, the fading light spilled its long shadows down the streets. She hung back for a moment, letting Mae's final gift to her sink in. She couldn't help feeling that Callum, absentmindedly tearing petals off a flower, was in some way also a gift.

She tapped him on the shoulder.

He grinned when he saw her. "How'd it go?" he asked.

As she told him the details, he put his arms around her waist. After she fell silent, they listened together to the children's laughter that echoed down the street. For the first time since Mae had passed, Hannah came face to face with the breadth of possibility.

Musicians were beginning to tune their instruments in one of the bars, and Callum whispered in her ear, "Let's buy something ridiculous."

They strolled along, hand in hand, pausing to peer into antique shop windows.

Thinking to tease him, she pulled him into a sex shop. She found herself giggling at his mystified smile as they walked through the racks of polyester underwear and padded cuffs. Her laugh caught in her throat as they reached the back of the store. Dim bulbs lit black leather masks, and they reached in unison for a beautifully sculpted, lace-trimmed mask.

"Will this do?" she asked in a small voice, holding it up to her face.

The black leather mask sat wrapped in pink tissue on Hannah's lap as Callum steered them back along the water, between forked trees that bore blackberries. She raised the collar of her jacket against the chill.

"Where are we going?" she asked, recognizing the succession of clearings.

"Back to my apartment," he said. "Why? Where do you want to go?"

Home, she thought, but said nothing. She looked over her shoulder at the tangle of trees that receded.

The swamp should have been frightening in the dark. There were too many creatures that slept in the sun suddenly clamoring for food, but the small lamp that winked above the boat's rudder turned the night into an intimate passage. The screaming birds and rustling reptiles fell silent in its beam.

Callum tied up the boat at the dock near his apartment. "Would you rather head home?" he asked her between puffs of his cigarette.

Hannah studied the grave moon above. "I'm not sure that's my home anymore," she answered honestly. "Home should be four familiar walls, but I'm starting to think it's made more by the people who share it with you."

Callum looked sad for a moment as he reached out and cupped her face. "You miss her," he said, and it wasn't a question. Her throat felt tight with tears.

Callum's bedroom was moonlit as he undressed her. Hannah glimpsed her pallor in the bathroom mirror as he tied the mask around her head, and saw herself transformed into a craved creature. She felt somber as she knelt before him, his moans something serious. Hannah could almost taste the guilt at her happiness, sharp and sour as a mandarin.

The next day, she went back to the house by the water, and saw that it was gathering dust. Graydon greeted her with wild, accusatory meows. Eventually, he settled into an uneasy sleep on her lap, and she drifted off on the couch. She dreamt of stairs without end, her feet wearying then bloodying on the eternal ascent.

On the nights without Callum, she felt her loneliness like something wresting inside her. She stalked the house and barely ate. She wondered whether it was her imagination that the wallpaper seemed to have lost its color, that the spices seemed to have gone stale in their jars.

Whenever she saw Callum, it was as though life rushed back into her body. She ate heartily and laughed loudly.

Their Christmas was modest, and as she watched Callum light a candle at either end of his table, she thought of her Christmases with Mae, making pecan pie and pralines and listening to carols on the radio. How Martha would often stop in, with a covered dish full of steaming crab claws.

Callum and Hannah watched the faithful head to Midnight Mass from the fire escape, and she said a clumsy prayer for Mae, not quite knowing what words would claim the attention of whatever was listening. She admitted to herself that despite the wealth of loss, she was in the grips of a happiness much greater than she'd ever thought possible.

January's chill came and went, but it barely seemed to

touch them. Even the tips of their ears were warm with the constant blush of what Hannah was still reluctant to call love.

One night, they arrived back at his apartment after a night of drinking. Hannah kicked off her shoes and collapsed onto the couch. "You're mighty comfortable here, aren't you?" Callum asked, teasingly.

Hannah sat up, blushing. "Sorry," she stuttered. "I don't mean—I just thought—"

His laugh interrupted her. "No, no. I like it. In fact, I think it's high time I gave you this. I'm miserable as a wet cat when you're not here." He held up something shimmering.

Hannah walked over to him and plucked the key from his hands. "Are you sure about this?"

He nodded.

"Thank you," she said softly, and moved into his arms. "Nobody has ever given me a key to their house before." She held the key as though it were a precious gem rather than metal. "I'll get you a key to my house, too."

Callum flicked her under the chin. "No, silly. I want you to live here. With me."

Hannah's eyes widened. She couldn't imagine leaving her home. Who would stoke the memories that still lingered there? How could she move into the town that had so viciously exiled her as a child? She worked her thumbnail over the knotted copper bracelet.

"That's a lot of thoughts that just rushed through your head," Callum said, studying her.

"It's a lot to think about." Hannah saw a lightning-quick expression of hurt rush across Callum's face and tried to explain. "I'm still tied to that house. Besides, this town hasn't been very welcoming to my family."

Callum's brow creased. "Who hasn't been welcoming?"

Hannah searched his eyes. He'd more than earned her trust several times over, and yet she still hesitated to tell him about her history. Would he understand the townspeople's reaction, perhaps a bit too well?

"It all happened a lifetime ago. Let's just say folks on this side of the river don't take to people who are different from them."

"Trust me, it's not just this town. It's a global epidemic. You can't just run from it, though. You've got to work to change their minds. And who wouldn't love you?" He brushed her hair away from her face, his fingers lingering. "Give it some thought," he urged. "There's a lot that could be done with the money you'd get from the house. And you have a home here, whenever you want it."

After Callum fell asleep that night, she stared fixedly at the foreign ceiling that had somehow become familiar. She tried to match her own jagged breathing to Callum's steady breath. There was an immense amount of comfort in something as minute as that sound. Tentatively, she touched Callum's bare back. She faded into a dreamless sleep with the sensation of his warmth against her palm.

Hannah itemized the things she couldn't live without and sent Callum to retrieve them from the house by the water—certain books, spices, and Graydon, who mewled and hissed as soon as he was deposited in Callum's apartment. She was surprised by how small the list was. Her love for the house didn't live in its contents.

In return, Hannah tossed out bags full of take-out containers from Callum's apartment, and she grilled whole fish, then sat straight-backed with excitement as he moaned his approval.

While he was practicing music or out on his boat, she composed recipes. Mae's dominance of the kitchen had been so assured that Hannah had assumed there'd be more recipe books, but there were just a few notebooks with handwritten scrawls, mostly for teas, broths, and suggested pairings of ingredients.

When Callum was overworked, she fed him chicken and okra gumbo, sensing instinctively that the smoked andouille and celery-infused chicken would revive him. Persillade, a simple mixture of parsley, garlic, and olive oil, scented his breath as he sang to her on his small balcony. If she squinted just so, the colored Christmas lights still wound around the fire escape became a galaxy, wreathing them.

Hannah discovered the effects of ground cayenne and paprika for herself. The giggles, the pervasive good mood. The wetness that welled inside her. She doused the apartment with heady fumes of Scotch bonnet peppers, dark roux, and salted pork, and paced the apartment until Callum came home. He learned to recognize the smell, as sure as a pair of red garters dangling from the doorknob.

The night she prepared sarigue in oregano and hot sauce, she left moist handprints on every wooden surface. He bent her over and she angled herself by straining on tiptoes. They awoke the next afternoon, limbs sore.

Her life before Callum was beginning to take on the quality of a dream, until she found a photograph of her and Sarah Anne in an old, water-stained copy of *Grimm's Fairy Tales* that Callum had retrieved for her. The terror-izing sweetness of first friendship was written all over Hannah's face. Shame closed the back of her throat.

They'd met at Sunday school, one of the few activi-ties in town that Mae had readily permitted as Hannah entered her teen years.

Sarah Anne had once been as saccharine as her name, all blonde hair, pale lashes, and limpid blue eyes. She had moved through the congregation in a cloud of white lace and curls, and although she was new in town, the towns-people took to her instantly.

Beside her, Hannah was plain and awkward, with dull hair that couldn't commit fully to either blonde or red and eyes the color of a half-laundered grass stain. The congre-gation stiffened their backs and cast suspicious sideways glances at her.

In the middle of a lesson, something about suffering little children and lambs, Sarah Anne had passed her a neatly folded note. "Hi Hannah," it said, and when she looked up, Sarah Anne flashed her a radiant smile.

By that point, Hannah already knew about the cruelty of other children. How they'd snare her with false sym-pathy only to trip her or throw rotten eggs at her feet. Hannah tossed the paper to the ground.

Sarah Anne watched the paper fall with an eerily adult expression. A smile twitched at the corner of her mouth, like the tail of a lazy house-cat. "I've heard what they call you in town," Sarah Anne whispered. "And let them talk,

I honestly don't care. I think it's interesting. I'd like to be your friend."

There was not much to say to that.

After the class ended, Hannah kicked at the marshy ferns that grew by the side of the water, watching Sarah Anne's dress eddy around her thin tanned legs as she walked. Hannah's arms remained crossed in mistrust.

"Do you like ice cream?" Sarah Anne asked. She leaned down and briskly wiped dust from her patent shoes.

"Yeah." Hannah looked down at her own shoes, brown Mary Jane loafers that had cost Mae five dollars from a second-hand bin. There was a patch by the heel where the leather had worn down that Hannah colored in with a Crayola marker. In the summer rains, she trailed a muddy stream of brown ink, quick as a wound.

"Good. Let's get a scoop. My brother has an appointment this afternoon so I'm free for a few hours."

"Where did your family live before?" Hannah asked.

"North Carolina. We moved here because of my brother and his," she hesitated, "head problems. We've tried doctors, we've tried priests, and now my parents are giving herbalists and voodoo a shot." Sarah Anne wound her arm around the crook of Hannah's elbow. She did this silently, moving closer until their shoulders touched.

Hannah looked carefully at Sarah Anne, her arm shaking from the effort of being kept perfectly still. "Voodoo?"

Sarah Anne waved the question away. "Well, it's technically not voodoo. He has a regular head shrink, but a year ago my mother started looking into other remedies. She's been taking him to a, what do they call it, a Yoruba priest." When Hannah raised her eyebrows, Sarah Anne added, "They thought the orishas might help. So here we are. Just us and the bugs."

Hannah studied the girl's profile. "You don't think that's dangerous? Calling on spirits?"

"Maybe." Sarah Anne sniffed. "I told you, I know what they say about you. I think you'd know better than me what's dangerous." Hannah turned her head and felt Sarah squeeze her arm. She pointed to the left as they reached the edge of the town square. "That's my favorite ice cream shop. If you lick it slowly in front of Phil, he'll give you another one for free. It gives him a boner, I think."

"Right," Hannah said weakly.

"I touched one, back in North Carolina. I told this boy I'd give him a hand-job, because I'd heard the older girls talking about it, but I didn't really know what it was. Neither did he, I don't think. I just ran my nail along it, like this." She demonstrated by tracing a vein on Hannah's arm, and something clapped open in Hannah's stomach. "He made this terrible face, like this, and I thought I'd hurt him. But then it started spurting this white stuff, like a little volcano. I got a bit on my dress." She giggled and tossed her hair. "It looks a bit like a giant tapeworm, don't you think?"

"I don't know," Hannah said, peering into the sunlight.

"I think so. Anyways, he looked kind of scared afterward, and gave me all his cash. It ended up being nine bucks." Her voice turned wistful. "He never talked to me again after that. Too bad, really." Sarah Anne paused, then said suddenly, "I like you," with the fearlessness that Hannah was just beginning to attribute to the beautiful.

"You don't seem to care too much about what people think of you. Why do you even come to Sunday school?"

"My mother sends me."

Sarah Anne rolled her eyes and unwound her arm. Hannah felt a film, an afterglow, where it had been. "My mom sends me, too. But I think she'd kill herself if she heard I wasn't participating. My immortal soul is really important to her. It's this one," Sarah Anne said, pointing to a storefront. Hannah had seen the shop before, but never been inside. She paused at the door, but Sarah Anne tugged her forward.

"My mother doesn't talk much about my immortal soul," Hannah said, hanging back as Sarah Anne hopped onto a stool, and all five sets of male eyes in the shop swiveled to her bare knees, which she was knocking together impatiently. Sarah Anne seemed to have the uncanny ability to convince people that she was older, or younger, as it suited her.

"Hi Phil," Sarah Anne said, her voice rising in pitch even as it softened. "Two vanilla soft serves," she raised her eyebrows at Hannah, and Hannah nodded, "dipped."

Phil was bushy-browed and teenaged, his arms like fresh summer sprigs sprouting from beneath his short-sleeved uniform. "Coming right up, honey," he breathed.

Sarah Anne patted the stool next to her. "Maybe she doesn't believe in it."

"Who? What?"

"Your mother," Sarah Anne said softly as she began to tear a napkin into strips. Hannah noticed that several of the girl's cuticles were bloodied. "Your immortal soul."

Callum made it his mission to ease her fear of boats. She grew to like being on the water, the green hyacinth patches that spread like a shifting carpet.

Still, she watched the small waves bob the boat, knowing that any disturbance of the moss could be an alligator warring in the dim.

Callum guided them down tributaries she'd never seen. She glimpsed the white-shingled roof of a mansion. Sparse notes, piano and cello and sometimes steel guitar, floated down from the summer homes. She wondered if Sarah Anne was in one of them, waiting for her, but she'd lost the piece of paper with the woman's address.

"Why did you come here? To Louisiana?" she asked Callum one afternoon.

"I was driving around the South with a couple of high school friends, pretending that we were a proper band, and I met a girl here. She said the touring life wasn't for her, so the band went on without me. Yoko was the least of what they called her. She was trying to make it as a photographer, and when she was called away on a job up north, I went with her. We tried for a while, but it didn't take. I'd always liked it here, so when that death knell sounded on our relationship, I came back. It turned into a joke, how everyone left me for the world, but I left everyone for Louisiana."

"Did you love her?" Hannah asked, struggling to sound casual.

He turned off the motor. The silence was instant and

absolute. He rested his elbows on his knees. "We're here. I've been up and down these waterways, but this is the most beautiful clump of trees I've seen."

Hannah looked up into the gray, sun-stroked canopy, fragile as ancient lace.

"I come here to be alone sometimes. That's Spanish moss hanging from the trees. Its closest relative is the pineapple, of all things." Callum paused. "I did love her. And of course, it couldn't last. We didn't know that, at eighteen. People tell you, but you think you know better."

"Can it last now? Is there a magical age?" Her own questions frightened her, as did the possible answer, but she found that she now hungered for comfort. Her life with Mae had been so insular, so self-sufficient, that she'd rarely given thought to sharing her life with anyone else. Even Sarah Anne, who'd flitted between boys, had once made a makeshift scrapbook for her future wedding. Rose petals preserved in hairspray were pasted carefully between faded ivory satin she hoped to one day be swathed in.

Callum drew a deep breath. "It's possible with the right person."

"Do you still love her?" She instantly wanted to take back the words.

He gave her a tender look. "It was a lifetime ago."

"I was eighteen two years ago," Hannah said, squinting at a large estate on a hill, the moss trailing down toward the water. "Short lifetime."

Moving slowly, he lowered himself on top of her and pinned her arms against the edge of the boat. "Over ten years for me. That's a fifth of a life in some parts." Hannah opened her mouth but he growled against her lips. "Shut up, smartass."

He settled in beside her as she snaked her arms around his neck, and the current made them undulate against each other. They closed their eyes and slow danced against the bottom of the boat, changing rhythms as the current drifted them past snippets of music.

Hannah moved through the grocery store aisles, keeping her head down. She massaged the pimpled flesh of grape-fruits and added stalks of asparagus to her basket. The amount of food available in the small town shop was still incredible to Hannah, who'd grown up purchasing pro-duce from nearby houses.

"Two of those salmon filets," a woman told the man behind the seafood counter. "No, those ones there."

Hannah risked an upward glance and her breath caught in her throat. She turned quickly on her heel and pretended to be unreasonably fascinated by a head of cab-bage.

"Hannah?" Sarah Anne asked tentatively.

Hannah looked over her shoulder and managed a wooden wave.

In a sweater and tight denim, Sarah Anne's twenty-year-old body looked almost sickly thin. "Fancy meeting you here. I was wondering when we'd run into each other."

Behind the counter, the man packed up Sarah Anne's filets, studying Hannah from under heavy lids.

"On the swamp, Mae used to mostly buy from farmers and fishermen in the area. She said it was fresher."

Sarah Anne mouthed "thank you" to the man and bounced the filets in her palm. "Maybe I'll learn how to fish while I'm here." She peeked through the cellophane and shuddered daintily. "Maybe not."

The man took a corner of his apron to the glinting edge of a blade, his eyes still on Hannah. The message was clear. Clearing her throat, Hannah backed away, picking up a bundle of squat carrots.

"So what brings you here, then?" Sarah Anne asked, oblivious to the man's knife.

"I'm—" Hannah stopped. The group of people who knew about her and Callum was so small that it felt like a secret. A private cubby into which only the two of them could fit. But she felt a girlish urge to gossip with Sarah Anne, remnants of a childhood cubby of their own. "I'm staying with a man in town. A musician."

Sarah Anne's jaw dropped theatrically and she clapped her hand to her chest. "Why, Hannah. I do declare." She laughed. "That's fabulous. Older? Younger? Hot?"

"Older." Hannah smiled. "Hot."

Sarah Anne sighed loudly. "What I wouldn't give to trade lives with you. My uncle's spending more time here than I thought. His idea of a great night is Scrabble and spiked lemonade. I swear, he handles me like china sometimes. I've barely had a night to myself since we got here."

"He's probably just worried that . . ." Hannah paused, swallowed hard, then finished in a small voice. "He just wants to make sure you're okay, being back here and all."

Sarah Anne raised an eyebrow. "You know how you make sure someone's okay? Quit annoying them to death."

They reached the cash registers and Sarah Anne fluttered her fingers over the glossy pages of magazines. "This?" she asked, tapping a photo of a blonde-bobbed celebrity. "For my hair?"

Hannah shrugged.

The wall of white teeth encased in crimson lips, black lashes like the multitudinous legs of centipedes, made her uncomfortable. The art of massaging red into her cheeks, perfuming the hollows of her neck, and ironing the kinks out of her hair was another gaping hole in Hannah's education.

"Maybe," Sarah Anne mused, squinting at the photo. "I cut it short once, and regretted it. It'd look good on you, though." Sarah Anne brushed her fingers through the ends of Hannah's long reddish hair.

"Next," the cashier urged them, gesturing with her hand.

Hannah laid out her items one by one, then noticed the cashier's arms remained crossed. Behind her, Sarah Anne hummed bits of an almost recognizable melody as she studied the back of a can.

"Next," the cashier repeated and Hannah looked up into her flat, unapologetic eyes. A dark mole sullied the woman's tanned face, and her lips cracked through pink lipstick.

Sarah Anne snorted. "You haven't done hers yet."

"I don't serve her kind," the cashier said simply.

"What would it hurt?" Hannah asked the woman, hating her doleful voice.

The cashier stepped back from the register. Hannah

thought she saw an expression of regret flash across the woman's face. But then she jutted her chin toward the door, as if Hannah were some dumb animal undeserving of speech.

Hannah set down her empty basket and moved toward the door, even as Sarah Anne called her back. Christobelle's words rang in her head, telling her to keep strong and close herself off, but all she felt was shame.

Sarah Anne caught up to her in the parking lot. "What was that?" she asked, her own groceries abandoned inside.

"They don't want me here," Hannah said, blinking back tears. "They want me in the swamp, with the reptiles. Where they think I belong."

Sarah Anne moved to stand in front of her. "You should tell the manager. They have no right to treat you like this."

Hannah stared bitterly out at the street. "You don't understand what it's like, being turned away anywhere I go. You can't know how much they hate me."

She felt paralyzed by the knowledge that others might turn on her even in the brief walk back to Callum's apartment. She was beginning to understand Mae's fierce protectiveness and how necessary their waterside exile had been. In that moment, she ached for the easy life that Mae had constructed for her.

"I don't care who your family is, money is money. Money is blind."

"Not my money. They don't want anything from me. Everything I touch is tainted."

She thought of Callum and the unburdened simplicity of his life before she'd come into it. How long before the townspeople found out who was sleeping in his bed? Or worse, maybe they already knew. Maybe they'd already confronted him, a wall of thick-armed men encircling him on the docks, his own small form eclipsed by their menace. There was nothing more terrifying than precarious happiness.

"Hannah, that's not true." Sarah Anne touched her shoulder. Hannah flinched away from the woman's hand.

"Now you're tainted, too," Hannah said, aiming for levity, but her voice came out dry and heavy. "I should go."

"I'm sorry," Sarah Anne said. "I know you must be going through a lot. Why don't you come over? Let me make you dinner one night, and we can catch up."

"Sure," Hannah replied, but she was already waving as she turned away. She'd imagined seeing Sarah Anne again many times over the years, and had rehearsed long apologies for abandoning her that night so long ago. But now she'd had two chances, and fallen short of contrition on both occasions. Maybe the finest gift she had to offer was to shut herself off.

So distracted was she by her thoughts that she bumped shoulders with the old woman standing in the middle of the street. "Sorry," Hannah mumbled. She caught a glimpse of white hair framing milky brown eyes as she passed, and when she looked over her shoulder, the woman was still there, watching her go. She noticed the varicose veins streaking the woman's legs beneath the hem of her pale blue shift dress. Hannah's shoes slapped the concrete as she walked away, and she thought of a hunted animal, moving inelegantly through the brush.

When Callum was gone, Hannah was restless. Her new life was different from her previous uncomplicated fascination with books, herbs, and fetching simple accents for Mae's dishes. It had been a small life, but comfortable in its simplicity and reassuring for seeming so secure. Now her future stretched in front of her like a chasm, specked with terrible moments of anger at Mae for coddling her, for not pushing her toward university, for not teaching her the basics of finance.

"What do you know how to do?" Callum asked her, then grunted. "Aside from being sexy as hell."

"Excellent," Hannah muttered. "An exciting future in prostitution awaits me." She cocked her head, considering. "I know how to cook, I guess."

"I'll say. You're incredible in the kitchen."

"No restaurant in this town would hire me, though," she said, squeezing the juice of a halved lime into her glass of water.

"Come here," he scoffed and wound his arm around her waist. "You don't need an income right this second, so stop stressing so much and just enjoy it. Slaving away for your bread and butter isn't all it's cracked up to be." They danced clumsily across the living room. "Jesus, woman, would you let a guy lead?"

Hannah stepped hard on his foot. "I would, if he knew how."

As he picked her up off the floor, she squealed. Beneath her trailing toes, his feet moved smoothly. "How's this?"

Her laughter answered him.

"Give yourself some time. You're young, still." He ran his finger alongside her eyes, over her lips. "No lines yet," he said, softly. He guided her finger across the same route on his face. "See? This is what they call expiring goods."

Eventually, they made their way to the bed, where he mapped her body with his tongue, his lips murmuring against her skin as if she were his harmonica. His hands moved with teasing slowness along her body and she answered his plucks and plumbs with her truest notes. Afterward, they lay beside each other, their faces mashed by pillows, and talked softly.

"How can you even afford this place?" Hannah asked him, running her eyes across the molded trim along the ceiling. The bedroom's large windows opened like doors onto the starred sky.

"Renting an apartment in the middle of nowhere can be remarkably cheap. I make do with the occasional gig. And my parents died," Callum added, his voice unemotional. "My mom first, a quick cancer, then my dad drank and smoked just enough to rot his stomach straight through."

Hannah was surprised that he hadn't shared this with her earlier, and found herself yearning to hear someone else's experience of loss. "I'm so sorry. Were you close?" She stroked his cheek, trying to coax out grief, but he gave a wry one-sided smile.

"Not really. I flew the coop at fifteen. They were fine enough parents, but a bit too right-leaning for a musical son."

"So why didn't you set up camp in Lafayette or Baton Rouge? Tourists are dying for a good swamp tour."

Callum shrugged. "You get your motor clogged with hyacinth, and they expect you to find them a gator nest. I'm brave in plenty of ways, but not stupid enough to taunt a momma alligator for the viewing pleasure of chubby kids in bucket hats. And the music's good in Lafayette, but I never warmed to the zydeco. I've been here for years, and still can't partner-dance to save my life. Anyway, my sister gave me the lion's share of what little our parents had saved up."

"You have a sister?"

Callum cleared his throat. "She's a few years younger than me. Was never too close with her either, but now she has a white-picket house in California and a little girl, and her husband is loaded. Sometimes it pays in unexpected ways, being a starving artist."

"You are starving," she teased, punching his ribs under the covers. "You're too thin."

"And you, my dear, are nesting." He turned her around easily, fitting himself against her back, and patted her stomach. She gasped and swatted his hand away. "Don't even," he scolded. "I love it. I love it all." His hand clutched hers. "What about you? Have you ever met your real parents?"

Hannah sucked in air and sat up. She could make out the unblinking glint of his eyes in the darkness. "My real mother's known in town. Or should I say, reviled. You've probably already heard about her, and maybe even made up your mind."

"Hey, you don't have to say anything at all. I was just running my mouth."

Hannah hesitated, then, taking a deep breath, decided to trust. It felt like counting on a slender rope to hold her against the appetite of gravity. "Have you heard of Christobelle?"

"That woman with the church? The spiritualist? I've heard a thing or two, usually from the too-good Baptist girls who heard it from their grandma. They say she's a voodoo queen of some kind, whatever that means." He made a scoffing sound. "Yeah, she's legend." Then, realization dawned on him. He sat up and slapped her knee in excitement. "Wait. That's your mother?"

"That's the one."

The silence was heavy. Hannah imagined Callum leaving the room without a word, the shuttered windows shaking in the frames as he slammed the door. She braced herself against rejection, steeling her limbs.

"Shit," he said, and drew her into his lap. She trembled with the effort of staying stiff, staying strong, then gave in. "That must have been interesting for you."

Hannah nuzzled gratefully against his cheek.

"We can be done with the conversation if you want, but—is there any truth to it? Speaking to the dead and all that?"

"Funny how the ones who know firsthand are never the ones gossiping." Hannah brushed back her hair and gathered it in a loose knot at the nape of her neck. It felt strange speaking out loud about things that she'd only ever turned over in her mind. "Who knows? After all, the power of voodoo is in the mind. You give someone a drink with crushed snails and sage, finish it off with a light psychotropic, and they'll see whatever you want them to. Some of these potions that people peddle have clay, black sand, or even ground-up bones in them. I don't know what she gives them, but from what I've heard, it's always men that go to her, and they end up sick. Or worse."

"What's she got against men?"

Hannah remembered the way Christobelle rested against Samuel, depending on his presence beside her. How she'd called him her partner. "I don't think she wants to hurt them," Hannah said slowly.

Callum whistled softly. "If I were you, I'd be so curious about it."

Hannah bristled. "She gave me up. Mae raised me, and that's all that matters. I'm no more a part of it than anyone else, no matter what people might say. I've spent my whole life strung up for things I know nothing about."

"Well, not nothing. Don't you ever wonder if you might have a bit of her in you? More than, say, her eyes or her nose?"

"You think it's catching? Talking to the dead?"

"I'm just saying that if there are people on the other side, it might actually be charitable to start a conversation."

"I don't put much stock in it," she said, trying to keep her voice steady as she lay back down and burrowed under the covers. "I don't really see how it's easier to blame a toilet flushing in the night on some angry, constipated ghost than faulty plumbing."

"That's some pressing unfinished business." Callum stretched out beside her.

"So?" she asked, trying to sound tougher than she felt. "Have I finally done it? Have I scared you away?"

"Oh, definitely," he said, a smile in his voice. "I'm shaking in my boots." His breath dripped down the whorls of her ear. "A little thing like you? Who could you possibly scare?"

That night, she dreamt memories. At six, she'd found shadows burned onto walls in the daylight, then wiped away at night. When she was nine, a very short man with filmy white eyes that looked as though they were wrapped in spiderwebs had come out of the water and offered her a fish. She'd been startled awake on dry land, alone, but the fish had been beating its death rattle on the ground beside her.

Then the dream changed. She was back in the house by the water. Hannah knew she was grown from the heaviness in her belly, the dull ache on either side of her breasts. Christobelle sat beside her on the living room couch. She held a handkerchief in her cupped hands, soggy and dripping blood.

"Do you need this?" her mother asked. The blood drops were perfect and pristine as cherries on the rug, and Christobelle wadded the fabric in her mouth. Her cheeks turned convex with it.

"Yes," Hannah cried, diving to her knees at Christobelle's feet. She pulled the handkerchief out of the woman's mouth, but it was a dry, dusty pink. Her own initials were embroidered in one corner.

"Whose blood is this?" she asked, and felt the handkerchief disintegrate in her hands. When she looked up, it was Mae lying on the couch, and the handkerchief was on her face. Rising and falling with wheezing breaths. Her hands worked furiously in her lap, slippery on a long strip of skin. She was on the seventh knot.

Hannah stood carefully and moved away. Something

scurried, something moving with four-legged agility under the dining room table.

Hannah turned resolutely away. "No," she said to it. A low scraping, like mussel shells against hardwood, answered her. She knew, without looking, that it was dragging toward her.

A warm, wet claw closed on her thigh and she looked down to see the back of a bald head, sun-bleached and ridged down the middle like a walnut. It was facing the floor, its claw roving blindly toward her stomach. Small, sniffing sounds filled the room.

"Wake up," Mae intoned in Christobelle's voice, the handkerchief seizing on her face. Her fingers flailed over the eighth knot. "Wake up now."

The claw closed, its thick fingernails sliding through the white skin of her stomach as if it were cream. Hannah heard a pop and felt something burst inside her, like a grape between teeth. Blood rushed out.

Below her, the thing turned its head and the blood struck it squarely between its white eyes, flat and polished as marble. The blood dripped down its tapered nose. A tongue, coated in white fur, slid out to taste it. It hummed between her legs.

Behind her, Mae screamed.

Hannah opened her eyes to blinding light and Callum kneeling beside her, shaking her furiously. "Christ, it's everywhere," he cried out.

The sheets were dark with clotted blood, slick as an oil spill. "I'm sorry," Hannah whispered. "Your poor sheets."

"It's too much," Callum groaned, gathering her. "Hold on to my neck. I want to get you into the bathroom."

Callum set her down in the bathtub, stuffing towels between her legs. "Hold this," he urged, guiding her hand. He disappeared and Hannah watched the white towels fill with poppy blooms.

"I have an emergency. My girlfriend is bleeding." She heard him on the phone outside the room. Hannah stretched out a red hand past the filmy shower curtain, toward his voice. "No, it's like a period, but it's very heavy. No, it started out of nowhere. It was hard waking her up and she seems confused. I don't think she can stand on her own." There was a long pause. "Thank you."

Callum sat on the edge of the bathtub and stuffed two pillows under her waist. He stroked her hair roughly. "They're coming, and they said to elevate you a bit. Are you okay? Can you talk?"

Hannah looked up into his face. His teeth seemed askew between ill-fitting lips and his eyes were wet. "Don't worry. It's just a dream."

"Oh, honey."

Mildew veined between his shower tiles, and she pointed weakly. "Bleach," she tried to say, but the room was slipping, siphoning into a single point of light. The pressure in her belly stopped.

Hannah came to in a bright room painted in khaki tones. A blue plastic curtain was pulled to one side. Soft beeps, slight as insects, surrounded her.

"Hey there," Callum said, scooting his chair closer to the bed.

"Where am I? What happened?" A dull ache shot over her pelvis. All she could remember was a handkerchief, and the suffocating smell of wet pennies. She leaned over the metal edge of the bed, gagging slightly. The linoleum floor shone like water, undisturbed.

"Let me call the doctor," Callum said. "He should be the one to explain everything to you."

Hannah grabbed his hand. "No. Please tell me." She noticed her wrist was bare of Mae's copper bracelet. "Where's my bracelet?"

"The doctors couldn't find a clasp so they cut it off when they needed to put your IV in." Callum winced. "There was a complication with . . . Well. You're pregnant. They said it's just over a month old."

Hannah shrank down into her pillow. Blind panic surged through her. "They must be wrong." Even as she said the words, she questioned them. She thought back over the last few months and was met by memories of care-free passion. Any of them could have been the moment of conception. Her fingers moved under the sheet to feel her stomach. The terrain was suddenly unknown.

"Is it—" He coughed and turned away. "Is it mine?"

"Either that, or an immaculate conception," Hannah said. "But I seem to remember us getting busy once or twice." Warm relief spread through her chest when he smiled.

"I thought we were being careful."

"I took my birth control," she said, defensively. "But, I guess, it's a truth from elementary school. Nothing's safe except—"

"Abstinence," he finished. "But where's the fun in

that?" Callum's smile slipped as his eyes traced the white sheets. "I was scared."

"I'm sorry." Hannah ran her thumb along his lip. He looked tired under the hospital fluorescence.

"They said you almost lost the baby."

Hannah's attention snapped back like a rubber band. "I didn't? I'm still pregnant?" Hannah could feel Callum tearing loose threads from the sheets.

"Yes. And I know it's too soon to talk about this, but I was wondering if we could keep it." The words raced out of him. Then, he reached forward and covered her mouth gently. "Don't answer right away. Please, think about it."

She did. Over the rough skin of his fingers, she studied him. What should've taken months, or years, she compressed into seconds. But the question that rose above all others was whether she could envision a life for her child without Callum. Could she even imagine her own life without him?

"How can we know we'll last? I don't know anything about being a mother."

"Look," he said, sitting up. "It feels right with you. I'm not saying we get married tomorrow—" His mouth tightened. "Although if you wanted to . . ." He trailed off as she shook her head, smiling. "But we could give it a try. Hell, I care about you. A lot."

Hannah licked her lips. Did he love her, though? She wondered whether it was a prerequisite, whether she'd be satisfied without it. He began to stroke her hair, and she felt his hand shaking through the gentle, rhythmic movement. Maybe love was just a word, standing in for a sentiment as irrepressible as the ocean.

"Okay. We can talk about it," she said, then the panic returned. "Oh, God," she whispered, and began to cry. "I'm not ready to be a mother."

Callum stood and leaned over her. He squeezed her shoulders and his face centered in her vision. "Well, we've got eight months to get ready." The blue eyes that had eased the ache of her past few months now showed his fear.

"What will we do?"

Callum laughed suddenly, despite the tears shining in his eyes. "Fuck if I know," he said, then switched gears when she sobbed harder. "We'll figure it out together. I don't think anyone really knows what they're doing when it comes to raising another person. It's instinctive, Cro-Magnon stuff. I'll fetch the meat and pelts, and you'll tend the hearth." She almost smiled.

"Where, in your apartment?" she asked, wiping her nose on her sleeve.

"Sure. Or we'll get a new place. We'll pick a spot of our own."

Hannah fell silent. Some part of her had always wanted to leave the silence and the water that frightened her with its ever-shifting surface. Hadn't she always envisioned a city somewhere, where she might open a café and spend weekend afternoons potting geraniums over a rickety fire escape? But in that moment, she realized that the land she'd been raised on pulled her still, drew her with its hazy mystery, its loon calls seeping into her morning dreams like a half-heard conversation.

And how long before the townspeople noticed the bloat of her belly? Who would be the first to push her to the ground?

"What if we went back to my house?" Hannah paused and considered her words. "It has more than enough room for three."

Callum frowned. "Is that really what you want?"

It was. "I'm not sure." Or she thought it was. The two were interchangeable for the moment. "Maybe?" She wanted her child to be born knowing the scent of oregano and patchouli that had seeped into the very wood of the place. She wanted to create the same sense of safety that Mae had forged for her.

Callum cupped her face and freckled her with wet kisses. "Maybe," he agreed.

CHAPTER
FOUR

At ten years old, while they made cookies one afternoon, Hannah had asked Mae about babies.

"What fool question is that? You're a child still."

Hannah shrugged. "I don't want one now. I just want to know what it's like."

Mae glared at her. "I suppose you already know where they come from. No good telling you tall tales about storks?"

Hannah dipped her finger in the sweet cookie batter and sucked. "I know a bit about it."

"Well, then, you know as much as me," Mae said, and slapped Hannah's hand away. "Have you washed those busy fingers lately?"

"Why did Christobelle give me to you? Was it because she didn't want me?"

Mae's jaw clenched, a hinge rocking back and forth. "Why, you don't like me anymore?" She let out a strained laugh.

Hannah ran her nail through the maze of wrinkles on a walnut shell, then stuck her hands in the pockets of her denim overalls. She waited.

"That woman experienced whole lifetimes worth of hurt. It's not that she didn't want you, but she knew well enough to know that she wasn't fit to raise you. She thought she was doing right by you, and frankly, I think we've done alright here, you and me." Mae fiddled with the metal clasp of Hannah's overalls. "Her actions aren't for us to understand, or to judge. The day will come when she'll answer for all she's done."

Hannah chewed her bottom lip, considering. "What about my father? Did she love him?"

"More than you can imagine, and losing him was more than she could bear." Mae ran the spoon, speckled with batter, under the faucet and scrubbed hard. Hannah had to step forward to hear her over the water. "Truth is, when the spirit world decides that things have run their course, you can't cite fair or unfair by our human standards. It doesn't work that way."

"So how did you get stuck with me?"

"Lord, child, you've got questions today. That's enough, unless you don't want dinner." Mae gestured to the fragrant pot of crawfish and pork-liver sausage, hot sauce belching out between pockets of rice.

"Please?" Hannah asked, knotting her fingers under her chin.

Mae rolled her eyes. "When I met you, you were still in

the womb. Your mother came to me because I had a reputation for midwifery." Hannah frowned and Mae waved her hand. "I helped women birth naturally at home. You were a real kicker, feisty even then. After you came, well, Christobelle trusted me by that point. She realized she couldn't take care of you properly, and didn't give much consideration to how much experience I had. Figured since I'd gotten the babies into this world, I could probably raise them, too. Come here." She jostled Hannah's collar into submission.

Mae's eyes were a deep earnest brown. New lines, thin as cat hairs, appeared each day, whiskering out from her mouth and eyes. "I know it's not a perfect life, but no life is." Hannah looked at Mae with her chin raised haughtily, knowing even then she was being told only a fraction of the story.

Mae stepped back and studied her. "And at least there are cookies. Get busy with those nuts."

Now, something stirred inside Hannah. Some *thing* because of how it writhed, clapping against the walls. It felt like a gator, rousing in the marsh of her belly. Callum rested his ear on her belly for a full hour, listening patiently, but there were only the stomach gurgles that preceded another bout of morning sickness.

Dr. Merrick, who'd given Callum his card at the hospital, had called to remind her of a scheduled check-up but Hannah refused.

"They said it looked like a healthy fetus," Callum assured her, but they wouldn't have known what to look for. The shadow of her mother's hand hidden in the oscillating black of her womb, the toothed mouth of a nightmare creature. "They need to make sure it's growing properly." Callum pulled her onto his lap. Together, they watched a wasp circle a honey-sweetened cup of tea. "Which I'm sure it is," he added quickly. "Dr. Merrick said you might be scared. Something about it suddenly being real once you see it."

"I know it's real. The pissing every hour was a tip-off. I'm so bloated I could take off my shoes and fly away."

"Do it for me," Callum cajoled.

"You'll owe me big for this," Hannah muttered, raising her right cheek for a kiss.

The hospital gown was lime green and left a visible sliver of bare skin in the back. While they waited for the doctor, Callum fiddled with the ultrasound machine. He lifted the probe from its holder and used it to nudge her thighs apart. "How much time do you think we have?" he asked, and slipped her feet into the stirrups as if she were Cinderella.

"Not much."

His face disappeared below the table.

There was a deep throat-clearing from the door. Dr. Merrick, clumps of white hair rising from his bald pate, closed the door behind him. "Condoms are in the drawer."

Callum smiled sheepishly. "I bet this happens all the time."

The jelly was cold as the doctor smeared it over her belly. "Let's have a look-see. Now, don't expect too much. This will be one of the less exciting ultrasounds. You'll hear a heartbeat and see something that looks a little bit like a crawfish curled up."

Callum settled beside the bed and braided his fingers with Hannah's against the cold metal. The room filled with the sound of a heartbeat, steady but submerged. "Is that it?"

"No. That's the mother's. Are you nervous, Hannah?" Hannah shrugged, and the doctor put a gentle hand on her shoulder. She felt safe then, a circuit closed by these two men touching her. "Don't be. There it is."

Hannah shut her eyes. Against the dark theater of her eyelids, she saw a hiccup of static on the screen, a moment of shadowed confusion. While the doctor fumbled with his machinery, Hannah would glimpse webbed feet and a long, tapered tail. Beady eyes affixed to hers through the thin skin of her belly, through the wavering screen of the monitor.

As soon as she'd begin to make sense of it, it'd be gone.

To her right, Callum let out a single burst of laughter. "That's wild," he said. She rolled her head to the side and looked at him. His eyes were wide. This was what a waking dreamer looked like.

The doctor squeezed her arm. "There," he said, and with a rough draw of breath, Hannah followed his finger. There, a little seed. Dr. Merrick punched her arm lightly in congratulations. "Healthy as can be."

It was real. Relief and fear rushed into her. Her speeding heartbeat echoed through the room. Her every experience of love had ended in pain, but now she let herself consider the possibility that she might be safe.

Callum ran the back of a finger under her eyes. She

hadn't felt the first tear, but he was ready and waiting to catch the second.

That night, Callum sat in bed and studied the sonogram they'd received.

"What are you doing?" Hannah asked, lying beside him.

"Imagining what it'll be." He illustrated how the shape might grow graceful dancer's legs or the hands of a pianist. With a dreamy swirling of his finger, he described the brain of a doctor who'd spend his or her nights poring over the intricate mutations that flowered into cancer and would awake one morning with the cure plain to see in the scribbles. Hannah could only look up into Callum's joyous face. *Our child*, she thought, still not quite believing.

Eventually, Callum's eyes closed. Hannah took the photo from his limp hands and studied the cloudy black and white. It was like a Rorschach. Blink, and it was a snail arching under layers of silt. Blink, and it was a seed uncoiling.

Something fell in the kitchen.

"Graydon, knock it off," she called out. A sleepy meow sounded from the corner of the bedroom.

She got out of bed, squinting into the darkness beyond the bedroom's open door. Callum snored below the covers as she inched into the hallway.

In her mind's eye, she could almost see the creature ahead of her, snouting the floor. Her hands closed into fists, although she wasn't sure how much good they'd do against its ribbed back. She'd seen it in bright sunlight and in the vague dark, but its reptilian muscles had rippled like a promise since she'd first glimpsed it as a child.

But what she heard was the fast patter of bare feet hurrying through the kitchen. "Callum," she cried out, almost exhaling in relief before realizing what the sound meant. "Someone's in the apartment."

"What?" Callum asked sleepily from behind her.

To her left, she caught a glimpse of a shape ambling awkwardly into the bathroom, white hair trailing like a puff of smoke.

"Someone's here," she whispered roughly.

Callum creaked on the floorboards behind her just as the woman burst from the bathroom, something glinting in her hand. She moved with shocking speed, and Hannah felt herself being pulled backward. Callum flung her behind him with such force that she fell onto the bedroom floor. As she lifted herself, she saw Callum wrestle the woman to the ground. A pair of scissors dropped from the woman's hand.

Callum turned on the hall light and stood over the woman, his chest heaving. Her dress was pushed up to reveal tangled threads of varicose veins. "Who are you?" he yelled at the woman. "What are you doing here?"

His fist hovered above her head, and Hannah wanted to call out for him to stop, but couldn't find her voice.

The woman's eyes rolled back into her head and she hissed two simple words, "We're coming." It sounded like wind circling through eaves.

"Who's coming?" Callum asked, punching the wall above her.

The woman slumped and said nothing more.

"Jesus," Callum breathed. "Hannah, call the police."

Hannah stood up in a daze. She dialed the number but stuttered over the words. "Someone broke into our apartment," she finally said. The woman wouldn't look at either of them, but instead stared steadily at the wall in front of her. Dimpled flesh hung in hammocks from her slender arms, and every so often, she parted her lips to show a toothless mouth.

Two cops with holstered guns arrived and hoisted the woman into a car, making note of the dropped scissors. "She's not talking, and I'm not sure I'd hold my breath waiting on her words," one of the cops said on his way out. "She might not be all there, you know? Do you want to press charges?"

Hannah shook her head and closed the door behind the cop. She was certain that it was the same old woman who she had bumped into in the street that day, who'd then bided her time. Hannah knew that she shouldn't be surprised. Her happiness didn't equate to safety.

Callum's shock, however, was obvious from the way he paced the apartment. "She came in through the fire escape," Callum repeated to himself, an echo of the cops' earlier verdict. "Why?" He directed the question at the room, rather than at Hannah. He stared at the spot where she'd dropped the scissors, as though that square inch of worn wood held the answer.

Hannah let him stalk the length of the apartment until she felt weariness sag her body, then gently patted the couch. "Come sit," she said.

He kept walking, still filled with nervous energy. "We're not safe here, obviously."

"No," she said simply, and something in her voice made him finally stand still. "I saw that woman in the street a few weeks ago. She must've followed me here."

Callum scratched his ear impatiently. "I don't understand. Why would an old woman do that? Why would anyone?"

"The town doesn't want me here." Hannah nudged a glass of wilting purple wildflowers back from the edge of the coffee table in front of her. *We're coming*, the woman had said.

"One crazy old broad bursts in and you think she speaks for the town?" His voice had an edge to it.

"One crazy old broad running at me with scissors, yes." Hannah shrugged. "Maybe her husband went with Christobelle," Hannah's voice rose as Callum shook his head, "or maybe it was her son. Maybe nobody she was even particularly close to, but I'd bet anything that it was a hatred of my mother that brought her here tonight." Hannah put her face in her hands and breathed in the sweet chamomile hand lotion that Callum had bought for her earlier that week. "No, that's not quite right. I won't bet this baby."

She didn't lift her head until she felt Callum's weight on the couch beside her. His arm clasped protectively around her shoulders. "So what do we do?"

In the early morning light, his skin looked waxy. She thought if he smiled in that moment, his face might crack. "We?" she asked. With that one word, she gave him a way out.

"We," he agreed, and touched her stomach. "The whole lot of us."

For several days, they ferried his life into hers by the swamp. Then a heavy morning downpour barricaded them in his dusty, mostly emptied home, and he laid a tattered red blanket on the floor. The rain brought sleep easily, but Hannah was startled awake by thunder. She rolled over to see Callum on his back, his eyes wide open, a vacant expression on his face. "Callum?" she asked, and felt an electric shock when she touched his chest.

Callum blinked rapidly and shook his head. "Sorry, I was spacing out. Guess it's just this sleepy weather." He reached down and massaged his right thigh. "In fact, my leg's still sleeping."

She plaited her leg with his, pressing her toes into his shin. "Is it all happening too fast?" she asked, giving voice to a fear that had plagued her for weeks.

He didn't answer and the stretching moment panicked her. "It's not the usual order of things. First comes love, then marriage, *then* the damn baby carriage, but that's a flawed schedule. Ask me, it's for cowards who need exits at every turn."

Hannah considered his words, then went back to the basics of childhood friendship. "What's your favorite color?"

"Green. Yours?"

Hannah closed her eyes and saw a deep maroon. She tried to describe it, but Callum wrestled his way on top of her. "The real question is, what's your favorite breakfast? I'm ravenous." He gummed lazily at her neck.

On the last day of the move, she sat on a tree stump by the water, watching bullfrogs bloat and belch while popping blueberries into her mouth.

"That's the last of it," he said, kicking a box of records. When she smiled, her teeth were black.

He approached her and peered into her mouth. "I've heard that women let themselves go after they've found themselves a man, but good God."

"I'm practically dating a pirate. I've heard you don't have the highest standards."

"Pirate?" he exclaimed. "Try expert navigator of these here dark waters. International waters, stern and bow, hull . . ."

"Even I know those nautical terms, Mr. Expert Navigator," she said, and yelped as he lifted her into his arms and walked unsteadily to the back door, declaring he had to carry her over the threshold.

Later, Callum made a cacophony of metal against metal in her kitchen drawers. "Where am I going to put all this stuff? Mae was so well stocked, there's barely room for me in this house. Could I try the shed out back?"

Hannah suddenly remembered what she'd seen in the shed, and even months later, it set her heart racing. "No, not in the shed," she said quickly. She toed a pot on the floor. "The shed's full of emergency supplies. Water, canned goods, things we'd need if we were ever stranded here."

"You have your very own boat captain now," he said in a booming voice, flexing his chest. "There'll be no more stranding for you, missy."

Hannah raised an eyebrow. "Oh, captain, my captain,

who can't use a pan to save his life." She plucked at a piece of plastic still wrapped around a frying pan.

"Pretty young women tend to find me when I'm hungry, and are more than happy to oblige." He fit her face between his hands and eased the scowl off her face with callused thumbs.

On her way upstairs, she stopped by his guitar stands and ran her fingers down the necks, frets like the ridges of a spine. She tried to pluck out a melody, but the sound came out wry and stilted, as if the guitars were mocking her attempts.

She'd never had a knack for music, and as had been the case during the last few months, the list of things she didn't know seemed to be growing longer. Knowing how to catch a frog and cook it, or how to pick out tarragon in a dish, had always seemed like enough for now. She'd toyed with a half-formed notion of going to college someday, but the thought of leaving Mae alone in the house had seemed unbearable. Mae had always listened patiently to Hannah's far-fetched plans, then gently changed the subject. Someday was transforming into a future with priorities she'd never imagined for herself, but maybe this was what it meant to live. An equation forged through the summation of choices.

Callum moved Hannah's dresser and desk into Mae's bedroom while she stripped the bed of its sheets.

"It's time to let go of her." Callum took the sheets from Hannah and stuffed them into a black garbage bag. "My sheets have seen better days, so let's just get new ones. I was thinking pirate ships," he joked.

"It's a waste of money." She'd always liked nestling against the daisy pattern after a powerful nightmare.

"I don't want to sleep on a dead woman's sheets. If you think about it carefully, I think the creepiness will dawn on you, too," he said, hoisting the bag over his shoulder. Then, seeing her smile shrink, he lowered his voice. "I'm sorry, that was glib. I wish I'd known her."

"She would've liked you, I think." Hannah squeezed the corner of a pillow as he pulled it from her hands. She watched it disappear into a black bag, and imagined several strands of Mae's hair going with it.

James visited with tools—"Some things Callum asked me to pick up"—and bagfuls of peaches and strawberries for her. He congratulated her on the pregnancy, hugging her tentatively and slapping Callum forcefully on the back. He looked different, softer, in khaki shorts and a blue polo shirt as he awkwardly handed her a bouquet of sunflowers.

"You know that bugs nest in here?" Hannah shook out the flowers gently.

"As long as they're not carpenter ants, they're welcome to join the parade of fat spiders and millipedes I've already spotted in this house," Callum called from the hallway.

She poured James a glass of iced tea as he looked around the kitchen. "We're still adjusting," Hannah explained, seeing the disorganized room through his eyes. She wasn't used to playing host.

"Looks good," James assured her, then added, "You're really doing this? The two of you together?"

"Stranger things have happened." Hannah halved a ripe peach and removed the fat black pit. She handed him half, then shrugged when he shook his head. "I wouldn't have planned this for myself. I thought twenty years old meant years yet to think about it."

James fingered a dried vine hanging from a hook above the sink and released the smell of herbs. "People say it always happens when you least expect." His eyes stalled on the melted candle on the windowsill. Hannah had found she missed their warming light, and it comforted her to echo Mae's habit of setting out candles at the beginning of each week.

"You think you'll stay in this house?" James asked.

"We're safer here than in town."

James sighed. "I heard about that. Mallory Thames was her name, if that means anything to you. We found a very expired driver's license in her pocket. She's been shipped off to a mental institution. The old bat kept babbling about things tying her to the bed at night, entering her body during the day. She used the old 'the voices made me do it' defense. Schizophrenic, must be."

"She scared Callum."

"Not you, though?"

Hannah flicked the black peach pit into the sink. "I'm used to it."

James stepped back to lean against the counter and sipped his iced tea slowly, deliberately. "I can promise we'd keep an eye on you in town, and I can give Callum the name of a top-notch security system. Ask me, I'm not convinced bringing a pregnant woman out to the swamp is exactly 'safer.'"

"And why's that?"

"Rumors," James said quickly. "You know, people

running their mouths. If the swamp alone isn't enough to spook you, then hell, crazy things come out in holding cells or in the drunk tank after a few hours of quiet contemplation. Men claiming they've seen or heard things."

Hannah snorted. "What? Voodoo in the swamp? Bare-breasted women bedding gators? Yeah, that's old news." She gestured around the room. "As you can see, it's just timber and brick like any other house."

James laughed, dismissing his words before he even spoke them. "I know, I know. I've heard from various entirely untrustworthy, drug-addled sources that this house in particular is special. They say it's easier to call on spirits here, that it's some kind of summoning ground. They call it a crossroads."

"Are you really buying into the boogeyman?" Hannah raised an eyebrow. "Okay, I'll bite. What kind of summonings?" Hannah was curious. As a child, she'd heard the townspeople's accusations and snatches of their stories, but when she came home, brooding over some new bruise and full of questions, Mae would dismiss their words. Eventually, after the bullying in town became unbearable, Mae had pulled her out of school and limited her contact to others who lived on the swamp. Others who, probably at Mae's prompting, knew better than to bring up Christobelle.

"I don't know," he muttered. "The locals claim the space draws spirits, that there have been hauntings. Others say that Mae had the ability to speak to orishas. They say that's the reason she was so skilled at medicine."

Hannah crossed her arms.

James's laugh was wooden. "It's not that uncommon.

Conjurers are a dime a dozen here, all claiming to work break-up spells or bring fortune, but that's just voodoo. The orishas are something else. Those who believe say that most people have to be initiated. There's a whole complicated process to follow, but some people are especially suited for it." He looked away. "They said Mae was."

Orisha. The word was exotic but strangely familiar, as if she'd heard it echo from some corner of the house while half-asleep.

Then the rest of James's words hit her. "Really, James, is this Salem? Say what you will about Christobelle, but how dare you speak about Mae like that? A talented nurse can't be just that, she has to be cavorting with spirits?"

James shrugged his shoulders and played with a cat-shaped magnet on the fridge door. "I'm not saying Mae hurt anyone, or ever intended to. People are unnerved by what they don't understand. She lived in your mother's house; she raised you. Have you ever asked yourself why?"

"I was a child," Hannah said, hating how her voice broke. "The only mother I ever really knew raised me in a good house, where we kept to ourselves. We laughed, we cried, and never wanted for food or anything else. Why here? I don't know. The woman who knew why is gone."

They both fell quiet as a gust of wind rattled the windowpanes.

"I'm sorry. Interrogating people is a force of habit, I guess." James cast her a sheepish look and held out a hand toward her belly. "May I?"

Hannah shrugged. "Knock yourself out, but there's nothing there yet to feel. I'm just your average chub."

"Leah was heartbroken when she heard about this,"

James murmured to himself. He cleared his throat. "She's liked him for what feels like a very long time."

Hannah pressed a nail into a soft patch of rot in the other half of the peach, smiling tightly. Jealousy filled her throat as though she'd swallowed the pit.

After James left, Hannah hopped up onto the kitchen counter and surveyed the room. Callum's pots were balanced in an unsteady tower in one corner, and a plastic bag filled with extra cutlery was in another.

She could hear him walking upstairs, stomping and huffing from room to room with his suitcase of clothes. Comfort was stoking a cautious fire in her chest. She resisted it, knowing now how it felt to be without it.

A clatter startled her and she looked down just in time to see Graydon jump away from the toppled pile of pots. "What's wrong?" Hannah asked as she slid off the counter and bent down to scratch behind his fear-flattened ears. She followed his yellow gaze to a hole in the wall that tapered off into slivered cracks at either end.

"It's just a hole, little one." As she crawled toward it, she heard Graydon hiss behind her. Gingerly, she touched her finger to the hole and instantly recoiled. The plaster was warm as a wound.

"What are you doing down there?" Hannah looked over her shoulder to see Callum smiling at her.

"What are you doing up there?"

"Enjoying the view," he said.

Hannah shook her head. "Maybe you should find another home for these pots. Graydon's nearly blind and senile, and sweet though he is, he won't pass up the opportunity to knock things over."

"Yes, ma'am. Right away, ma'am." Callum saluted her and filled his arms with pots. Smiling over his shoulder, he tossed them noisily into another black garbage bag.

"Not what I meant," she teased.

As light drained from the house, Hannah prepared dinner.

"What in hell is that?" Callum watched intently as she dropped chicken gizzards into a pot of broth.

"Rice tossed in with livers, onions, and spice. Dirty rice, because it comes out colored."

"Racist," Callum grumbled. She was aware of him fiddling with pantry doorknobs behind her. He paced restlessly, unscrewing the lids of jars, tapping the tops of cans, pestering Graydon with impatient pinches.

"God, would you sit still already?"

"I'm hungry," he said from behind her. A smile entered his voice. "My woman's taking too long with the food."

Hannah shook her head. Even the familiar motions of grinding black pepper and tapping out paprika over the meat couldn't quite calm her racing mind. She felt most at ease in the kitchen but wasn't used to being rushed. She wondered if the silence of the house was too much for him. It was an acquired taste. What would he be doing on a Thursday night in town? Any answer to that question would be very different from what she could offer. The smell of smoke pulled her out of her thoughts.

The livers were crisped to black in the pot. "Shit, it's burned." She took the pot off the element and considered the rice crusted at its bottom. "We could add some more broth, and maybe a bit of lemon. Try to make some soup?" she said, mostly to herself.

"Oh no. Not our dirty rice," Callum whined. "Here, let me scrape out the worst of it."

Graydon fretted in a corner of the kitchen, pawing at the hole in the wall then tensing. "Really, Gray, have you gotten into the catnip," Hannah began, then squinted.

The crack had grown.

"Go ahead and take out whatever's burned beyond repair," she said, handing the pot to Callum.

She knelt in front of the hole in the wall and tried to peer inside. The plaster was raised on either side, like the lips of a mouth. Beyond the edge, all she saw was darkness. She took a deep breath and hesitantly poked a finger into the hole. Feeling nothing there, she shimmied the rest of her hand inside.

"Jesus, woman, that's a slow way to escape."

"I only just noticed the hole this morning, and it looks like it's already grown. It must've appeared while I was gone." Hannah wormed her hand in deeper. She was almost wrist deep.

"Nothing just appears," Callum said. "Something must've thought the house was up for grabs. Out with it."

"Just a second." Hannah felt something tickling against the tips of her fingers. She could imagine a fallen nest, a baby bird birthed in the dank tightness between walls, its voice lost behind layers of insulation. "I think there's something in here."

"Out," Callum barked. "I don't want you getting rabies."

Her eyes widened as something writhed up her hand. She barely managed to pull it out before the biggest silverfish she'd ever seen, legs like a sunburst, squeezed through the hole and scurried under the counter.

Hannah stood unsteadily and faced Callum, who slapped his knees as he laughed. "Good God, you raise them big out here."

The sensation of so many legs moving along her skin remained like an afterimage, and she rubbed her arms to dispel it.

"There, now. I'll seal it up tomorrow. Now, how do you feel about blackened chicken livers sprinkled over a frozen pizza? You're in for a real treat. Trattoria a Callum."

Hannah laughed as Callum struggled to tie the apron strings around his waist.

Later that night, their muscles sore from lifting and rearranging, they made slow love in Mae's old bed. Callum's touch was sleepy, exploratory, and she responded in kind. She saw the muscles of his neck tense above her and realized that this was the first of many such gentle nights. That in less than six months, there would be a child. She gripped his face tightly as he came.

They lay tangled together afterward, and Hannah felt her body flinch as she slid into a half-dream. Callum stroked her hair, speaking words that she couldn't quite understand. His hand seemed to tangle in her hair, pulling hard. She heard a child laugh from below Mae's bed, and her heart jumped from a jumbled mix of panic and happiness.

It was too soon, she thought, and then: *it's here.*

When she tried to sit up, she felt a great, pulsing weight over her belly. She glimpsed the child from the corner of her eyes as it ran out from under the bed, but no matter how she tried to draw its attention, it wouldn't turn to show her its face. Instead, the child bent down to touch the head of the shadowed creature that lay with its belly low to the ground.

The white tail curled around the child's legs. The creature's eyes were filmed as if blind, but when its tongue reached out, it found the child's hand with the surety of sight.

"Darling," Hannah called in a quavering voice, "come to me." The child ignored her, running its hand over the walls. Then, Hannah noticed the walls. Something moved in the shifting shadows.

The child laughed again and moved closer to the wall. Hannah peered closer, and realized that they were silverfish, crawling atop each other. Hannah watched as the child pinched one of the flailing bodies and put it in its mouth.

Hannah tried to scream but woke up with a moan.

"It's just a nightmare," Callum whispered. Below the susurrations he breathed into her ear, she heard pattering across the walls. Hannah opened her eyes and saw them, black bodies carried like offerings atop their thousands of legs. She strained her neck trying to see past the edge of the bed, to see whether the creature was waiting, yellowed teeth ready for her tender skin. "Callum. Turn on the light."

"Hannah, honestly," he began as he flicked on the light, "there's nothing there. We're safe."

Hannah looked from his questioning eyes to the bare walls. There were no smears, no trace of a single silverfish. She sat up carefully, still sensing the phantom weight on her chest, but the floor was empty. "Just a dream," she muttered.

Callum drew a deep breath and lifted his arm, waiting until she was planted with her back against his chest.

Callum had filled the hole in the kitchen, but she'd noticed others. Smaller and shallower, but she could swear that they were all fresh, if only from the warmth that emanated from the split plaster. Callum sealed each, but by the fifth or sixth, he began to patrol the hallways, testing the wall with the heel of his boot. "House osteoporosis," he told her, frowning. "You know these walls. Have you seen holes like these before?"

Hannah shrugged. "I don't think so, but it's a century-old house, at least. Isn't this par for the course?"

Callum grunted and knocked on the wall. Hannah half-expected it to give way.

After Callum left for work, Hannah read, feeling unworthy of the luxury of time she'd been given. She had to admit that the earthy fragrance of moss and wet soil that wafted through the house's open windows relaxed her in a way the town's exhaust fumes never could, but her childhood home didn't feel as familiar as it once had.

Graydon slept all day, a furred tangle of twitching limbs. Hannah watched him as she lay on the couch and felt almost like she was imitating him. Too often, afternoons sped by as she sat cross-legged on the floor, sorting through the plastic bags of photos she'd found wedged behind old coats and sour-smelling blankets in Mae's closet.

She didn't recognize some of the people—five black

women, faces crosschecked by veils from their Sunday hats, arms around each other in front of a fountain. Young Mae beaming from a wedding photo, then in overalls, hoisted over the shoulder of the man from her wedding photo. Hannah struggled to think of him as her husband, just as she couldn't imagine this bird-boned girl inside the hardy, wise body of her Mae.

Finding a rare photograph of Christobelle was a shock, her profile against a blurred background of trees, a curtain of red-tinged blonde hair trailing behind her. The slanted light hid her face, mostly masking her features, but Hannah thought she could make out a smile. She wondered how well Mae and Christobelle had come to know each other, and then, with a shock, whether it was Hannah herself that had driven them apart.

There were dozens of photos of Hannah. In so many of them, she frowned at the camera, as if suspicious that anyone would want to commemorate such a plain face.

There was a photo of her riding a horse during her only trip to Texas, baby-fat face sunburned and peeling, as the beaten beast huffed around the ring. She'd hated it, the knotted muscles and cramped cartilage clicking between her legs, the coarse horsehair in her fist. And Mae stalking her around the wooden pen, the black Konica affixed to her face like an eyepatch.

The white border of a Polaroid caught her eye, and she pulled it out. Three over-exposed faces grinned up at her. Sarah Anne, Hannah, and the blank eyes of Sarah Anne's older brother. She ran her hand over Jacob's face, and felt static shock gathering in a fingertip. She tried to steady herself by lowering her head to the cool floorboards. Her body followed, and guilt weighted her like another body atop hers. Jacob's long-dead body.

She didn't get up until she heard Callum's feet on the stairs.

"What are those?" Callum asked, leaning over to kiss her forehead by way of hello. The photos fell from her hands and fanned out over the hardwood. "Any of you when you were little?"

"Trust me, you don't want to see those. I look like a brat, and not a pretty one. You're home early."

"I have a show tonight, and I wanted to check in with the old lady beforehand. I trust that's acceptable?"

"Sure is," she said, and took his hand.

He groaned as he pulled her up. "You're getting big. That son of ours is going to be a linebacker."

Hannah buttoned up his shirt. "You look vulgar," she said, and laughed as he stared openly at her growing breasts. "Can we go for a walk or something? I've been cooped up all day."

He squeezed her shoulder. "I know just the thing."

"You're quiet," Callum said, walking through the long grass a few steps behind her.

"You're quiet, too." Mosquitoes settled against Hannah's bare legs, piercing the skin. "Goddammit." She slapped at her calves.

"So this sullen silence is tit for tat?" Callum fit himself

against her back. He followed her like a shadow. "I thought you'd be happier, being back in the house."

"The mosquitoes have been driving me crazy. I've never had it this bad before. I woke up this morning and there were a dozen at least, sleeping on my legs like satisfied leeches." The humming had been constant for days. She shook her head, trying to dislodge it.

He pinched her back and brought up a still-seizing mosquito, his fingers red with a smear of her blood. "Stay close, then. You're my own private citronella candle."

"Happy to help."

"Should I try to guess what's on your mind?" he asked, his voice laced slightly with impatience.

Hannah sighed. "I'm a little bit mired in memories. Have you ever heard of the orishas?"

"Bits here and there," he said. "Superstition and stories from some of the older guys. This one drummer I knew a while back lost his leg by an alligator but got a souvenir. The damn thing left a tooth wedged in his bone. After that, he got involved with a strange crowd. He claimed that he started having these out-of-body experiences, and that he needed sex at the strangest times, but I saw him have one and it just looked like a bad bit of acid to me. He swore that he was being—what'd he call it? ridden, I think—by one of those orishas, but others who knew more about orishas and the traditions around them claimed it was disrespectful to say so. They got upset, said it was something else affecting him."

The open field seemed to fall quiet as he spoke. "What did it look like?" she asked.

Callum cleared his throat. "Nasty. I remember thinking he might've snapped, the way his eyes rolled back and his voice turned hard. He recited every damn ailment his body had, from a bum wrist to, and this is gold, a shrunken testicle. It took a few big men to subdue him, and even then, he just watched us with this strange smile. Some whispers followed us for a while, about devils and the like, but I never put much stock in it." He shrugged. "Why do you ask?"

"Have you ever felt like you know less about yourself than other people do?" Hannah brushed back her hair, and tried to smile. "I guess I've been thinking a lot about this friend I had when I was younger."

Callum growled in the back of his throat. "A boyfriend?"

"A girlfriend, actually." Hannah let the word hang in the air, realizing after she spoke it aloud that it was true. "Her name was Sarah Anne."

Callum scrunched up his eyes. "I'm picturing a curvy little blonde. Correct me if I'm wrong."

Hannah was silent.

"Now I'm picturing the two of you and a room full of pillows."

"Nicely done. She was blonde and very beautiful, a textbook cheerleader in the making. Her older brother, too, except he was a bit off. Had been his whole life, but moving here changed him. I've been running it over and over in my head, and I think there was something else wrong with him. Maybe he was possessed."

"I thought you didn't believe in that stuff," Callum teased her.

The last day Hannah had seen Sarah Anne and Jacob

was branded imperfectly in her mind, full of holes and confusion. She stroked her belly, struggling to center herself. There was no greater comfort than being fully known and accepted by another, but would Callum judge her as she judged herself?

"There was a fire at their house. A terrible fire." Hannah found it hard to say the words. "Jacob died. Sarah Anne and I were downstairs, and we managed to squeeze out through a window, but he was upstairs." She frowned at the field. The verdant patches stood out in contrast to the thirsty brown grass. "It moved so quickly that we barely got out."

"Jesus." Hannah could see the questions hiding in Callum's eyes. "How old were you?"

"Barely a teenager," Hannah whispered.

Callum whistled. "You must've been terrified." He pulled her into his arms. "But that was a long time ago. Why are you worrying about it now?"

"Because of those photos I found today, and because Sarah Anne's back in town. She came to Mae's funeral. A part of me felt like I was being reunited with my best friend, but a bigger part of me felt like she's a stranger. Funny thing is, I keep finding photos of her, like breadcrumbs."

"You should see her," Callum suggested. "It'd be good for you to get out with some friends. I know Mae kept a tight leash on you, but you can make choices for yourself now."

Hannah missed the easy intimacy of her friendship with Sarah Anne. Her life, and her body, was changing day by day. She'd grown used to Mae's good advice, and now that the woman was gone, she had no one but herself to rely on. "As much as I miss Sarah Anne, I feel like that night will always be between us."

"I'm sure she doesn't blame you. You were just kids."

So was Jacob. Hannah didn't voice her thought. Instead, she whispered, mostly to herself, "They said later that the fire started upstairs."

"You think he started it?"

"I don't know what to think. Never mind my rambling." She swatted at another mosquito.

"Hey, you're almost due for another check-up. Should I give Dr. Merrick a call?" He avoided her eyes.

He knew how she hated doctors, how frightened she was of the prescribed tests, although he didn't understand why, and she couldn't explain it to him without sounding crazy. What would she say? *I feel like I'm cursed. I feel like my very genes are barbed and deviant. Crazy*, she thought.

"Everything feels fine with the baby. I'm getting fat right on schedule, no more or less than expected," she said. "Soon I'll be wearing a muumuu, and then in a short few weeks I'll need you to cut a neck hole in a tent for me."

"You're beautiful," he said. "Truly. Now more than ever."

She shook her head, dismissing his words. She was growing rustic in her pregnancy. With the near-permanent blush on her cheeks and her newly broad hips and chest, she'd pass for a milkmaid.

"Hannah," he started, and exhaled. She could feel him fidgeting. He scanned the clearing and when he looked at her again, his eyes harbored fear. "I love you."

Hannah took an involuntary step back. The buzzing

of the mosquitoes filled her ears, making the silence seem longer. She'd yearned to hear those words from him, but now that she had what she'd wanted, she felt only dread. The most terrifying thing about love was losing it. The thought that it could crust and harden like honey in a jar.

She didn't know what she'd done to earn it, and so had no idea how to keep it.

Hannah tugged him by his belt loops, wanting to be transported away from the hungry mosquitoes and her aching body. She wanted suddenly to be back in those first, uncomplicated moments between them. To be able to make the choice to accept his love and love him back without being bound by pregnancy.

Callum cocked his head. "Hannah?"

He was waiting for a response, and she found that she had none. He looked down at her as if she were some perplexing stain he'd just noticed. As if he didn't know her.

"Let's head back," he said, disengaging.

"Sure." She sounded eager and false to her own ears. "It's too hot, and I want to shower before tonight."

"I didn't realize you were coming." He was staring at the ground, lost in thought.

"I haven't seen you play in such a long time."

"I'd love it if you came." Callum tripped over the words, as if hearing the echo of his earlier words. "I'm just surprised."

He turned around, his palm a visor over his eyes, then walked past her.

The bar was dim and loud, and Callum seemed fitful beside her. He rubbed his hands together like a fly.

"They're late," Callum said for the third time. Beside the stage, the bar owner waved at them, then gestured to his wrist. "Fuck. This is why I need an actual band. Nobody's ever going to take me seriously if I'm playing with amateurs who can't even manage to be on time for a gig."

Hannah stalled one of his hands in her own, and made an empty shushing sound. Leah paced in front of them, kohl-lined eyes shining. Her dark hair hung halfway down her back. She was taller than Hannah remembered, in a dark crochet dress that showed a black bra.

"They'll be here," Hannah said, tickling his palm with her finger.

He squeezed her hand then let go, downing the shot glass of tequila that Leah handed him. "They might not," he sighed and slunk away toward the stage.

Leah watched him go, then took his seat. "This has been happening lately. He hasn't been playing as much, so people are forgetting his name." So close, Hannah could see the girl's pretty lipsticked pout. "He's been busy with other things, I guess."

"Where's Tom?"

Leah's eyebrows rose. "Cal didn't tell you?" There was a note of delight in her voice. "Tom's on to Florida now. He thinks he might be interested in surfing. Writing about it, or something. It happens often around here. People come down, then pass through."

"You're sticking around." Hannah meant it as a question, but it came out flat.

Leah smiled. "I'm more serious than most." She glanced at Hannah's belly, the hint of a curve beneath her green dress. "You're getting far along, aren't you?"

"Day by day."

Callum appeared through a break in the crowd, his hair beginning to stand up from having been fingered so much. He motioned them over. Leah sprung up like a mouse trap and followed him with a whispered, "I'll take care of it."

Hannah settled back into the booth, trying to quiet a wave of unease. The smoke in the club stuck to her arms and neck, which were coated in bug spray. She stank of chemicals. Earlier she'd watched, unbelieving, as a fat mosquito had stalked gingerly up the sheen of her freshly sprayed arm, and feasted.

For a while, she was happy to try to make out the music coming through the speakers. *John Lee Hooker*, she thought, surprised to recognize the tune. One of Callum's favorites. She closed her eyes and hummed along, half-listening to snippets of conversations and the salvo of laughter.

A short-haired girl in a man's striped shirt tapped on the table and asked if the other seats were taken.

"Yes. Wait, maybe not," Hannah said, realizing Callum and Leah had been gone for a long time. "You can take the whole booth."

"Thanks." The girl smiled sweetly and waved to a group of teenagers behind her, their piercings glinting, as Hannah stood and surrendered the table.

Hannah circled the club twice. A young girl two-stepped with a white-haired man, her head bowed to follow his complicated steps. He chucked her under the chin. "Don't look at my feet," the old man chastised.

Hannah stood by the bar on her tiptoes, and a familiar grin shone at her like a beacon.

"You're Callum's girl," the man said with perpetual good humor. "I've been drumming with him for a while. I've seen you at some of our shows. Name's Stuart."

"Right. I'm Hannah," she said and took his offered hand. His wrist was thick with a garland of veins. "How's it going?"

"I was slated to be in the band tonight, but I just got the call from the rest of the crew and they're pulling out."

Hannah's heart fell. Callum needed this. More than money, more than the joy of playing onstage, he fed on adulation. The energy of the crowd satisfied a need that was separate from what she could give him. "That's awful." She sighed. "I'll go find him."

"Hey," the drummer pulled her back gingerly by the arm. "I know it's not my place, but Callum hasn't been looking too good."

"What do you mean?"

"He's looking skinny, you know? Like he's on edge. Is he into drugs again? I only ask 'cause I caught the tail end of it last time, and he had a hell of a time pulling himself out."

Hannah flinched. "How long ago?"

"A couple years. He had the same hungry look he's got now."

Hannah took a deep breath, trying to rein in her suddenly galloping heartbeat. "What drugs?"

The drummer fidgeted with his drumsticks, tapping

them on his thighs. "I'm sorry, but it's not really my place to say. You should ask him."

She searched the man's face, but it was guileless. "Thanks for the concern," she murmured, as the owner of the club came to stand beside them, nodding briefly at Hannah.

"The rest of your band never came. It really fucked us," he growled to the drummer. "Look, Cal's a good kid, plays a good solo, but y'all need to work out your schedules. I had to take back the advance. We've already had complaints."

Stuart sighed. "It's not his fault. This gig meant a lot to him. It's these young kids . . ."

"Don't matter to me. You're here, you get paid. You're not, fuck you, too."

"We could do a real stripped-down set? Just vocals, guitar, and my drums?"

"Something tells me Cal's not in any shape to carry a set right now." The man grimaced. "He's getting shit-faced with that girl out back. Ask me, she's bad news." Stuart cleared his throat, his eyes darting toward Hannah, but the club owner kept speaking. "She wanted to buy a bottle of tequila. That dumb bartender I hired last week saw a bra strap and handed it over. Now I have to fire him and that's another thing Cal's cost me. Last I saw they were taking turns sucking the last few drops from it."

Hannah moved through the graffiti-speckled hallway, past the kitchen, loud with Spanish curses and thick with grease smoke, and stopped at the open door to the back alley. She had to crane her neck to see them fully, lit by a car's headlights against the brick wall.

It hit her like boiling water, searing down her chest

and pooling in her stomach. She felt it sloshing there. Callum's hands lost in the nest of Leah's hair, their tongues fighting, an image that would never fade.

She said his name. Rap music rang out from a car in the parking lot and the sound of chatter squeezed out past her. But he heard her. He turned around and his mouth, moist from Leah's, quivered like a sound wave.

Hannah retreated wordlessly. She knew he would follow, even if Leah pawed pleadingly at his chest. She knew he would follow and she couldn't bear to look at him.

Their boat ride home was silent. Each time he tried to touch her, she struck him with a force that surprised them both. The moment the boat docked, she rushed off, almost tripping in the dark. She slammed the back door behind her and raced up the stairs into their bedroom, where she allowed herself to keen for several seconds. Even having seen it, she couldn't quite believe it. The image of them together seemed like a half-remembered scene from a nightmare. When she heard his steps outside the bedroom door, she rushed into bed.

He lay down beside her and she kept her gaze fixed beyond his shoulder, on the moon outside Mae's bedroom window. Months later and the room still felt borrowed. Some mornings, she still woke to the feeling that her feet had been warmed between old hands.

"It's not what you think," Callum said in a low voice and wormed his body closer. His hand clutched hers.

"You wouldn't know what I think," she answered.

"I can guess. Can you let me guess? She really is nothing," he began. "No, that came out wrong. Maybe there were feelings once, but they were never real. They don't even come close to touching what we have here. This," he said, tightening his grip on her hand, "is real, this is what I want. That was a mistake that will never happen again. All you saw was a moment of weakness and too much tequila."

"Is that all I saw?"

She waited through his silence. He was fitting together words in his mind, casting off the rotten ones, those that had been proven wrong. There were too many words, but still too few to balm the ache inside her.

"Yes, definitely. Say something," he urged.

Hannah shook her head in the darkness. She couldn't parse through all of her feelings. "Are you on drugs again?"

His hand released hers, then quickly squeezed it again. "How do you know about that?"

Anger throbbed through her, so strong that she felt it like an injury. Warm to the touch and red, across her breastbone. Anger that he would do this, anger that he would do this after having put a child in her. As she thought this, the anger became almost indistinguishable from fear as she touched her belly. It was the fear that kept her in the bed, even as she shrank back from his damp touch.

"Well, I certainly didn't hear it from you." Hannah turned her body into the mattress.

He gave chase, lifting up her slip, and pressing his thigh against hers. "Because there was nothing to tell. It was a rough time, but it's long over. It has nothing to do with this, with us."

They were two furnaces, drawing from each other. She felt mosquitoes crawling sluggishly along her skin, poisoned by the layers of bug spray but determined.

She swatted his leg away.

"You've been so distant," he began, and she stiffened. She heard him hesitating, cutting off words at the roots. "Sometimes I think you don't want this. Me, I guess."

"Because I didn't say it back? That I love you? So tonight was, what, payback?"

"You don't even want to marry me," he insisted, propping himself up on his elbow.

"I do," she hissed. "On both counts, I do. Just don't rush me. Can't you be patient?"

"Yeah, but don't write me off and don't shut me out. I'm sorry." His voice broke. "I'm so sorry. It was a mistake."

She turned her head and his mouth was waiting, a warm salve for her chapped lips. "There's something good here," and their lips were so fastened that although Callum spoke, the words seemed to come from both of them.

She pulled away from his mouth, and saw his wide, frightened eyes. "I don't know," she said, very quietly, and immediately knew it to be true. After several minutes of silence, he began to snore but she remained awake.

She felt with a sudden ferocity that she'd never really deserved this love to begin with, but still she was angry at having been fooled. And below the anger, shame. At her own dumb hope that her happiness might last. Happiness was meant for saints. Jacob's face, smiling and complacent, appeared before her eyes, a piercing condemnation.

"Come over and meet my friend, little bear." Sarah Anne had called from the foyer of her house. "He likes to hide." Sarah Anne closed the heavy wood door, inlaid with stained glass, behind them, then took Hannah's hand.

"It's okay." Nerves danced along Hannah's shoulders. "Let's not bother him."

"It won't."

"Sarah?" A blonde boy wearing faded denim and a long-sleeved tee appeared in the hallway. Hannah sucked in air. He was beautiful, otherworldly. His eyebrows and eyelashes were pale, which brought out the teal of his eyes.

"Jacob, this is Hannah."

Sarah Anne's brother, several years older and towering over them both, brushed a lock of blonde hair from his forehead. "Hannah," he intoned, by way of greeting. His arms, thick with fisted muscles, should have been hoisting Southern cheerleaders over his head. His arms were the sort that made old men revise their own histories, retrieve false memories of hunting and wrestling in the rain.

"Hi Jacob," Hannah said. Something flickered in the boy's face, as if he were a turtle at the bottom of a deep well, roused by a pebble.

Sarah Anne moved fluidly to her brother's side. "What have you been up to?" she asked him.

He moved away, and with a shrug, Sarah Anne followed him into the backyard.

The backyard smelled of freshly cut grass. A green and white striped patio set was planted in the middle and

Sarah Anne plopped down on the chaise, kicking off her shoes. Wildflowers were scattered along the fence.

"This is his favorite thing," Sarah Anne called back. "He's pretty good at it, don't you think?"

Jacob's work sat in the shade by the back fence, neatly ordered rows upon rows of carefully constructed birdhouses and birds' nests. "Wow," Hannah breathed.

Jacob sat down cross-legged in front of a large wicker dome. Rocking back and forth, he resumed building.

Hannah moved through the rows, resisting the urge to touch the structures. They were impeccable. Birds' nests more perfect than those that any bird, imprinted with the knowledge from birth, could ever make. Speckled eggs sunned themselves in some, and a squawk startled her. A starling unfurled its flinty, polka-dot plumes from a bed of straw. Three pale turquoise eggs sat beneath it.

"This is amazing," Hannah said.

Jacob squinted up at her, and chortled. The bird turned to him and chirped in response.

"Yup," Sarah Anne said, sounding bored. "We have a whole menagerie. Our parents are so thrilled." She clasped her hands behind her head.

Hannah leaned in close to the starling, holding out a finger. It opened its beak, and a daddy longlegs struggled to escape. She spun around slowly, seeing beaks open all around her like the vulgar lips of lilies.

"We're like a foster home for them," Sarah Anne said, knocking her knees from side to side. "We feed them, give them nests, and then they fly away. My mom calls it practice for when Jacob and I fly the coop."

Hannah stretched out a finger, dangling it over the

starling. Black eyes reared back in its head suspiciously as she touched its wings. They were soft and smooth, slightly moist. She shivered.

"How long have you had these?"

Sarah Anne yawned. "He's been doing it since we got here. My father's sort of impressed by it. I think he's got visions of architecture dancing in his head. My mother hates it."

Jacob braided wicker with quick fingers, his face calm and concentrated. At each errant chirp, his eyes scanned over the nests.

"Anyways, you'll be fine here, little bear," Sarah Anne said as she stood up and walked over to her brother. Her fingertips hovered over his head.

Jacob turned suddenly and grasped Sarah Anne's thigh with one large hand under the hem of her white cotton shorts. Hannah took a step forward then stopped.

"Stay," Jacob said. A private look passed between the siblings.

"We're going to get some ice cream," Sarah Anne said, pulling his fingers from her skin one by one. As soon as she was free, she trotted quickly toward the house. Hannah followed, sparing a backward glance for Jacob. He sat surrounded by wicker, his fingers lost between the wet red of his lips. His eyes, however, were lucid. Predatory.

In those days, Sarah Anne's great pastime was ice cream in the uneven shade by the river. Hannah watched as Sarah Anne licked the last bead of frothy ice cream from her hand.

"He breaks everyone's heart," she said. Her cherry-red toes bobbed in and out of the murk. "The other day, he turns to my parents and says, 'I'm sorry I won't be able to take care of you when you're old, because I can't have a job.'"

Hannah swallowed hard, a chunk of cookie dough still lodged somewhere in her chest.

"That's the worst part, I think. It's bad enough to be wrong in the head, but somehow so much worse to know it." She rolled up the cuffs of her shorts and rubbed the gooseflesh down. "As my mother always says, 'It is what it is.'"

"She sounds easygoing."

White birds swooped lazily from the willows. It was one of those beautiful moments, when Hannah could almost believe in the church of nature, in the holiness of light seeping through holes in the canopy as if God himself was punching through from above.

"Not when she's sober. My mother drinks," Sarah Anne said, and shrugged. "I figure I'll have that to look forward to. It runs in families, I've heard." Sarah Anne swallowed the last bite of her cone, arcing her neck back and gulping it down. "Do you want to go for a swim?"

Hannah shook her head.

"Come on," Sarah Anne goaded, standing up. She lifted her camisole up, flashing a sweet little potbelly ballooning from her ribs. "I'm bored, and too warm." Hannah could see the bright red lines of Jacob's fingers still on Sarah Anne's thigh.

"You have goosebumps," Hannah said, around a mouthful of ice cream.

"And you never take your clothes off. What are you

hiding under there?" Sarah Anne tugged at Hannah's cotton shirt. "I'll show you mine if you show me yours."

Sarah Anne pulled off her top and Hannah stared at her training bra, edged in white cotton lace, supporting two budding mounds. Hannah turned away, crossing her arms over a flat, unremarkable chest. "Suit yourself," Sarah Anne said.

Hannah listened to the stubborn shedding of clothes, the muffled whine when Sarah Anne touched a toe to the water, and then the loud splash. She glanced over her shoulder and stifled a gasp. Two more unmistakable hand spans, purple fading to a hurt yellow, marred Sarah Anne's back like wings.

Sarah Anne was frowning into the depths of the water. "What do you suppose is down there?"

"Lots of things. Garbage, clothes, vengeful spirits." Hannah leaned over the edge of the water and grabbed Sarah Anne's shoulders with a harsh "boo," but the other girl barely reacted.

"Do you really think there are spirits? That might leave the swamp?"

Hannah had seen women laughing as they walked on swamp water from her bedroom window. Men pulling fishing lures from their cheeks. A stark white alligator, following her always.

"There's bones, too," Hannah said, then clamped her mouth shut.

Sarah Anne made a sound of disgust. "What kind of bones?"

Hannah stood up and brushed off her pants. "Gator skulls, mostly. Birds and lizards. Maybe a horse skull or two."

Sarah Anne's face blanched and she moved carefully back toward the bank, her palms skimming the murky water's surface. "I had a horse once," she murmured.

"Have you ever seen a horse skull?"

Sarah Anne shook her head.

Hannah had. The day she'd first met Christobelle, she'd seen one hanging on the wall. Hannah only had to see it once, half-lit by the dim light sliding through filmy white curtains, to have nightmares for weeks. "You don't know what you're looking at, at first. There are holes for eyes and ears, but the rest is smooth like an anteater's face. The mouth and nose look like a beetle's jaw."

Sarah Anne splashed her. "Enough. Help me out."

Hannah offered her hand, resisting the brief urge to let go once Sarah Anne was braced against the muddy bank.

"You're so weird," Sarah Anne added, as she put her clothes back on.

Hannah averted her eyes, secretly pleased, and looked out over the bayou. What she didn't say was that she dreamt vivid dreams of human skulls lodged beneath several layers of mud and silt. Worked into the curve of a discarded tire, wedged under a rock by the tide or a strong boot. Whole skeletons could be constructed from what lay under the water—a humerus too small, too young, for wide shoulders, and tibias too long for frail knees. Somewhere down the factory line, a gator skull would fit perfectly into the hook and eye of a strong, lean spine.

"Hey, snap out of it." Sarah Anne's shirt was see-through where her wet bra touched it.

"Okay," Hannah said, and took a deep breath. "You have bruises on your back."

Sarah Anne gave her a flat look. "Jacob's strong. He doesn't know his own strength." Her fingers traced another faded curve of fingerprints between the dip of her breasts as though adjusting a necklace. Then she smiled slyly. "I knew you were a perv, checking out my body."

Hannah laughed. "If your mother could see you now."

Sarah Anne shrugged. "I'd say it was your bad influence." Her face was unreadable, her rosebud mouth as still as plaster.

CHAPTER
FIVE

Hannah placed slices of apple into a glass dish and sprinkled them with ground cloves. Every few seconds, she'd dip her face close to the fruit and sniff deeply. The smell of licorice and star anise was wafting from somewhere in the kitchen, below it the sure, sweet scent of something rotting.

"Something's spoiled," she muttered to herself and heard Callum stir over his pile of scattered papers on the table behind her.

They'd been circling each other warily. The previous night was still vivid in Hannah's mind. Every so often, she'd tried to understand his side of it, tried to put herself in his skin, but found she couldn't. And yet, if she searched herself, she knew her love for him was strong as ever, although cowed.

Throughout the day, she'd stood outside whichever room he was in, about to speak her mind. But what would she say? How would she explain that the sense of safety and succor that he'd given her was gone? He might tell her to grow up. Worse, he might be right.

"I'm thinking of selling the apartment," Callum said tentatively. "It'd give us some extra cash, to get ready for the baby."

Hannah slid the dish of fruit compote into the oven, then rubbed her swollen belly. She was still amazed at the firmness she felt there, and how the skin stretched to accommodate it. "You should."

"I could plant a pear tree out back here, and we could make jam. You could sell jars of it, if you wanted." They sounded like the words of a man gingerly trying to create a glossy vision of the future.

"I like oranges better. Besides, orange trees will grow better out here."

"Oranges, then. So, I'll be living here? Unless you'd rather I get myself a nice big appliance box and put down some blankets, park myself somewhere under an awning in town."

"Haven't you already been living here?" Hannah asked, breaking open an egg. Yolk oozed out through the serrated crack. "I could've sworn you have." The image of Callum and Leah together flashed in her mind like a rogue reel spliced into a film.

"I was also thinking about some additions to the house. Maybe add a little wooden wraparound porch? We could stick some rocking chairs out front and be proper Southern old-timers."

How many times had she wanted a place to read in the shade? She had a pleasing vision of herself in an apron, bending over as she served him sweet tea, but she wasn't ready to give ground. She tried to summon up the trust that had come so easily just days before, but found only a meanness that worried her.

"Have you given any more thought to what we talked about last night? Marriage, I mean?"

Hannah carefully worked a mound of fresh, ripe mozzarella against the grater. "As a concept?"

"Don't be evasive," he said quietly. She felt him behind her, his breath as slight as a butterfly's wings, and as strong as a gale. "I know we've been quick about everything, and I know I fucked up, but I want to know it's something we can talk about. Unless it isn't."

Hannah drifted, almost feeling the veil, edged in white rosebuds, outlining her satin-clad, rounded body. She imagined Callum standing tall and anxious in a penguin suit, beaming when he saw her. Her ring finger tingled, and she let it slip against the edge of the grater. "How can you ask me that right now? After what happened?" The words tumbled out.

"I'm so sorry. It shouldn't have happened and you have to know it won't ever again. Hannah, I'd take it back in a second."

The sizzle of the oil was deafening. She watched the egg solidify, and touched her stomach again. A deep, self-sufficient strength would be necessary to raise a child alone. Mae had it, but she couldn't count on having inherited it.

"Of course we can talk about it," she said, through gritted teeth. "I guess we should, eventually, for when the baby comes." The concept was still abstract for her.

He rested his chin on her shoulder and she smelled grappa, pungent and rich, on his breath. She wondered how much he drank, and how often, and remembered the drummer's words.

"Good. I just wanted to venture. Poke around a bit," he said, tapping the side of her head, "in this busy head of yours."

Callum's eyes were milky from a week of post-midnight shows, and she'd spied him massaging his head with a grimace. She wondered how often he'd snuck away with Leah when Hannah hadn't been around to stop him.

"This busy head is filled with some unpleasant images," she said. "It'll take awhile to erase them."

"I know," he said, and squeezed her waist. "However long it takes. You just have to keep talking to me."

She turned her face so it rested against his. It felt so simple to turn a bit more, run her lips over his soft beard. "Poke away," she whispered, inching her hips back. He rolled his head back and she watched his neck working, valves closing and veins pumping like a hydraulic machine.

He lowered his eyes abruptly and looked beyond her. "The omelet's burning."

"Shit," she muttered, flicking the stove off. "Can you take the ice cream out of the freezer? It's a weird dinner, I know." She squeezed her legs together, dampening frustration.

"One day, we'll stop burning food, I promise." His lips

on the small of her back made her whole body convulse. She broke out in goosebumps. "I can take the ice cream out," he conceded, and lifted her skirt.

The next day, affection came easier, at least outwardly. The day after, Callum skipped a show, and massaged her feet as they sat on the couch and played cards. Time healed wounds, Hannah realized, or at least scabbed them. The trust was still gnarled, like a tree grown wrong after a lightning strike, but it held. With each day, Callum's small kindnesses warmed her heart and even coaxed her into returning them.

"I can go get groceries," Callum said, his head hidden under the kitchen sink. "Just let me tighten up these pipes."

Hannah shook her head. "I'm stuck in this house all day, every day, while you get to sail the whole damn South. Let me."

"You're supposed to lie supine while I feed you grapes and fan you with palm leaves."

"Nine months of that sounds like prison. I need to get out a bit."

"Want me to come with?" he asked, sitting up.

Hannah gathered her purse against her chest in answer. Callum's sleeves were pushed high over his elbows, his face flushed. A Band-Aid dangled from one of his toes. "No. I want to come back to this, to you looking just like you do now."

But the closer she looked, the wearier he seemed.

Bruised half-moons hung from his eyes, and even his lips were white-tinged and parched. *Serves you right*, she thought, thinking of them moving against Leah's iridescent mouth, then regretted it.

"Have you been sleeping okay?" she asked.

He scratched his arm. "Not the best, no. I've been having bad dreams."

"What about?"

"Oh, you know," he said lightly. "Losing you."

"You haven't yet," she said, and kissed him gently on the forehead.

The back of the house sloped quickly onto marshlands, while a saunter out the front door showed woods, broken up by the occasional road or grassy clearing. Beyond the miles of trees and wet sod were other houses that valued their privacy and wanted for little. They grew what they could and took the boat into town for what they could not. The small stretches of crops were well camouflaged by the greenery, but fat Creole tomatoes winked through wire cages, and she spied the copper hue of sweet potatoes, unearthed by some animal, under green leaves.

The path to the main road was easy to find amidst the yellowing grass, and she touched the landmarks as she passed them. An old cypress with a deep gash in its side, a toppled fence with neon piping tied around the fence posts, a fallen tree that had been hollowed out by wildlife.

She thought of the first time Mae had led her up the trail, holding her hand, Hannah's eyes fixed on the backs of Mae's taut calves. Bold yellow flashed between the green then as now, and Mae had taught her how to spot Cercosporidium blight on Leyland cypress trees.

"Blight is right," Mae had said, stroking the rotting wood. "It becomes pandemic. The fungi travels through airborne spores and affects the lower branches first." Wherever her fingers touched, the sickly yellow needles fell like rain.

Almost immediately, she thought of the last time she'd crossed the fence for Mae, and felt an irrational pinch of panic for Callum.

A branch cracked to her left and she jumped.

"Just me," Martha said, her braid flipping back as she pulled a canoe down the wooded slope. "Can you help me put this in the water?" Martha dropped the rope and fit the paddle into the hull.

Hannah took a step forward, then eyed the exposed roots. She rubbed her belly. "I'm not sure I should."

Martha's eyes widened as she followed the movement of Hannah's hand. "Since when?"

"About three months."

Martha stepped forward, her arms extended, and Hannah sunk gratefully into the older woman's arms. They'd always been a poor substitute for Mae's, but Martha knew where to circle her palm to ease the knots in someone's back. She cupped Hannah's head as though supporting a baby's, and Hannah smelled fish and ginger on the woman's neck.

"Sweet child. Congratulations." She pulled back and pursed her lips. "Who's the father? I hope you know."

Hannah blushed. The woman had known her all her life, and had steered Hannah in her straight-talking, fisherman's way. She found that she feared Martha's anger, which was legendary for being so rarely seen. It was solemn, unbending, and filled with that worst of adult feelings: disappointment.

"The father's Callum. You would've met him at Mae's funeral. He ferried people over." Hannah bit her lip.

Martha raised her eyebrows but only said, "That was fast."

"Would she be cross with me?" Hannah asked.

Martha shook her head, chuckling. "No, child. You've got to be careful who you let into your life, but he's handsome and looks to be strong-armed. There are far worse ways to make a living in the bush than driving a boat. You just make sure he's got an even temperament. I cooled real fast on my ex after a few months of his ups and downs." Martha winked at her. "Good for you, but why are you out in the woods where you could trip on any damn thing?"

"I insisted."

"Do me a favor, honey." Martha leant in. "Insist less. Come on, this can stay here for a bit. I'll walk you back."

"We need some things for dinner," Hannah said. "Please, I want to go."

Martha looked sideways at her, then sighed. "Far be it for me to try and tell you what to do. You're nearly a mother yourself now, and I remember how restless I was in those final months, being trapped in the house. Be careful and be back before dark." She gathered the rope in a fist and hoisted the paddle under her other arm. "Mind me, child."

Hannah nodded and waved. She stood in place until the red canoe was swallowed by the general green.

When she reached the road, the sky was darkening. Hannah had the sense of being watched, although she knew to expect the eyes of birds and crickets and maybe even young bears that couldn't help but mark her passage. She whistled softly under her breath to distract herself, some half-remembered playground rhyme. The wind picked up as if in answer and bent the trees down toward her. She glimpsed it then, a swipe of white in the dark woods.

Hannah whistled louder and fixed her eyes on the road ahead, walking faster. In the silence between breaths, she heard a tree groan. *Look ahead,* she commanded herself but her shoulders trembled with the effort. The road seemed to lengthen before her.

There was a noise behind her, like teeth chattering, like a tongue clapping against the roof of its mouth. The sound was sucked from the woods until all Hannah could hear was the clicking.

Hannah. The two syllables stretched out through the hush, and she sped up. The voice repeated her name, and Hannah nearly tripped. It was patient, amused. She spotted a fence, half-hidden in a high bush, and steered toward where the house would be. Branches rose up to meet her, slapping her arms and face. Adrenaline numbed her to the sting. She ran the few feet to the clearing in front of the house, where she could see a group of four men sitting around a spit of meat. The smell was unmistakable.

She burst into the clearing, trailing ferns torn from their roots. *Go,* it whispered in her ear, then the sound tapered off. The men looked up from the fire pit.

"Can we help you?" Richie Lardeau asked, sluggish with whiskey.

Hannah smoothed down her hair and managed a smile. "I was looking for Doug. I guess I took a wrong turn."

"You sure did," another man offered from a striped lawn chair. His heavy cowhide boot was resting casually on the decapitated head of a large alligator. "Doug's three houses west of here."

Hannah inched forward. The men scanned her bare legs, studied her breasts, and she stepped into their scrutiny, away from the patient watcher behind her. Its gaze bored into the back of her head, with an itch that felt like larvae stirring along her scalp.

"What'd you need Doug for?" Richie asked, coaxing the embers with an iron stake.

"Some berries," she said, her voice faltering. "Maybe some eggs."

Richie smiled benignly at her. "Jodi!" he yelled, his eyes never leaving her face.

"What?" a woman's voice called from the house.

"Be a peach and bring this nice lady some eggs."

There was a silence. "We barely have half a dozen." Then, "What lady?"

His smile widened, pristine white teeth winking at the corners. "Jodi, honey. Be a peach." Each word fell from him like venom.

Another man rose unsteadily from a lawn chair. He pulled off his baseball cap and silver strands tumbled loose above thick glasses. "It's Hannah, Jodi," he called into the house. "You all remember Hannah." The men looked to him, expressions confounded by alcohol. "She lived with the black woman. Child of the cultist. Yes, sir."

Imogen Jarrod had hunted alligators for decades, and

was known for his vicious killings. Hannah remembered him. Eleven and shopping in town, she'd heard Mae cry out and a gaggle of sour laughs rise up around her. Mae had bent over in the street and picked up something white and wet. Imogen had been sitting in the back of a pick-up truck.

"I've got my eye on you," he'd said, pointing at her with the alligator's other eyeball.

Hannah shrunk back from him now. Muscles still flexed under his tan, wrinkled skin.

"You consort much with your kin these days?" Imogen peered at her with his obscenely magnified eyes. "I bet y'all just visit each other in the night, riding on broomsticks."

"Can't say I've ever had the pleasure," she said with bravado she didn't feel. The smell of gator flesh was rising.

"Let me tell you something, girl. I've been living in this parish since I was born. That's my grandfather's house behind me. My brothers left for Baton Rouge when they were teenagers, but I took to this life easy enough. It's quiet. It's decent. Folks know to leave other folks alone." He squatted down over a dead alligator and, keeping his bug eyes fixed on her, dragged his knife through its belly. "Most folks, that is."

Hannah's hands fluttered as they moved to cover her stomach and her mouth.

"And then," he continued in a low voice, "your bitch of a mother comes along with profane ideas. Things have been different since. And I'm not just talking about those fools that go straight to her. She showed up and we had three men killed by gators. Three, when we hadn't had any in years. One of them was my nephew."

"I'm sorry about that," Hannah mumbled. "But I don't know anything about it." Jodi appeared in front of the house, shielding her eyes. She held a carton.

Imogen rose, all the fat stripped from his old body, and strolled toward her. The knife hung from his fingers. "I'm sure you are." He lifted the knife and sniffed it. "Gator blood smells a little different, a little sharper." He looked around at the men. "Others kill them with a bullet behind the eyes, but I'm getting up in years, and I don't have the steady hand to find an alligator's pea brain. You feel it more, when you use a knife."

Hannah knew the scent. Old alligators would some-times drift up to the bank behind the house and smaller prey would set upon them, chewing wildly as if knowing this inversion of the natural order was temporary.

"That's enough, Im," Jodi said, slapping him lightly on the back of the head as she passed. "Here. Three's all I can spare." She wrapped an arm around Hannah's shoul-ders and turned her toward the woods. "Say goodbye now, y'all." Then, in a lower voice, "They've been drinking since noon. You know how it is with men when you get them in packs over some roasting meat. They get like wolves."

Imogen called out, "Stay on your own goddamn land."

"Thank you for this," Hannah whispered to Jodi, clutching the near-empty carton.

"No problem." Jodi let go of her at the edge of the trees and cast a cursory look into the deep shade. "You better get home quick before the sun goes." She shook her head. "I hate these goddamn woods. They spook me just about every other day."

"Do you ever see things? Out in the trees, or on the

water?" Hannah whispered. Leaves shivered like feathers. The whole tree line a sleeping bird, with claws made of roots.

Jodi blinked. She pulled the elastic from her short dun hair and fanned it out around her ears. "Oh, sure, but it's just your imagination playing tricks. The sorts of things you see with your mind's eye. But these old eyes explain it all away."

"Have you ever seen a white gator in the woods?"

Jodi's eyebrows rose. "A white gator? Who ever heard of a thing like that?" Then she squinted into the trees. "But you know, the land here's always full of surprises. You can never be too sure what it's going to spit up from day to day."

Richie whistled from behind. "Thanks for the visit. If you women are done clucking, the gator's nearly smoked. Lady, you'll understand if we don't ask you to stay."

Jodi shoved her. "Go on, lucky duck."

Hannah stumbled back through the woods, walking quickly. As the shadows gathered, she noticed how many hiding places there were for something ill-intentioned to lie in wait. Each snap of a twig made her heartbeat race.

By the time she finally arrived at the house, she was soaked in sweat and almost wheezing for breath.

"Good God, what's wrong?" Callum cried when he saw her. He sat her in a chair and fanned a newspaper over her warm skin. "What's happened?"

"Just got spooked," she said shrilly, and leaned on his shoulder. She massaged feeling back into her fear-numbed legs. "I thought something might be following me." Her words sounded ridiculous to her own ears. "Never mind me. I feel stupid."

"You are," he said, soothingly. "You're stupid to go headstrong into the same woods where you told me alligators make their dens, but I'm the bigger idiot for letting you go. I hope you know I won't be making this mistake again."

"It's fine," she said. "Really, it's nothing."

He opened the carton and shook his head at the eggs. "Well, we needed everything from carrots to bread, and you came back with three eggs."

"I know those woods well enough to walk them in the darkest night, but somehow I got turned around." She willed her hands to stop quaking. Graydon hopped up on the back of the chair and nudged the nape of her neck. Slowly, her breath became even.

From that day on, Callum took over all the chores that required traveling any significant distance. As summer set in, Hannah planted herbs behind the house and sometimes sat cross-legged in the dew-wet morning shade amongst them, sniffing deeply, wondering if this would be the baby's first experience of chicory and basil.

Hannah was heating tomatoes in a skillet one afternoon when she heard the sound of a large motor coming toward their dock. Her stomach sank as she saw Samuel rise from a boat.

She said a small prayer of thanks that Callum was out, that the two halves of her life could remain separate for a while longer, and waited in the back doorway as Samuel hobbled toward her.

"Why are you here?"

"Don't be tiresome, child." Samuel spoke in a low voice. "She hasn't been feeling well. She wanted to speak to you. Where should we put her?" He rose on tiptoes and peered past Hannah into the living room. A stack of fresh laundry teetered on the edge of the sofa.

"Wherever you please, but get on with it."

"She was hoping you'd come to her, you know," Samuel said.

"I know," Hannah said sharply, and kicked off her slippers. "But I hoped if I waited long enough, she'd forget about me."

Samuel's mouth tightened. It pocked his cheeks into craters. "You'd best respect your mother—"

"Do something or don't, but do it quick. I have my own chores to look after."

His oily eyes still on her, he raised a hand into the air and gestured behind him. Christobelle was pulled gingerly from the boat by three solemn men, and Hannah saw that her mother had shrunk alarmingly. Her linen shirt hung off her body, and her long skirt was fastened around her waist with a worn leather belt. Even in the heat, she clutched a scarf tight against her neck. Christobelle suddenly doubled over and Hannah saw a thin line of spittle fall from her mouth.

"Not a word, child," Samuel warned.

Two of the men half-carried her into the house, while the other waved a newspaper to fan her and knelt to remove her shoes. "Never mind that," Christobelle muttered.

For the first time in a long time, Hannah felt unafraid. She led them into the living room, then planted her feet firmly and imagined she was an oak tree, bred to with-stand. "Set her down there," Hannah said, gesturing to the couch.

There was fussing for another minute punctuated by groans and coughs, all done so quietly that if she closed her eyes, Hannah could almost imagine it was some house down the street being eclipsed by her mother's presence.

And then there was perfect silence, and a tableau. Her mother in repose, her feet neatly side by side beneath the hem of her floor-length violet skirt, and the men standing around the perimeter of the couch like fence posts.

"Well then," her mother said, smiling with effort. "Is there lemonade?"

Hannah crossed her arms over her chest. "Samuel, would you?"

He blinked. A squawk of air left his mouth. He met Christobelle's eyes, which narrowed at him.

She shrugged. "My daughter and I have things to dis-cuss. You might make yourself useful. The rest of you should go by the water and cool yourselves."

They bowed their heads and sidled out of the house, squeezing past Samuel. Their blind obedience unsettled Hannah.

"There's a jug of iced tea in the fridge," Hannah said evenly to Samuel. "Lemons are in a bowl on the counter. There's no ice, but you could make some." She unwound her apron strings, and webbed her hands over her belly. "Depending on how long you're planning to stay."

Her mother stared fixedly at Hannah's hands, eyes boring into the bump beneath them, her expression filled with appetite. "Child, your temperature's high."

"It's summer. Not all of us are blessed to live in the shade of half-life."

Her mother's mouth twisted into something like a smile. She stretched out her legs and played demurely with the hem of her skirt. "Today the shade's thin."

Hannah sighed and pulled a magazine from the pile under the coffee table. She sat across from her mother and fanned her halfheartedly. "Samuel mentioned that you're not feeling well?"

Christobelle scanned the living room and paused when she saw the guitars set on their stands. The woman's hair had grown in unevenly since the last time Hannah had seen her, and she spied bare scalp beneath the mix of strawberry blonde strands and icy-white tufts. "I've been feeling a bit faint lately. I've had to extend myself further than I'm accustomed to, but it's nothing for you to concern yourself with." Her eyes closed against the meager breeze. "I waited, thinking you'd come visit me. Hoping that you'd have questions now that Mae is gone."

"Visiting is for people who have relationships," Hannah said coolly. "As we don't, I didn't think it'd be appropriate, although you seem to disagree."

"This was my house, child," Christobelle said. "Don't forget that you're only living here because I granted it to you. Besides, you're barely of age. I was concerned."

Hannah remembered studying her profile as a child. The same feline cheekbones sat before her now. They had the straight, stately nose in common, and a deep basin above their mouths, but her mother's lips were thin and tinged in purple. She touched her own hair now, wondering if the woman's bald spots, white scalp like bone under fur, lay in her future.

"But the house isn't the reason for my visit," Christobelle said the last word deliberately. "I've heard things. All manner of things."

A pair of Callum's boxers hung off the edge of the couch. Hannah moved to hide them, then shifted back, reminding herself that she was a grown woman. Her life and her body were hers to do with as she pleased. "Which side was talking?"

"Both," Christobelle said. She watched Hannah with unfocused eyes, but Hannah felt that if she tossed an orange from the bowl on the table at the woman, a strong hand would whip up to catch it. "The living are usually less reliable, but when both sides come together on a story, well, there's not much wiggle room."

"Why have you come?"

Christobelle looked pointedly at Hannah's belly. "That's a stupid question."

Hannah patted her stomach. "I thought your business was death." She was surprised to see a bead of sweat grow at the edge of her mother's nose. The woman's touch had always been arctic. The sight of sweat on Christobelle's skin, and the blush rising above her scarf, were unusual.

"Right now, my business is you. Who fathered the child?"

Mae had told her little about Christobelle, but she'd always implied that the woman had an omnipotent knowledge of Hannah's life. Hannah had grown up with the sense of being watched from a distance, which was infinitely worse than being watched from proximity. There were no corners to hide in.

"I would've thought you'd know all about him, being so well informed."

Christobelle massaged the knuckles of her left hand. She ground her teeth in even, measured spurts. "He's hidden from me. Veiled." The room filled with the aching sound of enamel flaking away.

"I appreciate the concern, but it's none of your business."

"It is precisely my business!" The yell was masculine, enraged, and Hannah shrank back.

To calm herself, she pulled a few socks from the laundry basket beside the couch and began pairing them. "Callum. You might've seen him at Mae's funeral."

"The blue-eyed man? The light-haired one?"

"That's him," Hannah said, rolling her shoulders. "He's a good man. He's taken good care of me."

"I see feathers," Christobelle muttered under her breath as she rubbed her forehead. "Only feathers around you." She squinted around the room as if seeing it for the first time.

"Anyways, there's been talk of marriage, but we're taking things as they come. We agree there's no need to rush into things. We're happy here."

"You're going to keep it?"

Hannah tossed the balled up socks aside and stood up, her hands clasping around her elbows. Although in her darker moments, she still sometimes wondered if she'd made the right choice, the idea that she might not have kept the child, now that she'd grown used to the heaviness inside her, felt foul. "Of course."

"That's a mistake." Christobelle spoke slowly. "It will weaken you. It will come out wrong, child, if it comes out at all."

"My baby is a mistake," Hannah repeated in a flat voice.

"You cannot imagine the sacrifice it took to bear you or the effort to protect you all this time. At least I had Mae to bolster me. I fear it will be the same for you, and you need your strength for yourself. "

Hannah plastered a smile onto her face. "Samuel," she called into the kitchen, "time's up."

Christobelle spoke over her, intoning each word carefully. "You are my child. You are my blood. You can ignore it, but you cannot avoid it. Things transfer."

"I'm nothing like you," Hannah said, her smile tightening.

"They are gathering around you, child. You're wide open, and lit up like a flame. If you cannot control it, they will consume you—" Her hand lashed out, palm straining for Hannah's belly, and her irises disappeared upwards. The whites of her eyes were tinged with yellow. She chanted in a low voice.

Hannah backed away. Hissing came from behind her and she turned to see Graydon, his old teeth gnashing. She rushed down the hallway on unsteady legs. "Out," Hannah called. "Right now." Christobelle's incantations still came in whispers from the living room. "I want you out."

The men lined up in front of the door, expressionless. The youngest was in his teens, his unlined skin hanging loose from a skeletal face. Hannah couldn't assign an age to the oldest, whose back stooped like a grandfather's.

"Go and get her," she said to the men, but they continued to stare straight ahead, frozen like wax statues.

Samuel and Christobelle materialized in the half-light, their arms wound together. Hannah looked away as they passed by her, but her mother's sharp-boned hand closed around Hannah's chin and swung her head around.

"I could stay, child," Christobelle whispered, her breath musty as swamp water. "This is still my house. But I'll go, because I'll relish it more when you come to me. And you will." Hannah wiggled in her mother's strong grip as her face came closer. Between words, her tongue wiped the front of her teeth. "Do you remember Jacob?"

Hannah flinched. Her legs began to shake, her own body's weight suddenly too much. Christobelle leaned close and licked the palm of her hand, her tongue flicking up over several fingertips. Before Hannah could stop her, she pushed up Hannah's shirt and ran saliva-wet fingers over her stomach. A long line down, and a shorter line across. "You are not alone," she whispered as Hannah pushed her away and all the men exhaled in unison, a scent of sweet rot lingering briefly in the air then dispersing.

Hannah stood in the open doorway, wiping her stomach, long after the boat disappeared beneath the trees. She tried to understand Christobelle's words, but what made her heart pound was that somehow her mother had known about Jacob. Her greatest shame.

Sarah Anne's bedroom had been blindingly white, and a blown-glass vase on her nightstand held a bouquet of yellow roses. At home, Hannah's own dingy striped blanket was smeared with peach jam and cornbread crumbs.

"It looks impressive, doesn't it?" Sarah Anne asked wryly. She ran her hand over the top of her dresser and showed Hannah her clean fingers. "They have a maid clean it three times a week. My mom's a little bit obsessive compulsive when it comes to the house. She feels weird about being a stay-at-home, but really, what else could she do? Bag groceries in town?"

Sarah Anne pulled out a thick hardcover book of fairy tales. "My mom likes to pretend she doesn't drink, so she chose our maid very carefully." She cracked the book's spine to reveal a cutout chamber with a large rectangular flask inside where the pages should have been. There were worn initials carved into it. "She doesn't snoop."

Hannah shot her foot out behind her to close the door.

"It's absinthe." Sarah Anne ran the open flask under Hannah's nose. The fumes made her head spin. "I met a boy in town who gives me a bottle every once in a while. When he doesn't come through, I fill it with rum from the cabinet downstairs."

"What does he ask for in return?"

Sarah Anne raised her eyebrows and took a small sip. She wiped her mouth daintily and smacked her lips. "Nothing too scandalous." She handed the flask over and Hannah tipped it into her mouth. It tasted a bit like anise and she felt a thrill in her pelvis.

"I've never really made out with a boy before." Hannah sat on the bed, running her hand over the silky cotton. A year back, there'd been a pale boy with glossy hair who had offered her a crown woven from cattails, but they'd gone no further than a wet, uncoordinated kiss that had left her feeling anxious.

Sarah Anne hopped onto the bed, covering the opening of the flask with her thumb, and crossed her legs. "Why not?"

Hannah avoided the question. "Why do you do it?"

Sarah Anne took another long sip. "It's fun. It gets me things, but I wouldn't do it if it wasn't fun." Hannah flinched as Sarah Anne's nails touched her cheek. "You really are pretty," she mused. Ignoring the jerking muscles in Hannah's face, Sarah Anne pulled a tube of lipgloss from her pocket and ran it across Hannah's lips. "Smack for me," she instructed, and Hannah tasted synthetic strawberries. "You have an unusual face."

Hannah grabbed the flask. "Unusual. Exactly."

Sarah Anne ran a finger down one of her pin curls, straightening it to its full length. She studied its crisp, slightly frayed end. "It must be nice, not trying so hard all the time."

Hannah took a long gulp of the absinthe and her shoulders slumped. It made her giddy even as it sapped her body of strength, and the rain began to fall in a soothing rhythm, turning the world outside to watercolor.

Sarah Anne yawned as she rose to close the curtains. The darkness was immediate.

"The rain always makes me so sleepy." She punched Hannah's leg. "Scoot over." Hannah sat clutching the flask as Sarah Anne fidgeted out of her skirt and lay in bed. From the corner of her eye, Hannah saw long tanned legs crossing and the fading yellow splotches high up on the thigh. "Are you going to have a nap, too?"

Hannah looked around the room. Shadows swam across the walls. They looked like wingspans, extinguishing the light. "What about your brother?"

"He's fine. He can entertain himself."

"Don't you ever worry, leaving him alone?"

The silence prompted her to turn around. Sarah Anne was staring at the ceiling, biting the inside of her cheek. "Jacob is much stronger than people think. Sometimes I think the rest is an act he puts on to be left alone, and I—I almost understand it." The corner of her mouth was wedged between her teeth. "Look under the bed."

Hannah leaned over the edge of the bed and glimpsed a dark pool of shadows, and a spider dangling from the bedframe. It seemed out of place amidst the perfect order of the bedroom. When she lifted the bedspread, it dropped onto the floor and scurried away. "Why?"

"Look."

Hannah lowered her head to the plush carpet and saw small mounds laid out in a circle. "Are those stones?" she asked, and when she touched them, they were warm.

Sarah Anne's voice was gruff. "I had to ask around town for a while before someone told me about that." To Hannah's bewildered face, she whispered, "They're for protection."

Hannah swung back onto the bed. "What I saw the other day, Jacob grabbing you like that—" She hesitated. Sarah Anne's expression was pained, and she didn't know how to finish the sentence. "I don't think stones are going to solve it. You should tell someone."

"It's not him," Sarah Anne said quickly. "At least, not always. I wake up in the night and—" She fisted her hands against her sternum. "Something's sitting here, holding me down. I feel like I can't breathe. The woman in town called it a cauchemar, a spirit. She said they can't count, and stones in a circle will keep them busy all night."

"Sarah Anne," Hannah began, then stopped. She could hear her friend's conviction, and she watched as the girl scratched at her cuticles intently.

"I know it sounds silly."

Hannah sighed. "Do they work?"

"Some nights, but then it comes back, and I think maybe it's just toying with me," Sarah Anne said distantly, then shook her head. "I'm so tired. Let's close our eyes for a bit."

Hannah sunk back against the pillow. The scent of vanilla and liquor was cloying. "Just for a bit," she said cautiously. "It's like I'm in a bowl of potpourri."

Sarah Anne nuzzled her curls, solid as a starched collar, against Hannah's face and Hannah forced herself to lie still as Sarah Anne inched closer. "The maid sprays everything. Some days it smells like a garden. Other days, it's muffins."

Hannah listened to the rain pounding against the window. She could feel Sarah Anne's heartbeat against her arm. "Does he hurt you?"

Sarah Anne clutched Hannah's hand. "We're friends, aren't we?"

Hannah nodded.

"He's been different since we moved here. My parents don't like to talk about it, but I know." Sarah Anne squeezed her hand. "It's not him anymore." Hannah didn't know where to look. The whites of Sarah Anne's eyes were absolute. "He's someone else now."

"Sarah, he's still your brother," Hannah said gently, but the girl spoke over her.

"When we first moved here, our furniture was a week late. My brother and I slept on air mattresses downstairs." Her eyes glazed over. "It started out so slow. He'd make these sounds in his throat, and they sounded so small. I went to touch him and he woke up, but he was crying. He asked me why I didn't hear him screaming." Sarah Anne paused and sucked in breath. "Then he said he couldn't move, that someone was sitting on top of him, running blunt nails up and down his chest all night. It sounds like such a silly detail, those blunt nails, but he showed me what they can do, if they have hours to scratch. Then he stopped talking. The priest that we came here to see, the one that was taking care of him, has given up on him. He says it's too late. Jacob only speaks to me now."

"What does he say?" Hannah asked in a choked whisper.

"He talks about what it feels like to die. He says you can feel it, when your heart stops."

Hannah swallowed hard. "Did someone hurt him?"

Sarah Anne nodded, and then added casually, "He talks about you, too."

"Me?" Hannah asked, bewildered in the trance of absinthe. "What about me?"

Sarah Anne sat up. Hannah could feel the girl's toes flexing against the mattress. "Something whispers your name to him at night. I've heard it, too. Sometimes I can't tell who's speaking, whether I'm awake or asleep. It feels like a fever. Like my body isn't my own anymore." Sarah Anne pulled distractedly at her cuticles as she spoke.

Hannah looked pointedly at the bruises on Sarah Anne's thigh. "You need to tell someone about this."

"No." Her voice was low and urgent. "I thought you of all people would understand. It's like I'm communicating with another world through him." Sarah Anne's eyes were wide, imploring. "You do understand, don't you?"

The shadows were coalescing again, their feathered tips brushing along the wall. "Sure." Hannah squeezed the girl's hand.

In a quick movement, Sarah Anne straddled Hannah. Her eyes were wild. "When it comes in the night, it holds me down, just like this," Sarah Anne leaned forward. "Do you want me to kiss you?" she asked. Hannah could see the line of her jaw, the edges of her white teeth, the inside of her nose. A complicated bouquet of peppermint, berries, and licorice rushed out with each breath.

"No," Hannah said slowly, but she wasn't sure she meant it. There was something magnetic about the other girl's intensity. Curious, she touched a pulsing vein in Sarah Anne's throat.

Sarah Anne's eyes widened. The pulse quickened under her finger and Hannah could almost feel the girl's heart palpitating behind her thin ribbed cotton top. "Come on," she goaded. "You can practice on me."

Their lips touched, although it seemed like neither of them had moved.

In the dark, anything was possible. The bed seemed to fade beneath them, the dimensions of the bedroom

changed. They could've been in a field, crushing strawberries and mites as they writhed. Red seeds braiding themselves into their hair. The tongue pressing for entry, then
sending a live-wire charge through the tip of her own
tongue, could have been a caterpillar.

Hands slipped under her back and began to roll up
her shirt, and still she didn't open her eyes, didn't feel the
smallest twinge of self-consciousness as her young nipples, flat and brown as moles, touched bare skin.

Thunder cracked to their right and Hannah had time
to open her mouth wider, ready for the fall of rainwater,
before an inhuman grunt sounded.

"Jacob," Sarah Anne said calmly.

Hannah wiggled out from under the girl, pulling down
her shirt. The dreamy high veered into nausea.

To Hannah, it looked as though rage was moving
across Jacob's face like bruised clouds. The absinthe had
set down barbs in her mind. Hannah noticed the door was
splintered where he'd forced it open.

Jacob opened his mouth and let out an animalistic
howl. Hannah covered her ears and turned away just as
Sarah Anne dove off the bed and rushed toward him. He
caught her in his vast arms, and turned her around like a
rag doll by her right hand. He mashed her face against the
door so quickly that her whimper of hurt was cut off.

Jacob held Hannah's gaze as Sarah Anne struggled
under his grip. Her efforts barely registered in the muscles of his arm.

Hannah held out a plaintive hand. "Jacob, calm down,"
she pleaded.

His head jerked back and forth as if he was being tugged. The light coming in through the hallway backlit him; Hannah had to squint to make out his features.

"Go," Sarah Anne said to Hannah, and when Hannah hesitated, she screamed the word.

Hannah stumbled to her feet, unsure what to do. "You have to let her go," she began, flinching as he pummeled his other fist against the door, barely missing Sarah Anne's ear.

"Leave now. Go." Sarah Anne's voice was different, echoing, and Hannah realized that she spoke in time to the thunder that was growing closer. When the lightning struck, the blue light picked out tendrils emanating from Jacob's mouth, little sprigs of light sprouting from his head.

"Please," Hannah tried again, and dropped to her knees, "I can't leave until you let her go."

Risking a glance upward, she saw Jacob release the girl's head as if it were a sack of groceries. The effort she'd used to brace against his hand brought her backward against him. She slumped briefly, her face hidden by her curls. Hannah nudged forward to touch Sarah Anne's leg. Too late, she saw Jacob's foot lift. And move backward as if Hannah's hand were a canebrake rattlesnake. As if Jacob feared her touch.

A hiss filled the air and it took her a moment to realize it was coming from Sarah Anne.

"Are you alright?" Hannah whispered urgently.

Sarah Anne righted herself and shook out her hair. She looked down at Hannah with an expression of contempt. "Of course," she said, patting Jacob on the chest. A red ribbon of blood trailed from her nose, and she lapped it with her tongue. "Christ, can't anyone hold their liquor?"

Hannah tottered as she stood. Her eyes moved between the siblings and the door, which wore a small spatter of red.

"Come with me," she said under her breath to Sarah Anne. The dizziness was overwhelming. She wanted to flick away a bit of clotting blood from the girl's nose, but Sarah Anne's expression was so imperious, that Hannah's hand dropped weakly to her side.

Sarah Anne flicked on the light switch. Jacob rolled his neck and staggered against the doorframe. He looked at Hannah with his usual sweet blankness, and his lips quivered just short of a smile.

"You should go," the girl told Hannah, and snaked her arm around her brother's. "My parents asked me to make lunch for Jacob, and I guess I forgot. Are you hungry?" A charged, private look passed between them. Jacob nodded.

"Sarah Anne," Hannah said slowly, and then looked around the room. Everything was unchanged. Porcelain figurines of ballerinas remained ordered on top of the dresser, fenced in by a rainbow of nail polish bottles. The bed was slightly mussed, two fuzzy white teddy bears toppled in the white waves of the duvet. Even the thunder was receding, taking with it the last hints of menace. When she turned around, she was met with twin expressions of flat, polite curiosity.

"What are you waiting for?" Sarah Anne asked. She seemed unaware that she stood on one foot, the other flexed against her shin. Her red toenails scratched insistently.

"Something happened," Hannah said dumbly, and Sarah Anne shook her head.

"Let's not talk about it anymore. Sometimes girls are

stupid. We got a bit drunk," she explained, giving her brother a sheepish half-lidded look. His mouth committed to a smile, innocent as a baby's.

"I mean, what happened afterward—"

"Enough," Sarah Anne said firmly, and then lowered her voice. "Let's not make a thing of it." Her eyes crinkled sympathetically as Hannah opened her mouth and found only silence waiting in her throat. "I have to take care of my brother now. You know the way out."

Almost in a trance, Hannah stood stiff-backed as Sarah Anne maneuvered around her and returned with a windbreaker from her closet.

"Here," Sarah Anne said, hinging the jacket over Hannah's shoulders. The fabric didn't feel real against Hannah's stunned body. She waited for something else, some explanation or reassurance, but none came.

"Okay," Hannah said. She felt her lower lip begin to tremble, the twitch moving up her cheek and into her quickly flooding eyes. "I'll see you around."

Hannah ran from the landing, almost falling as her bare feet slipped on the carpeted stairs. At the door, she hurriedly put on her shoes. Faint conversation trickled from upstairs, Jacob speaking calmly. "It's not her time," she heard him say.

She was halfway down the driveway when she remembered the windbreaker. As she slipped it on, the pelting rain a welcome wake-up call, she turned back to the house and squinted at the upstairs window. The blinds were drawn.

CHAPTER
SIX

Hannah woke at dawn to a sky swollen with storms. Gently, she unclasped her hands from Callum's. Her legs felt populated, and when she lifted the covers, every inch of bare skin was dotted with mosquitoes—swollen, sated, and dead. The sheets were stained with a constellation of blood.

Cringing, she rushed to the bathroom, where she lay her head on the lip of the bath as if she were guillotined and turned on the faucet. The mosquitoes drifted even from her hair, dozens of dark bodies. They clumped in the drain. She sat on the edge of the tub, her feet hovering over the thick river of mosquitoes parading down the ceramic, and ran warm water up and down her legs, then cleaned her arms with a washcloth. The fabric became a landscape of slight wings and slender legs.

The house was hushed and expectant, waiting for the thunderstorm. Hannah moved down the stairs, stroking her fingers through spiderwebs and dust. When the swamp held its breath, all the birds and crickets watchful under their temporary truce, Hannah felt like a ghost, moving through some unpopulated middle plane. It was a beautiful privacy.

Standing at the kitchen window, she opened her robe and looked down at her nipples, inflamed as the rest of her. Her hands moved down to her stomach, and she held her breath, wondering when she'd feel the next kick. The child's birth had once seemed so far away, something she wouldn't need to worry about for much longer, but the day was rushing closer.

Would she be ready?

Hannah looked up as a bolt of lightning veined the sky. Birds began to scream in the swamp, and she ran her hands over the urn that held Mae's ashes, unmoved for all these months. All she could hope for was that she'd be a fraction of the mother Mae had been, no matter how unprepared she felt for that level of selflessness.

She spun the spice rack like a roulette wheel and chose three spices at random. She turned on the oven element and poured herself a cup of coffee, then tapped out ground chicory root into the steaming black. A halved peach sizzled against the element for several seconds, then she spread a thin layer of fresh-churned butter into the hole left by the pit. She colored the melting smear with cinnamon and nutmeg. The peach released a stream of butter, spice, and its own sweet flesh into her mouth.

"It feels strange, waking up in an empty bed. Every-thing okay?" Callum asked from the doorway, yawning loudly. Hannah noticed his shirtless body had shrunk. The storm light cast shadows under his ribs.

Hannah closed her terrycloth robe and walked to him. She pushed a piece of peach into his mouth and he moaned his approval.

"It's going to storm soon," she said, ignoring his ques-tion.

He squinted out the kitchen window. "Looks like it's going to be a bad one. Should I go shutter us up?" His hands moved absently over her belly.

"I don't think it'll do much good," she said, surprising herself.

The petal touch of his lips against her cheek made her shiver. "Come now, doom and gloom. It's just a thunder-storm." He sniffed, and made a face. "Chicory coffee, huh? I never took a liking to it. Back to bed with you and I'll take care of things. What would you like for breakfast?"

"I'm not sleepy." She was thrumming at a low fre-quency, all her hairs on end. If someone leaned in close enough, they'd sense a buzz, like telephone wires in the high of summer heat. A gale wind struck the house, rat-tling the windows in their frames, and Hannah moved instinctively against the wall as a knock sounded from the back of the house.

"What's wrong?" Callum asked, smoothing the worry lines along her forehead.

She cringed. "Nothing." There was a known sound of glass and wood struck together, a friction that signaled weather. But what she heard now was unknown, some entity stirring in the shed. She wondered if something blanched and hairless was crawling through the waving grass. "Come back to bed with me. It's Saturday. Let's go under the covers and sleep through this together."

He laughed. "I will, but do you really want a house full of broken glass?"

She worked her plush body against his sparse one, trying to coax him.

"Don't worry," he breathed into her ear, and unclasped himself. "I'll be right back."

Hannah stood with hands gathered nervously at the nape of her neck. The kitchen door slammed shut, and she saw Callum move shirtless through the wind toward the shed.

She moved on tiptoe toward the stairs, interlaced fingers moving to guard her belly. Each step made the whole house groan, and no matter where she looked, she couldn't find her own shadow against the white wall.

As her feet touched the bottom step, the stairs began to shake. She turned to the window just in time to see a crow's dark mass speeding toward it. The bird disappeared below the sill with a muted thud.

Hannah grunted as she lowered herself onto the bottom stair, a quiet ache blooming in her right side. At the back of the house, Callum began to hammer wooden boards over the windows. The sound seemed to come from a great distance.

As clouds filled the sky, darkness spread along the house. Hannah leaned her heavy head against the banister and watched the darkness seep through the curtains then constrict around the petals of her white orchid. It grazed picture frames, splayed itself across the armrest of Mac's favorite chair.

Just as she closed her eyes, her breathing unnaturally slow, a sharp hammering began at the door.

"Callum, use the key," she called out, but there was no reply. With a moan, she stood up and swayed toward the door. The doorknob was warm and clammy to the touch. *I'm inside a wound.* The thought seemed to come from outside her mind, and sounded almost like *womb.*

She opened the door.

On the doormat was the crow. Its neck was stretched and it peered at her from beneath one wing. One leg was strained toward the sky, talons pulsing open and shut like a fist.

Hannah backed away. She sighed deeply, knowing suddenly it was a dream, and recognizing the viscous quality of sleep. Her spine seemed soft, as if she might bend back like a weary stamen, her head rubbing gently against the ground.

Behind her, the thudding of Callum's hammer continued. It, too, had slowed.

The crow followed her, balancing on one leg and its beak, black and gleaming like a crab's pincer. The wings made a terrible rustling sound against the wood.

"What do you want?"

The crow paused, and one immense yellow eye blinked at her. It reminded her of the feathered bodies that had once made their nests in Sarah Anne's backyard.

"Jacob, is that you?" Hannah asked in a low voice.

The crow began speeding toward her, and the

pounding of its beak hurried her steps. She tripped over a stair and fell backward. The pain was real, a deep bruising in the small of her back. The crow stopped at her feet, then fastened its talon onto her leg. Blood beaded around the edges of its bite.

"What are you?" she whimpered, and before she could finish, the crow began to expand. Hannah shrunk back. Bald patches marked its swollen body, and they were speckled with crusted rot. Beneath the cover of feathers, its wings were tipped in pincers.

Still watching her, it planted its beak into her distended belly button through her robe. "This," it croaked, long and deep, and Hannah had a moment to wonder what it meant, before the beak punctured the puckered skin. Hannah began to scream.

Her cry seemed to go on for a long time before she opened her eyes to Callum's startled face. He was calling her name.

"Where were you?" she asked, trying to regain her breath.

"Outside, putting shutters on the windows." Callum studied her face. "Jesus, woman. What's wrong? You can't just scream like a bloody banshee for no reason. Not after what happened at the apartment."

Rain spattered the floorboards through the open front door as she stared at the empty floor in front of her. She'd just conversed with a disfigured crow that wasn't there. A shudder wracked her body. "I fell down, but I'm alright."

"You scared me shitless. I thought that old crony was back." Callum frowned at the door. "Was someone here?"

Hannah shook her head. "No, I just thought I heard something out there. Probably a branch." Then she felt under her robe, where a wet bead sat in the basin of her belly button. Her finger came away red.

"What's that?" Callum asked, pawing at her robe. "Is it the baby?"

"The baby's fine," Hannah said with a certainty she didn't feel. "I must've scratched myself in my sleep." With a last glance outside at the sheets of rain that sprayed a fresh, green smell through the house, she stood and headed upstairs. "I think I'll take you up on that nap."

Callum looked up at her, exasperated. "Is it just me or are you a bit crazy these days?"

Hannah feigned a smile. "Might be," she said. She looked beyond him toward the door, and felt a sneaking suspicion that though it was open, she couldn't leave. It'd been years and years since her nightmares had felt so vivid, but this was the first time they'd actually left a mark.

"Well, stop it." He massaged his temples. "Okay. Let me finish boarding up the house, and I'll be up with some tea. Are you hungry?"

"You don't need to do that anymore," she said evenly, pausing at the top of the stairs. She looked down at Callum, her frightened penitent, and sighed. "It won't do any good."

In the bathroom, Hannah studied her belly button under the fluorescent bulbs. The cut was very small, but it leaked a slow, steady flow of blood. She pasted a Band-Aid over the tiny wound and sat down on the edge of the bathtub, caressing her belly.

At least the cut was proof that something had happened. There'd always been the real world that others saw and dwelled in, and then another, filled with pale shades. But something improbable had stepped through and made its malice known.

CHAPTER
SEVEN

Hannah huddled in the back of the boat as Callum pulled it ashore. The storm had brought flooding, and many of the marshy beaches along the shore were now submerged.

He'd questioned her decision to come here, and why wouldn't he? After she'd so firmly distanced herself from this part of her life, it must seem to him like another example of unhinged behavior.

"You don't have to come," she'd said to him.

He'd snorted. "How do you plan on getting there without me?"

"You're not the only one with a boat." She'd been halfway to the front door when he'd barred her way, arms raised in a gesture of surrender.

"Sorry, sorry." He didn't sound particularly apologetic. "But you're right. It's your family, no matter how

171

estranged. You have a right to reconnect. I'm just not sure I understand why you'd want to, after everything we've been through. Do you really want to give the crazies in town more ammunition?"

"I doubt that the townsfolk will be watching the woods with their binoculars," Hannah insisted, but found that she didn't trust her own words.

"Well, good. As long as you doubt it."

They'd boarded the boat and made the choppy journey in silence, Callum focusing on steering to avoid fallen trees. She hadn't known how easy it would be to find her way back to where she'd first met her mother until they were on the water.

He stretched as he got off the boat and extended a hand to her. "Coming?"

Hannah nodded and looked beyond him to the large barn in the clearing. A single oak tree stood beside the barn, and the sun poured through its boards like divinity itself. A wide dock had extended the land so a corner of the barn seemed to float in the flood-raised water.

She spotted her mother by the barn, looking over the water.

"I can't wait to meet the parents," Callum said dryly as she stepped carefully off the boat and into his arms. He ran his fingers lightly over her neck. "I just want you to be safe," he murmured.

Hannah squeezed him back, enjoying the moment, until she remembered where they were and why they had come. "Can you give me a few minutes? I want to talk to her alone first."

His brow furrowed. "Will you be alright?"

She answered with a kiss.

A murder of crows, their feathers coated with an inky sheen, fell silent as she passed the tree. Their yellow eyes followed her, necks craning in tandem from their perch on a branch.

The first time she'd visited, she hadn't known what to expect, but she found herself surprised now by the lack of pagan constructions. There were no upside-down crosses hanging from the lush green branches. The lawn was cut and unusually fertile, all weeds seeming to respect some unmarked border at the edge of the clearing. Even the water seemed cleaner, sparkling without murky undertones.

"So you've come," her mother said, without turning around. A shirtless old man straightened at the edge of the water. There was an angry red lash where the rope he held had cut into his shoulder.

"I have," Hannah said, staring at the ground. She felt strangely humbled, and it was uncomfortable. Hannah noticed that Christobelle looked healthier than she had the last time they'd met. A windblown blush rode her cheeks.

"You're immense. I see you ignored my advice, but I suppose that shouldn't surprise me."

"No, it shouldn't."

Christobelle shook out her black dress around her legs and sighed heavily. "The water's rising, child, and the land's disappearing. Someday, there'll be no one left here. Just echoes. But for now, we're still standing."

The man in the water groaned as he hoisted the thick, frayed rope. Silver hair plumed at the sides of his head, and his chest shook with each tug, but muscles still flashed under his hanging belly.

"We should've settled in the North, found a decent parish somewhere. That's a lesson for you: always find higher ground."

"It's stuck in the mud, ma'am," the man called out, his face slick with effort.

"Get someone to help you, then." Christobelle's face was grim. "There are still more relics after this one."

"He's an old man, he shouldn't be straining so much. Do you want to give him a heart attack?"

"No, child, I don't want that." Christobelle inspected the man. "But we all die, whether it suits us or not. Some of the more able-bodied men turned tail at the first sign of the floods and there's work to be done. That damn storm nearly sunk the property. We were huddled inside while the wind and lightning did their business, and it's not over yet, not by a mile."

The man was panting in pelican honks, but Christobelle only rubbed absently at her mouth. Eczema was spreading around her mother's pale lips like lichen. Hannah had seen it inflamed, a septic red that made children's eyes widen in horror, but now it was subdued, a needlepoint only slightly darker than her fair skin. A fine coat of antique lace. "We'll take what we need, and the rest will drain down the river. I suppose you'll be leaving for town now?"

Hannah blinked. The thought of the house, left empty in their wake, had never occurred to her. She imagined the windows hollowed out like pocks. "The house is fine," she said slowly. "Where's Samuel?" Hannah had never before seen her mother without him.

Christobelle flicked her head like a horse sensing a fly. "He's unwell."

Below them, the man finally pulled the statue free. Hannah was surprised to see that the figure resembled Mother Mary, her robes coated in thick grime, her clay hands full of mud and torn roots. He rolled it onto the bank and bent over, hands on knees. With each rapid breath, his ribcage appeared and receded.

"We'll keep rebuilding," her mother muttered as she dropped down into the wet earth and began cleaning the statue's face with the hem of her skirt. "What a thing, to birth a savior."

Hannah closed her eyes as an unfamiliar pity and the ever-present anger crested in her, rolling over each other, frothing like surf.

"Come inside," Christobelle said, straightening suddenly. She looked toward the boat dock and nodded to herself.

Hannah hesitated. She took a step toward the kneeling man, whose head lay against the wet earth, his hair filled with peat, then followed her mother into the barn through a side entrance. The thick wooden door was inscribed with scrolls and blank, knowing faces. "What are these?" Hannah leaned close to study an open mouth, toothed and black. She imagined the sharpened points would prick.

"They impress the uninitiated," Christobelle said, with a sly backward glance. "We bought the land, complete with the barn, from a recluse. He was what people might call a medicine man, or a shaman. He had his ideas about the order of things, and thought this was a sacred space. A place well suited to conversing with the other side." Christobelle tapped the feet of a carved figure, a hunched woman in heavy robes seated at the top of the door. She seemed to preside over the faces carved below. "This is Nana Buluku. She goes by many names. She stands in for the creator in many religions."

"Isn't God supposed to be a man?" Hannah asked, and immediately remembered being twelve, Christobelle unexpectedly out in the town streets, flanked by her entourage. How Hannah had stopped dead in the street, so suddenly that Sarah Anne and her mother stumbled into her. How distrustful eyes had followed Christobelle from behind half-closed shutters as if they were in a scene from a Western. How Christobelle had stood stiff-backed to the side, hands clasped at her waist.

"Hello, children," she'd said in an unfamiliar, saccharine voice.

"Move along, Hannah," Sarah Anne's mother had urged.

Christobelle's unblinking gaze had slid smoothly to Sarah Anne. "You two look to be good friends. Where did you meet?"

"At church," Sarah Anne had answered. She'd raised her eyebrows at Hannah.

"I myself am not especially devout," Christobelle had said. "I prefer to worship at home."

"Where's home?" Sarah Anne had asked sweetly, tossing back her mane of curls.

Hannah had pulled on the edge of Sarah Anne's jacket as Christobelle's eyes affixed to the girl's rapidly atrophying smile. "I think you know."

Now, Christobelle clapped her hands in front of Hannah's face and studied her. "Speak to many people and you'll find they have many ideas about what God is, and many names for him. Or her. They find comfort in religion, or science, until they encounter something that cannot be explained by either. And there are such things."

Hannah's eyes struggled to adjust to the dim as they stepped into the barn. Sleeping bags and crude ceramic washbasins sat against one of the walls. Another lined with pews.

"I quite like crows," Christobelle said, seemingly out of nowhere, "despite their reputation. They gossip among themselves, and remember the faces of those who have wronged them. It's why scarecrows are so effective," Christobelle said, waving her hands toward the ceiling. "Dark little rumor-mongers whispered something in my ear last night."

Hannah looked up into the rafters, hearing the flutter of wings. The sagging beams of wood were shedding yellow hay. "It's funny that you mention crows. Was it you?"

Her mother cocked her head. "What?"

Hannah squinted. Light squeezed through holes in the ceiling, like a pinhole camera. "Was it you," Hannah repeated, "who sent that bird, that *thing*? Were you trying to scare me?"

Christobelle gingerly bent at the knees and plucked a large, thick-legged spider from the plush hay. "Here you are in my house, girl," Christobelle said lightly. "It is a place of worship, where those who are willing can see beyond the limits of sight. You speak when spoken to, and listen well." She took a step toward Hannah and extended her arm. The barn spider sat on her middle knuckle, its striped legs fit to the trenches made by tendons in the woman's hand. "I pity you, having grown up lost. The world must be so frightening when you know so little of what comes next." A slight tremor went through her hand and the spider stirred, tiptoeing up her finger. "I imagine it must make you feel helpless."

Hannah straightened her shoulders as Christobelle's hand brushed her collarbone. Her whole body quivered. She felt the spider hesitate against her neck.

"Child," Christobelle said, her voice velvety. "It's just an insect. It's a fraction of your size. You kill them without even noticing, without giving it thought."

"It's repulsive."

"Is it?" Christobelle looked down at it as if admiring a ring. "I find it pleasing. It's one of nature's many indulgences."

With great effort, Hannah forced herself to brush her mother's hand away. "I'm too old to be receiving lessons from you. Especially on what I should and shouldn't fear."

"But you are afraid." Christobelle placed the spider onto her shoulder and fanned out her skirt. Hannah saw the papery skin around her mother's ankles. "It comes off you like an odor." A shade of sadness passed over her mother's face, quick as a door closing.

"Nature is against me." Hannah sagged forward. A stroke of color caught her eye. Below a rough hill of hay, she could see a patch of dark red staining the floorboards.

Christobelle breathed a long sigh. The blush seemed to drain from her cheeks as her eyes pouched inside violet-veined skin. "Leave us," Christobelle said softly, and Hannah scanned the room. Two men rose, as if from a deep, confused slumber, from the hay stacked in the dark corners of the barn. They seemed like shadows come unstuck, stepping through the back door and into the sunlight.

Christobelle turned back and stared at Hannah's stomach with ravenous intensity. "What's happened?"

"I had a dream that wasn't exactly a dream." The words sounded ridiculous. "A crow came into the house, but it was wrong, wrongly made somehow. It attacked me here," she pointed to her belly button. "And it spoke. Or, I thought I heard it speak."

Christobelle frowned. "It came into the house? I saw it circling when I was last there. An unusually large one."

Hannah's mouth opened, then closed. "It attacked me," she repeated. She'd expected more, having forgotten not to expect anything. "Something's wrong. It's in the air, in the floorboards, everywhere. Everything feels threatening."

"Because you are threatened." Christobelle moved forward over the bleached hay, seeming to float. Nothing rustled beneath her feet. "The child is distressed," she whispered. She pulled a small vial out of her innumerable layers and handed it to Hannah. "Drink."

"What is it?" Hannah asked, not reaching for it.

"It's for the child," Christobelle said evenly. "To calm it." Then, exasperated, "You came for help, and this is it. Drink."

Hannah took the vial, then hesitated. She held it up to the light. The liquid inside was dark and thick, and sat over a layer of black sediment, but even after she opened it and breathed in, she couldn't guess what it might be. Hannah gagged slightly against the few drops that slid down her throat, metallic and sour as spoiled meat.

Christobelle locked her hands over Hannah's stomach

and the chill permeated deep into her gut, sinking though her bladder. A low pain began between her legs. Hannah groaned and the sound hung between them. "It's time to speak the truth, Hannah, all of it. Some things are written on your face, so tell me."

Hannah's body felt constricted, as if all her veins were bathed in frost.

"What else have you seen?"

The child kicked inside her and Hannah looked into Christobelle's face. Her irises lowered as she blinked. She'd felt it. "It's something I used to dream about when I was young." Hannah's voice cracked. There would be no unspeaking this. There'd been an implicit treaty of silence, some sense that acknowledging it through speech would make it real. "A recurring nightmare that always started the same, in a house that wasn't mine, but I thought was mine through that strange dream logic. I always felt watched."

Christobelle nodded impatiently. The long, patrician nose was inches from hers. So close, Hannah could see the filigree of dark purple veins clustered across her cheeks, along her chin. There were flecks of gold in her mother's eyes, just like hers.

"I'd hear it first, a swishing across the floor like a fish dragging itself toward water. Then I'd see a flash of white out of the corner of my eyes. Not a pure white, but yellowed. Organic. Its movements were reptilian, like an alligator. It never felt threatening, just watchful. In my dreams, it never came close to me, just circled me. But lately . . ."

"Lately?" Christobelle prompted.

"I've seen it," Hannah said in a whisper. "Out in the

world. Not even in a half-sleep, but out walking in the woods."

"I see." Christobelle backed away. She bent at the waist and gently set the spider down onto the hay. It scurried away from her long fingers.

Hannah waited for more, but her mother turned her back and stood staring at the rafters. The words rushed out of Hannah. "I did wrong against someone when I was younger. A boy named Jacob. You said his name the other day, and I feel—punished. Ever since Mae died, nothing feels safe."

"Child," Christobelle said gently. "You have never been safe. We are all always at the mercy of the world, this one and the next, but fear serves nothing. Fear gives power to shadows, even though they can only exist in the presence of light. As for this boy, this Jacob, he was not what you thought. He would've harmed you. Guilt can be as dangerous as fear, if it's undeserved, if you take on too much of it." Her mother's head shot up sharply, her fingers flexing at her sides. "He's out there." Christobelle said.

Hannah rubbed her eyes. Having said it, having had it dismissed, lightened everything. Excuses and explanations suddenly soothed her like medicine: it was the hormones from the pregnancy and the grief at Mae's death mingling in her chemistry. The mind was susceptible when surrounded by so much quiet. "Callum."

"Callum. I'd forgotten about the name. It means dove. Don't you find that interesting?"

"Should I?"

Christobelle shrugged and turned back to face Hannah, a half-smile haunting her mouth. "I'd like to meet him."

Hannah saw her teeth grinding back and forth "Will he be my son-in-law?"

Hannah gathered her hair into a loose bun at the nape of her neck. She'd been waking up to find long strands of her hair mottling her pillow, coiling and knotting in her sleep. "I'd have to be your daughter by law first."

"Law. Doesn't mean much out here, as I think you're starting to learn." She gestured for Hannah to lead the way out.

Callum stood with his back to the barn, his hands in his pockets.

"Welcome to our swamp." Christobelle said softly, stepping up to him.

Callum turned. "Thanks, but I've already been here for a while." They watched each other like hawks circling the same mouse.

Callum searched Hannah's face. She tried to keep her features steady, despite the painful loosening in her womb, like a valve split from too much pressure.

"But you're only just now being welcomed in return." Christobelle moved forward and gripped his face, her fingers sliding into his hollowed cheeks. "A cool reception, is it?" Her body reared suddenly, and though they barely moved, her hands shifted from clenching to cradling almost imperceptibly. Tenderness filled her face, and seemed ill-fitting. It made her seem younger. "I'm sorry, child," she said, in a whisper.

Hannah forced a smile. "For what?"

Christobelle hugged herself. Her bony arms looked as if they might clasp around her corseted waist. Bits of hay hung from the hem of her skirt like decoration. "I thought

I could, but—" Some realization had dawned on her. "I can't help him. I can't help either of you."

Hannah cried out as warmth seeped out from between her legs.

Christobelle shushed her. Hannah began to retch, but her mother only whispered, "Let it work." Hannah convulsed again.

"What's happening?" Callum asked, fear in his voice. "The baby?"

"Get the boat, boy," Christobelle said quickly, "and take her home. Put her in bed."

"What did you do?" he cried.

"I need you to remember this. She can't leave," Christobelle said quietly. "Not with the child inside her. The house may still offer some small protection."

"From what?" Callum asked.

Christobelle closed her eyes against Callum's desperation. "You must take her home."

Hannah met the eyes of the man on the bank, hoisting another cracked statue from the water. He fell to the ground with it, hugging its painted plaster. A greasy, browning vine hung from his neck like a noose. Hannah's moans didn't register on his face. Beyond him, she saw the two men from the barn, slumped in the grass. They shook their heads from side to side, raising and dropping their arms as though taken aback by the ability to do so. She saw their faces. Horror and amazement conjoined.

Callum stepped toward Christobelle, rage puckering his face. "You did this!"

Hannah doubled over, and she tried to focus her vision on something that might calm her. The kicks inside her felt bruising. Spit flew from her lips as she shushed sense-lessly. She meant it for the baby but addressed a beetle on the ground that thrust its horns impotently against a rock.

"What have you done to her?" Callum cried, moving as if to strike her mother. The two men rushed toward them as if they'd sprung up from the damp earth, waiting for a signal.

"Go home. All that is left is to wait." Hannah felt her mother's hands on her head, tangling in her hair. They pulled painfully as she stroked. "You should've listened to me. Now you're exposed."

"Come on," Callum urged as he pulled Hannah toward the boat. "What did she do?" Hannah shut her eyes, unable to speak. Unable to tell him that some small part of her had known, and had drunk. Callum folded her into the boat and gunned the motor.

"They have you," Christobelle called out after them, her head bowed like a willow.

CHAPTER
EIGHT

Hannah stayed in bed for days, her finger circling the small puncture wound in her belly button. Outside, the world moved feverishly as another storm descended and falling branches shattered windows. She watched the bedroom door, her pulse pounding in her throat, but there was only Callum calling out, "Just a window, honey. I've already locked Graydon away."

Cramps choked her stomach, signaling blood, but the sheets remained unmarked. It was only this that kept Callum at bay, even as he paced the length of the bedroom, threatening to call James, to rain down police batons on Christobelle's men.

"Your own mother," he repeated again and again, and Hannah was too weary to clarify that they were family only in the barest sense of the word. He brought her ginger tea, his face worried. "Wake up, sweetheart," he cajoled, his voice increasingly fatigued, but she remained on her back, her limbs at once leaden and liquid.

She dreamt of the child excavating patiently through the red dome of her womb, braiding veins as it went, then swinging from the vines. Always, its hands were clawed. She dreamt of Callum lying on the floor outside their bedroom, her child's heartbeat resounding through the house. His body thinning, his very skin growing more transparent with each pulse.

Callum finally called Dr. Merrick. He kept his leather bag tight against his chest, the very picture of a small town doctor, as he moved around the room. He avoided touching the furniture and he gasped when a large black raven met his eyes from a branch outside the window.

"It's taken up residence," Callum explained, tapping on the window. "I think it's probably after all the dead frogs."

Dr. Merrick sniffed the air like a possum, frowning at the ammonic smell of her body. "Smell that?" he asked Callum, anger in his voice. "Smells like *Fetor hepaticus*, or breath of the dead. It's the terrible sweetness of a liver fighting too much toxicity in the blood."

No matter how Hannah turned, how she stoppered her face with pillows, the smell was pervasive. It inhabited her.

"Tell me the truth now," the doctor said. "Have you taken her to some traiteur on the bayou?" Callum regarded him blankly. "A witch-doctor, son."

Hannah slammed the heel of her foot down on the mattress and threw Callum a warning look.

"Of course not."

Dr. Merrick gently pulled back the sweat-drenched sheets to study her body. His eyes settled on her stomach. "What's this then?" Hannah rose onto her elbows to see the faint outline of a cross over her belly.

"Jesus, I don't know," Callum breathed, staring wide-eyed at Hannah. Dr. Merrick made a sound of disgust as he handed Callum his stethoscope and placed the end on her belly. Watching his face relax, Hannah could almost hear her baby's heartbeat.

"I can't figure it out." Hannah heard the doctor say. "That smell . . ." He hesitated. "When the chemicals produced by the body aren't filtered out anymore, they seep into the lungs. But her blood pressure seems to be fine, her circulation's good, and there are no clear signs of jaundice. What's she eaten in the last few days?"

When he only shrugged, the doctor considered Callum carefully. "You're looking a bit ill yourself."

"It's just stress." Callum's mouth tightened as he pointed the doctor's attention back to Hannah. "Sleep has become a luxury we can barely afford."

"It could just be a bad flu, but in the meantime, I'd like to get her in for some tests."

"No," Hannah groaned from the bed.

The doctor nodded to himself and pulled out a syringe and five vials. "Then we'll do them here. One way or another, young lady." Hannah glared at him as she extended her arm. He wiped down a fat blue vein, then plunged the needle in. Her blood was viscous, flowing slowly into the ampules. "Whatever happens," Dr. Merrick said to her in a low voice, "don't turn to folklore. It'll do more harm than good. Mae fooled around with it, but underneath it all was a foundation of medicine, pure and simple. You have more than yourself to think of now."

Hannah stared fixedly out the window at the cloud-laden sky until he left.

She knew the smell wasn't her body leeching poison, not entirely. It was laced with the pungent stench of fear, at what waited outside and what lay inside her. Christobelle had said that she couldn't leave with the child inside her. Hannah felt cornered, paralyzed by the sense that leaving the land, leaving the swamp, might cause the child harm.

Her own mother had given her what was, by her definition, a remedy. Lose the child and leave freely. Keep the child and live in fear. She didn't yet know the dimensions of her prison, but she was caught like a moth in a killing jar.

Callum sat back in the chair beside the bed. He massaged his chin with his thumb. "What can I do?"

Hannah shook her head wordlessly and rolled over, seeking the refuge of sleep. In her sickness, the memory of his kiss with Leah felt like an infected wound. She'd dreamt of Leah, unafraid, before a sea of men's hands and eyes. Many of the mouths that closed around Leah's were Callum's, his lips replicated and insatiable. She woke confused. While it might be sanded away, polished and painted over, it would never really fade. A careful touch would always find its edges.

At some point, the storm calmed. She woke to the gentle chime of trees shedding their last raindrops into puddles outside the open window. The air smelled laundered. And then the drumming started. Hesitant at first and deep inside her, her child began to tread water. Each kick pulled her into consciousness and the motoring of its legs felt like it was frothing her insides, all the heaviness of days past turning to spume. Hannah wiggled up onto her pillow.

"That was quite a storm," Callum said from the doorway. "I thought it might tear the whole house apart."

Hannah's eyes felt swollen, her throat parched. "Water, please." He hurried away and returned with a tall glass. She took the glass, then pulled his hand onto her belly. "Feel," she ordered.

Callum's laugh was half gasp. "There it is! God, he's strong. He's alright." His hand followed the child's movement, darting like a minnow. "You missed the strangest thing. There were frogs in our backyard. Dozens of them, all drowned."

"What are you talking about?"

"From the storm, I guess. Graydon was pawing at the kitchen window, meowing like mad. They were just bloated and washed up in the grass."

"How high is the water now?"

"It's risen but only by a few feet," Callum said. "There's a bit of flooding in the basement."

"It's testing us," Hannah whispered. "It was a warning."

Callum squinted at her, and licked his lips. She had the sense that he was summoning up patience. "Honey, you've been ill. There was a tropical storm down in Florida, and we've been getting the backwash. The critters got spooked. I bet every house around us for miles had some kind of fish or frog flopping on their doorstep this week."

Ignoring the protests of her body, she stood and walked to the window. They were still there. Swollen, slick specks bobbing above the shallow water that had crept toward the back door. "How did they drown?"

Callum shrugged and left the room. "I'm running you a bath, okay? What do you want, lavender or citrus?"

She parted her robe and looked down at the hard bulge of her belly, her skin irritated from the terrycloth. "I shouldn't have baths," she called back. "It can harm the baby."

The water turned off, the sound replaced by the bathtub draining. "How can I relax you? Anything you want."

She felt restless. With sunlight warming her skin, she found it hard to remember why she'd placed so much stock in her mother's warning that she couldn't leave the swamp. A test was in order, and even though the thought of boarding a boat and running the motor straight into the Atchafalaya and beyond drove a spearing ache into her gut, she ignored it. "I want to get out of here for a bit."

His face brightened, the corners of his mouth fluttering toward a smile. "Sure. I can make reservations for dinner in town. Any preference?"

She shook her head. "No. Let's go for a walk or something."

"The ground's too soggy right now. I don't want you to slip."

"I'll hold on to you." The need to flee was almost physical, a slingshot trembling for release. "Look, you asked. This will relax me." He came to stand beside her, his eyes sunken and dark. Each time she'd roused from her fever he'd been there, watching her. "You look tired. More tired than I've ever seen you," she said, running her hand through his beard. The white speckles had turned to full strands.

"I've been worried." He nuzzled his chin against her palm, then looked past her. "Scratch worried. Angry, maybe. Terrified, definitely. I've been having nightmares to set your hair on end. But Hannah, if there's something wrong, you have to tell me. You have to promise me."

How could she bring him into her world? He'd grown up in the light of the easily explainable, a place where the laws and medicine of men could tend to most harms. She thought of Mae, her poor neck strained, her face contorted by fear. Mae had died afraid, Hannah suddenly realized.

She couldn't help but feel that there would be more loss to come, but she knew that the ultimate loss, the one she wouldn't be able to bear, was him. Her selfishness dripped bitter down her throat even as she said the words, "I promise," her eyes unflinching.

She used the clause from childhood, the chant of *cross my heart* and crossed her fingers behind her back like a baseball sign. It was an old trick, done by looking at the valley between the eyes. "A walk will do us both good."

"I'll get your shoes," he said.

Hannah watched him go, then turned back to the window. The frogs lay on the ground below like an offering. From this high, Hannah could see what Callum had not. They were lined up in a watchful perimeter around the house.

Hannah struggled with her swollen, water-logged ankles, and it was an effort to keep up with Callum.

"It's true," he was saying, "everything's stranger on this little patch of swamp."

Hannah hooked her hand around Callum's arm. "It's

hard for me to imagine how it looks from the outside. People can get used to anything, if it's all they know. I think I'd find it stranger in a city, around all that concrete with greenery struggling to break through. I'd find the noise distracting."

"You should've heard the racket that damn storm made, breaking into our septic system. I used to think I was enough of a man's man, enough that my father didn't worry too much when I turned to music," Callum said, plucking at his light sweater. "But it hurts my pride to say I'm not sure I know how to fix it. There's sludge coming through by the fistful. A roughed-up carp bubbled up when I flushed the toilet the other day and Graydon lost his damn mind. He's still got some kitten in him."

"I would've liked to see that. Well, as appealing as a swamp sludge bath sounds, you should just hire someone to fix it up," Hannah said, focusing all her attention on stepping between the puddles. The land sagged with rain.

"I liked fixing up the windows, though, and I was thinking we could put in some stained glass to fix the one that broke. Add some character to the place."

Hannah snorted. "It doesn't have enough character for you?"

"It's a great old house. But we could really make something of it, once we're done getting the baby's room ready. What do you think of the room with the bay windows, the one that used to be yours? It'd need a few quick coats of paint and maybe some new netting on the windows." He shoved his hands in his pockets. "It would add to its resale value."

Hannah stopped and stretched, both hands digging

into her lower back. The symmetry was fitting: her room, where she'd wept and laughed and even tentatively masturbated for the first time, passed over to the baby. His last comment she doggedly ignored, even though she'd been expecting it. Callum knew normalcy. Of course he would want to return to it someday.

"Isn't it kind of big for a baby's room? I've been led to believe they come out small."

Callum retraced his steps, and pecked her ear with dry kisses. "The whole house is kind of big. We have more space than we know what to do with, and with the money we'd make from the sale—"

"You know it was Christobelle's house originally?" Hannah said, moving her head away.

"No shit?"

"She settled here when the movement was in its infancy. I guess the congregation was more manageable then."

"You mean to tell me there were services in that house? Real-life ghost conjurings?"

Hannah cringed into the sun and thought of the living room's tall windows pouring light into the slack mouths of men. "I don't know how real-life any of it is."

Callum stopped mid-stride. "I know it's not my place, but I have half a mind to go on up to that church of hers and ask her why she didn't lift a finger to help her own daughter. You collapse in front of her, and she stands there all-powerful like you're some stray. I can't believe those idiots she keeps around her don't see her for the charlatan she is."

Hannah thought of the men and their blank eyes. "You have more sense than that," she said. "Just leave it alone. For all we know, it was a stomach bug."

Callum's jaw tightened. "Sure. Must've been that arsenic stew we had last week. Hannah, she's not on our side." Callum pressed his hands on either side of her stomach as if packing a sand castle. "I used to trust that the rumors about her were just that, but now I think she's actually dangerous. And for the life of me, I can't understand the instinct that would turn someone against their own blood."

"Now who sounds crazy?" Hannah scowled. "Look, I'll admit that it was a mistake to go there. We were already so tightly wound. Maybe if we leave her alone, she'll return the favor." In saying the words, she wished them, wondering if they could be true. Under a cloudless sky and scorching sun, hope came easier.

Callum shivered suddenly.

"What's wrong, Cal?" she whispered, touching his skin. It felt like a skillet, searing.

"Ignore me," he muttered. "It's just lack of sleep. I've been dreaming about—well, never mind."

"No, what?"

Callum's shoulders heaved as if he might sob, but he only stared out at the trees with his increasingly troubled eyes. "My mother, collapsed in a chair, trying to pull herself up by tugging on the tablecloth. Over and over again. I thought I saw her this morning at the dining table. I thought I felt her." He wiped his mouth. "It's all just stress."

She burrowed her body against his, a small creature nuzzling for a moment of safety. "The mind plays tricks when you're so isolated."

"Then let's leave it behind, the isolation," Callum said in a rush. "Maybe it is just fear, and that's another thing my father would frown to hear me say, but it's poison all the same. Not just for us, but for the baby." He shook out his head. "Tell me you haven't thought about it. And what that woman said? About you not being able to leave? She's just messing with us. It's all about control with people like her."

Something buzzed in Hannah's head, more physical sensation than sound. "Of course I've thought about it," she trailed off.

Callum fingered his ear. "What's that sound?"

Hannah took a step back. "You hear it, too?" Something was coming over the hill in a pale and distant wave.

He swatted at his ears. "It feels like it's inside my head." Then he saw them, spreading like a dome over the field, their sonorous bodies blotting out the sun. "Are they locusts?" Panic was seeping into his voice. "Jesus," he let out a laugh that verged on hysteria, "is it a plague?"

"This isn't the Bible." Hannah unwound the cotton scarf from around her neck and tugged down the sleeves of her sweater. "We need to move quickly," she said. "They're usually harmless, but sometimes they'll try to feed."

"Feed?"

"They're cicadas," Hannah said calmly and tied her scarf around her waist. She took Callum's shaking hand and started to trot toward the trees. The sound was swelling, thousands of bodies clicking and strumming in concert. A kicking, of protest or celebration, started in her belly.

"There's so many," he said, craning his head as they ran.

"They live underground for a decade or so, then come in swarms to overwhelm their predators." Two women in jeans and white sneakers stood at the edge of the trees, pointing and shrieking. Hannah didn't recognize them. "Go back," Hannah called.

"Cicadas?" the older of the two called back.

Hannah nodded, out of breath. She grasped a tree trunk and rested her forehead against it. "I haven't seen it this bad since I was a kid. It's far too late in the year for them to come out like this."

The sound rounded over them and was muffled by the canopy. Behind them, the clearing was dim, a stream of cicadas settled like crusted caramel.

Callum stretched his arms out on either side. A few strays hovered above his trembling hands, darting down then retreating. "This is so fucked up," he cried, and seized as a cicada burrowed under his shirt collar.

"Nature's been strange," the older woman said, then pointed to the other woman. "Wasn't I just saying that the other day, Dina?"

Dina nodded eagerly. "We've been finding bloated bullfrogs in our gardens. Lined up in rows and most of them dead. The ones still alive so sluggish it took a dozen firm shakes of my broom to move them."

"I found a mound of grasshoppers, biggest I've ever seen, just climbing atop each other like they were pretending to be ants. They made such an awful racket that they woke up my husband, and that man will snore through anything."

"It's a strange time," Hannah muttered, rubbing her belly. The rhythmic beating continued unabated, like war drums.

"Oh, sweetie," the old woman exclaimed. "When are you due?"

"Around two months," Hannah said.

"May I?" The older woman stepped forward when Hannah nodded. It was a strange feeling, all these hands drawn magnetically to her stomach, settling there with a rapturous look as if she were miracle made flesh.

The woman whistled. "He's really going at it, isn't he?" She laughed. "We don't know the gender yet."

"When will they clear?" Callum asked, peering out past the trees. He'd moved in front of her, acting as a buffer.

Hannah stepped into his shadow, grateful for the protection. "It's hard to say. They'll migrate eventually, but until they do, we can move through them as long as we're quick and cover up."

Callum gave her a sideways glance. "You've seen this before?"

"Oh, sure," the older woman interjected. She massaged her bare arms. "There was another bad swarm fifteen years back. Farmers were locked up in their houses for days, with these darn insects covering up their windows. This looks to be much smaller than that."

"My father said we were being punished," Dina said quietly. She had a full, freckled face and plush red lips. The corners of her eyes looked like crinoline.

The other woman scoffed. "Your father was more superstitious than most old women I know."

"Well, we should be getting back," Callum said, offering them his hand. The older woman clasped it between both of hers.

Dina hunched her shoulders as they passed. "Whereabouts do you live? Have you had much flooding?"

"A bit. We're right down in the swamp," Hannah said quickly. "The house that slopes down to the water."

Dina's eyes narrowed. "The one that used to belong to the conjurer? That's a bad house. They call it a crossroads, where all the doors are open. Where all things are possible."

"Shush, girl," the older woman hissed and slipped an arm around her shoulders. "There's no such thing."

"That woman, the tall one that claims to speak to the dead," Dina insisted, her voice growing louder. Her eyes were muddled, terror and anger swimming together in her whites.

Hannah stood stiffly, taking in the woman's fear.

Dina's body went loose as a dropped doll. Her face blanched as she began to speak, low and quick as an incantation. "My father said it was her fault our crops died. My mother got sick in May, and by June they cut a tumor out of her that had teeth and a tail."

"Goodbye now," Callum said, then he was propelling Hannah into the clearing. Hannah began to walk, holding her belly like a bowl. The tension of so many wings held aloft faded to either side of her as she passed.

"See how she parts the veil," Dina said from behind her. "They're afraid."

Hannah quickened her pace and passed through the edge of the trees. There was a deafening clutter of wings, like a thousand tambourines circling the clearing.

"Hannah," Callum said in a low voice.

Hannah looked up. The cicadas hovered a few inches above her head, so close she could see their corded legs and the blue of their bodies. They were her escort back to the house. She knew suddenly that if she deviated from the path, their mouths, tubed like a butterfly's, would sink into her belly.

"Hannah," Callum urged.

It was true that cicadas swarmed from hibernation to overtake their predators, sometimes in numbers that could be called plague. It was true that they fed on crops and stuck to houses so they made a false night. But ahead of her, they were taking shape. They were clumping to form dark patches, arms and a torso atop long, thick legs. A face that Hannah almost recognized, blurry and wavering in the wings. And then it dissolved.

As she looked around her, she saw thousands of them, treading air and stationary. Watching her. And lower, she was conscious of a gulf stream, a quiet subcurrent of wings circling her waist, closing atop each other as delicately as petals.

"What do I do?" Callum tried to wave them away, then cried out as he was bitten.

Hannah looked down into dozens of eyes, polished like the butts of rifles. They had settled over her small bulge in layers, and she could feel their slight legs pinching at the fabric of the scarf wound around her belly. Her body thrummed with their vibrations and lower, deeper, her child hammered frantically. Hammered, then suddenly stopped.

They dropped from her body like leaves, shaken loose by each of her steady steps. She kept her head high, her eyes fixed straight ahead, and eventually they passed through the swarm. Callum matched her stride.

They were a few meters from the house when she leaned against a tree and lifted her dress up over her belly.

Callum gasped and moved his fingers over the marks, scores of small bites that had turned her white stomach red. "He's not moving."

"Baby's first cicada swarm," Hannah said. *Kick*, she thought at the baby, the word pounding in her head. "It's practically a rite of passage. Every generation gets a couple."

"He's okay, though?"

She nodded against him.

"I thought I'd jinxed it. You asked me to wait, but I couldn't."

Hannah's body stiffened. "What do you mean?"

"I'll show you, but don't be mad, okay? Take this as it was intended." He took her hand and led her up the path to the back door, kicking branches out of the way. The ground felt like quicksand under her shoes, more marsh than solid earth, and she stopped when she saw the frogs. Speckled bullfrogs and tree frogs, the pure green color of new ferns, littered the back slope.

"How was it intended?" Hannah asked, allowing Callum to take off her sweater then kneel to remove her muddied shoes as if she were a child.

"A reminder of my love," Callum said grandly as he led her up the stairs. They stopped in front of Hannah's old bedroom and she felt her stomach sink.

She knew before he opened the door, could almost picture the mobile twirling, but the reality took her breath away. He'd pasted transparent, colored films to the windows so the light filtered in as rainbows. A gleaming mahogany crib stretched against one wall, beneath two mobiles, one with flowers, the other with stars and moons.

The crib was lined with a thick white mattress and covered in a yellow fleece blanket embroidered with a lamb.

She gripped her belly. It would be that small, that

utterly vulnerable, when it left her. There'd be nothing to protect it from corners and stairs, from particles in the air and water, or from finer particles still, in the unknown spaces between worlds.

"Do you like it?" Callum asked shyly. He'd painted a faint question mark on the wall, large and confrontational, in yellow watercolors. "I was thinking yellow for the walls, if you decide you still want to wait until the birth to know its sex."

Hannah ran her hand along the edge of the crib, imagining all the sleepless nights she'd spend in that exact spot, her feet guiding her to it blindly in the darkness. Then she noticed the rocking chair in the corner.

"That was Mae's," Hannah said, lowering herself carefully into it.

She'd spent countless hours in Mae's lap being lulled by the ticking of the chair, the back and forth that always teetered under their combined weight without falling.

Hannah focused on the faint creaking as she rocked, fighting back tears. The carved armrests gleamed below her fingers. She imagined Callum bent over the chair, buffing and varnishing, with the single aim of welcoming their child.

The child that she'd recklessly, selfishly taken from the house. Put in harm's way, and for what? To confirm what she already knew. Whatever forces surrounded her, those that had always been there and those that grew stronger in pace with her child, would not let her go.

At least now she had a definite answer. Tears trickled down her cheeks as the cicadas settled against the windowpane, each body another brick on her prison wall.

She beckoned to Callum and he came to sit beside the chair.

Even in the dim, there was a yellow cast to his skin that worried her. How much had he been drinking? Had the stress pushed him to pursue other vices? She opened her mouth, wanting to ask, then changed her mind. "I take it as it was intended," she said, her voice choking. "Thank you."

He smiled wryly. "Well, good. Reports of how easy this was to put together may have been exaggerated." He dropped down onto his back and frowned at the ceiling. "Look, something's wrong here," he said. She tried to catch one of his bobbing toes, but he wiggled away. "I've never seen anything like that. Fuck, I've never heard of anything like that. A cicada swarm, fine. Weird, but documented." He arced his neck to see her. "But they were focused on you. On the baby. It was like they were sentient."

Hannah bucked her feet off the floor and rocked harder. "Of course they're sentient. They're insects."

"It's not just that. It's this whole house. I love you, I love it, I love that you love it, but maybe we can talk about finding another place. Somewhere that will bring us more luck." Hannah saw naked want on his face, and realized every- thing he'd given up. She'd been raised in the silence and was content to sit on the bank, watching hyacinth patches knit themselves into a lush carpet, then break apart. She saw now that he needed something very different.

"We can talk about it after the birth," she said slowly, hating herself for hiding things from him. "A big move like that would be stressful for me and the baby." Small thuds sounded behind her. She didn't turn, knowing the cicadas were pattering across the glass, shifting then settling to make room for more. Light drained from the room as they covered the window.

"I need to sleep," he said from the floor, and gripped the leg of the crib. "I could've sworn I saw them—" He stopped and shook his head. "I don't know. It sounds insane. It looked like there was someone in the swarm. As if they were forming a person." Callum laughed sharply. "Fuck," he whispered, rolling his face into the floor.

Hannah tried to laugh, then rubbed her eyes. "Maybe all parents feel like this," she said with a sigh. "The paranoia of everything that can go wrong."

"There's paranoia and then there's justified concern." Callum pulled his guitar from under the crib. "I've been imagining playing him to sleep when he comes, and this incredible peace settles over me," he said. "Well, him or her." His metal pick flashed like a razor in the growing dim. "How is it possible to love someone you've never even seen, someone who doesn't yet exist, so fucking much? I would never do anything to hurt either one of you, so if you think we need to wait until he's born to move, then we'll do that. But Hannah," his finger slipped on a fret, "after that, we start looking for somewhere safe to raise this child."

She rocked back and closed her eyes on hot tears. "Sure," she said, her voice breaking. *What will happen then*, she started to wonder but blocked the thought. She'd bought herself time to find a way out.

He set down the guitar and moved to hold her. She spotted the swollen spot on the back of his hand where the cicada had bit him and leaned over to kiss it.

"Mama," he said softly.

CHAPTER
NINE

From the ridge, the marsh looked like a robin's egg. Blue water broken by tussocks of yellowing grass. A long-limbed bird stepped gingerly through the shallow water.

Hannah drew her knees under her chin, her sunburned legs scaled as bark. Beside her, Jacob cupped his hands to his mouth and let out a single, mournful note. The bird raised its head and spread its wings. It regarded them, eyes black and unblinking.

"What did you say to it?" Hannah asked.

Jacob shrugged, smiling vacantly. There was something strange about the marsh, all the trees cracked in half and crowned in jagged spikes of their own bark. The sun had blanched Jacob's face and hair to the dry white of a skull. He seemed to fade into the landscape.

"Where's Sarah Anne?"

Jacob's eyes clouded. Confusion spread across his face. "Your sister," Hannah added.

"Not my sister. Me." In the flat silence, she thought she heard a rustle of wings behind her. "I saw you together." His face was wavering, changing so slowly that Hannah had the urge to rub her eyes, but she felt unsure that she could move her hands.

"I saw you with your mother. The dark one. I saw her alone once, too." His mouth opened and she saw the quaking pink tip of his tongue. On either side were nine black teeth, rotting and caked in mud. The smell of dead tissue and briny gator eggs rolled from his mouth.

"Jacob," she whispered, trying not to cover her face.

"I've been screaming underground," he said without closing his mouth. His tongue flailed like an earthworm.

The bird cried out below them.

"What did the bird say back?" she asked in a smaller voice.

His body began to convulse as a scream built all around them.

Sunlight stabbed her eyes as she woke. Callum sat on the edge of the desk in their bedroom and stared out at the water with deep concentration. Graydon watched him sleepily from the windowsill.

"How long have you been awake?" Hannah asked, rising stiffly from the bed. She paused to stretch out her lower back before walking over to him and laying a cool hand on the nape of his neck.

He flinched from her touch. "I couldn't sleep. I kept dreaming about swarms of birds, or insects. It was hideous." He cleared his throat as she gathered scrawled notes from the desk and eased herself beside him. "They were attacking you. I can't shake the sound of them chewing. It was *wet*."

Hannah followed his gaze to a black spot amidst the green leaves, some black carrion bird watching her from a branch. The bird opened its beak in a soundless squawk and pattered away in a dainty spread of plumage.

"You were dreaming, too, I think. You were making little sounds and kicking in your sleep," Callum said.

Hannah nudged his toes with hers. "I don't remember."

"Dr. Merrick called this morning with the results of your blood tests."

Hannah rolled her shoulders. "Oh, I forgot all about that. I'm doing so much better, don't you think?"

"Toxins." The word hung in the air, confounding. "He found a whole host of animal and plant toxins, all in trace amounts. He said, and I kid you not, that they amounted to poison." Dark circles shadowed Callum's eyes. Hannah plucked at the loose skin on his elbow, noting that it remained extended for a few moments.

"Mae's spices," Hannah began, but Callum shook his head and spoke over her. "Your mother, Hannah. That goddamn woman made you ill."

"I don't think she was trying to. It was my own fault. I asked her to help." The lies were difficult to speak, leaden in her mouth.

"Help with what?"

Hannah held up her palms. "I thought she could offer

some protection, something to ward off what's been happening."

"What, Hannah, poor man's witchcraft and cure-alls?"

"Mae's done the same before, relying on herbal remedies. They can be more powerful than pharmaceuticals in some combinations. I've been messing around in the kitchen, looking through Mae's old recipes and spices, and I found a few that are pretty strange. One called for menstrual blood."

Callum's mouth clamped shut. He squinted as if trying to make out familiar contours in her face, then took her hand. His lips ran an arpeggio along her knuckles. "Do you promise you're alright? I honestly don't know what I'd do if—" As his voice trailed off, a gust of wind rose off the water. "No more messing around, though. Promise me. It's not too long now," he said, hooking his arm around her shoulder. He nuzzled her ear. "I wonder what he'll be best at. Think we'll go fishing together?"

"Don't forget that it could very well be a she. I'd bet she'd cast a line with you." Hannah tried to smile. She felt brittle inside. Hatred was an unfamiliar sensation and though it left her dizzy, she embraced it. Her own mother. "There's been only girls on my end," Hannah added, and immediately tightened her hands into fist, her nails pressing deep into her palm, one by one. It was a private rosary, a prayer for protection, that whatever broken gene might have passed to her would end with her.

"You're sure you don't want to have it checked?"

"I'd rather not know." Hannah mapped his spine with her thumb. Those same ridges were materializing in her belly, a slender ladder whose rungs leaned ever so slightly to the left.

Callum gave her a thorough, plumbing look. "Momma's choice, I guess." He hopped off the desk and knelt in front of her, laying his head against her belly. "I always hoped I'd be here," he whispered. He sounded young, a little boy telling the story of his day as he drifted to sleep. "My own father was such a deadbeat that I hoped I'd get the chance to do it right with one of my own. My poor mother. I'd get mad at her sometimes, as though by staying with him, she was rewarding him. Like, her presence was saying, 'It's okay. You're still within the limits of okay.'" He paused, then craned his neck to gaze up at her. "But now I'm happy, and it feels like more than I could've asked for." His brows were bowed with vulnerability. "Are you?"

"Of course I am," she cooed. "This is *it. The* thing we're meant to do. The goal of everything."

He shuffled down so his head was resting against her thighs and looked beyond her, his eyes echoing the deep, uncanny blue of the sky. "What will we do?" he asked, "When it comes, I mean. What if," he swallowed hard, "I get sick and can't be around. How will we take care of the baby?"

Hannah chuckled. "Oh, you know," she said lightly, "the best we can. I'll mourn for a little while, then trade you in for someone younger."

She was still surprised by the sensation of something moving inside her, turning slowly through the snug confines of her womb. It didn't feel tethered, held in place by sinewy cables. She could tell by the way her belly bulged differently from day to day, by how the heaviness shifted and bundled itself in the night. A slow-motion game of cups was taking place underneath her curve.

You can't hide from me, she thought at it. *You can try to swim down to my ankles, or flatten yourself under my ribcage, but you are always in me.*

"I was thinking we could invite James over tonight. After all, it's Halloween. We've been so wrapped up in our own problems here, and it'd be good for us to socialize a bit."

"Halloween," Hannah repeated dumbly. Locals claimed that the veil between the living and the dead was thinnest around Halloween, but the elderly blamed unusual occurrences on local kids who used the night to try their unskilled, drunken hands at voodoo.

One Halloween, Hannah had dressed in an elaborate witch's costume, complete with a silver pentagram necklace she'd bought from an antique store in town.

"What are you playing at, child?" Mae had studied the synthetic black wig, the skintight black bodysuit, and the cheap nylon cape tied at the neck with fragile cobwebbed lace. "You can call it superstition, but do me this favor. Take it off. It's a game of chicken, impressionable children goading the other side."

"So, what do you think?" Callum asked.

"The house is a mess, and do we even have enough food for a proper dinner?" Hannah immediately began listing excuses. Then, "Will he bring Leah?"

Callum sat up. "Of course not."

"If you want her here, then go ahead," she said quickly and slid off the desk, trying to pick a fight.

"I don't. I swear it. I just need a bit of a break." Her

throat closed. "Never from you," he added. "But it's been stressful here. Living in town, all I learned is drunks are drunks from sea to shining sea. That, and crazies are sane enough to work a lock. Living here, by the water, is a very different beast."

"I've lived here my whole life. If you reject this, you're rejecting me." Hannah looked around the room. There was the dresser she'd picked out on her sixteenth birthday, which they'd moved into Mae's bedroom. She'd dreamt of filling it with beautiful clothes, opaque black stockings that would close tight above her knees. There was Mae's strong mahogany bedframe, which had withstood Hannah's jumps toward the ceiling and her acrobatic somersaults into a fort of pillows against the headboard. The memories murmured from every corner.

"I don't mean that and you know it. I'm saying," Callum said in a sigh, "that I've followed you into the goddamn murk and would keep at it into the deep bowels of the earth. I will even stay in the goddamn murk if you need us to. But we've been living in this dankness and it'd be so good to clear it out. Just a bit."

She picked at the cat hair on her nightgown, trying to keep hidden how his words affected her. "Fine. James can come to dinner."

"That's it?" Callum crossed his arms. "That's all you have to say to that?"

"I love you," she muttered, crossing her own arms. "Happy now?" He stepped toward her and angled her face up with the crook of his thumb.

"Say it again."

"I love you, idiot."

"Happy now," he agreed and kissed her deeply. His tongue dipped between her lips and swirled hypnotically. She felt everything mute around them and, for a moment, the calm pacified her.

Then her eyes burst open. "I need to get ready. What will we feed him? I can't believe Halloween snuck up on us like this."

"When you didn't mention it, I thought you'd forgotten. I took the liberty of outfitting you for this evening." Out of a nondescript cardboard box overflowing with peach-hued tissue paper, Callum pulled out a dress. He'd brought home elastic-banded cotton pants and skirts to house her growing belly, but this was something else. "I'll admit," he said, hovering over her as she fingered the low-cut bodice, the empire waist, and the pleated silk skirt. "It's not much of a costume per se, but a job took me into Baton Rouge last week and I thought you'd like it."

"It's too much." She could almost smell lilac and forsythia in its sheer purple folds. It was a perfect bloom, born from fabric. "It's not really me." Callum's face fell, and she shook her head. "No, I just mean, where would I wear it?"

"Tonight, of course. You can be my princess."

Licking her lips like a child before a dessert platter, she pulled off her nightgown and carefully slid the dress up over her naked body. Where the chiffon brushed against her nipples, it felt like a kitten's tongue. "Zip me." It fit as if it had been custom made, stretched around her belly and snug against her chest. "How do I look?"

"Beautiful. Do you like it?" Callum asked.

"I love it, but what will you be?"

"Your gallant prince," he said wryly and pointed to a starched white shirt, "who will look suspiciously like a waiter."

"You've done," James paused and did a theatrical turn around the living room, "absolutely nothing with this place." He handed Hannah a bottle of red wine and kissed her cheek. "That's quite the dress," he added in a whisper.

"Well, we're not really sure where we'll be settling down just yet," Callum said, avoiding Hannah's eyes.

"Nothing's quite been decided." Hannah smiled tightly. "We have enough change coming down the pipeline without adding to the stress."

A loaded silence fell over them, and Hannah smoothed the silk dress over her stomach.

"You're getting huge," James changed the subject. "And glowing. My God, how far along are you now?"

Hannah and Callum looked at each other and spoke at the same time. "Nearly eight months."

"That's a lot of baby." James sat down on the couch. Graydon lifted his head from Mae's old chair, surveyed the room, and curved into himself like a touched fern.

Hannah stood back against the wall. Being a hostess was not in her repertoire. Mae had fashioned a world from books in homeschooling her, and taught her to be whole in herself. Friends had rarely visited and she'd rarely wanted them to. Even around James, who had no expectations and would've been happiest with beer and cream cheese on crackers, Hannah found herself adjusting herself and her home. A strand of loose hair was immediately tucked. She moved the lamp in a senseless shuffle back and forth by centimeters.

She wondered how often Leah had entertained the two men. "Shall we open the wine?" Hannah said, her voice sounding taut to her own ears.

"I'll do it." Callum took the bottle.

She sat down beside James and palmed her knees. After a moment, she heard glasses clinking from the kitchen. "He must miss you, and the nightlife in town. I feel bad for that."

James blinked, then leaned over and pulled a stack of magazines from his bag. "Yeah. A few grungy bars and too much drinking. Really, what's to miss? I think he's in good hands here. I hope you are, too. I brought these for you."

Hannah's hands sagged beneath the weight as she leafed through the covers, a series of flawless airbrushed faces. Her finger lingered on the beaming face of a bride. She let herself consider the veil on the magazine's cover, committing each white satin rosebud to memory.

"That one's from Leah," James said. "I told her it might not be, well, you know." He muffled a cough. "Anyways. She insisted."

Hannah could feel her face flush. "She would, wouldn't she?"

"She's trying to be kind," he said quietly.

Hannah raised her chin and looked him straight in the eye. "I'm protecting what's mine."

"Believe me, I get it." James put his hand over her wrist. "But there's nothing for you to worry about."

"But," Hannah started, then noticed James's red cheeks.

It dawned on her. "You love her," she said slowly. She could feel the clamminess of his hand, and his fingers twitched as if a mild current was animating them.

"Her hair's brown under all that black gunk. We go back awhile. Everything was simpler then, back when we used to climb trees and smoke our parents' tobacco. When we used to feel free saying what we meant, piss-drunk off our parents' rye." His mouth clamped shut.

"Have you told her?" Hannah asked, lowering her voice.

James looked over to the kitchen, where Callum was rifling through the pantry. "We got older, Hannah, all of us. Mistakes were made."

Hannah bit the inside of her lip. "Did they," she cleared her throat, "together?"

James squeezed her hand and though she waited, breathing carefully, he didn't look at her. "It's the past," he said simply.

Hannah swallowed, and it sounded like someone falling over a gorge. She'd known somehow.

"It didn't mean anything to him, Hannah. Not really. I can promise you that."

"But it meant something to you," Hannah said.

James's smile was pained. "I've watched her hook up with an army of shits, and for some reason, I've stuck around. I guess you never forget your first love when, no matter how hard you try, the timing never works. But, still, you hope." His eyes closed for a moment.

Hannah withdrew her hand as Callum entered the room, his body half-arched to support the three wine-glasses.

"You, my dear," he said, thrusting his chin toward Hannah, "can have exactly one. A little one." He winked at James, not noticing his expression. "We men will luxuriate in not having a uterus."

At the dinner table, Hannah studied the spread of food that Callum had prepared. He'd moved with surprising speed through the kitchen, baking fragrant cheese-and-chive scones, as she'd given orders from her chair. She tried to summon up an appetite for the salmon speckled with pepper and parsley, but its dead eyes looked like props to her. Callum excavated the bones from the fish, then squeezed half a lemon over her pickled fennel.

"It's nowhere near as good as Hannah's cooking," Callum said.

"I believe it," James said, smiling, "but it's still a far cry from those awful nachos you used to live on. You've trained him well, Hannah."

She watched Callum move his food around his plate as James spoke. He seemed to be gagging deep in his throat whenever he looked down at the fish. She squeezed his thigh under the table and fought not to indulge the nauseating image of his hands entangled in Leah's hair, the two of them tussling on a mattress.

When they were left alone for a minute, Callum kissed her through a blazing smile and his cheeks felt warm. He massaged her belly. "I'm happy to be us."

"You're just drunk," she said, laughing, but hugged him to her neck. She tried to remember that his warm breath was hers alone. She looked over his shoulder, at the table littered with dirty dishes, the tablecloth freckled with crumbs, the quartered lemons limp and curling on the edges of plates. Somehow, she'd stumbled into a real life. A life that was hers, and growing inside her, a life that was theirs.

"There's something wrong with your plumbing," James said, knocking his shoulder against the doorframe. "It sounds like there's something in the pipes."

Callum leaned forward across the table. "Something *wrong* with the *plumbing*," he said slowly, making air quotes. "Code for quick, spray some air freshener."

"I'm serious." James squeezed the back of his chair and sighed. "I'm drunk, and I'm serious, and I should be getting home."

"I'll take you," Callum said, rising from the table.

Hannah waved her hands. "No one's going anywhere. James, sleep here. We have so much extra space, and no one to fill it with." She tapped her stomach. "At least not yet. You can sleep in the nursery. I'm sure we can find a sleeping bag somewhere."

The two men shared a private look and Callum chuckled. "We'll be by to swaddle you later."

"Shh," James hissed. A bang echoed throughout the house. "Listen."

The pounding came again, followed by a scurrying across the walls, and Hannah felt for a panicked moment that there was something pressing against the interstitial spaces of the house. "What is that?"

"It's just the pipes," Callum said, squinting at the ceiling.

"I told you they're clogged." James ran a finger along the wallpaper, a striped pattern that had faded and bled decades ago. "Want me to take a look at it?"

Callum yawned. "Tomorrow. It can wait. Besides, it's probably a frog that got in when the swamp flooded."

"Big frog," Hannah whispered and gathered a stack of plates against her stomach. She took them into the kitchen and by the time she ran the water over them, the hammering had stopped. Still, she thought she could hear a pulse between the peals of laughter from the living room, where Callum and James were opening a bottle of whiskey and cracking peanut shells.

Above her, the light flickered as if someone were screwing and unscrewing the lightbulb.

Hannah woke in the night to the clapping inside her and the thudding against the bedroom walls. She rolled over.

"I can still hear it."

"Go back to sleep," Callum said, his voice plaintive, and stroked her arm. She watched his face lose the luster of consciousness. After a moment, he started to snore.

Hannah stared at Callum's bowed head. She reached out a hand to brush his hair aside, but something stopped her. The angle was strange, the hair too long and covering too much of his face. Her heart began to pound and she thought that there might be no features beneath the darkness. A terrible, irrational suspicion welled up in her that it wasn't Callum lying beside her.

Another hammer tested the house's walls.

She sat up and tiptoed toward the door. As she peered into the hallway, fear dried her mouth. "James?" she called softly.

Silence answered her, and she snuck along the old floorboards. The door to her childhood room was ajar and she pushed it open. "James," she whispered into the room.

His face was half-lit by the moon, his features slack in sleep. He had collapsed in his clothes atop the sleeping bag, and he looked harmless, although she remembered a very different version of him pinioning her against a rusted pick-up when she was only ten years old.

"Who gave this to my little sister?" he'd yelled, dangling a twine necklace in front of her. A bone hung from the loop.

Hannah had gone limp at that. It was fear, she'd suddenly understood, that motivated him. "I don't know," she'd whispered.

A slap had sounded against the door of the truck, and they turned to see a waddling old woman in a crochet sweater. White wiry hair showed beneath her makeshift turban. "Hush up, boy," she hissed, "or I'll cane you like your mama should. That there's rabbit, and your little miss must be teething something fierce. You put it back around her neck, 'less you want her smile to grow up crooked. Go on," the woman had said, and slammed her bag of groceries against the truck again. "Git."

A thud against the wall startled Hannah out of remembrance, and she backed instinctively into the doorframe, hands closing like parentheses around her belly. In the moment, she had the wild sense of a womb around her, spasming with its own imperative.

"What the fuck?" James cried, struggling to his feet.

"I couldn't sleep. The pounding was so loud and I was trying to figure out what it was."

James massaged his head as he came to stand by her. "I slept through it. That whiskey was potent. Where's Callum?"

"Asleep."

James sighed, the edge draining from his voice. "I hate to say it, but you might have a burst pipe." He flicked the light switch on and the house remained dark. "Please tell me that idiot bought flashlights."

Hannah shrugged. "I don't know. We have lots of candles downstairs. Mae was a big believer in candlelit everything."

James fit his fingers between hers and stepped into the hallway. "Tread carefully. He'll never forgive me if anything happens to you." They made their way down the stairs, both grasping the banister. She wanted to take the lead, to tell him she'd practically slid up and down these stairs on moonless nights her whole life, but she kept quiet. Sounds still bubbled up throughout the house, and when she put her hand on the wall to steady herself, she felt a pounding behind it.

"We need matches," he said, and disappeared into the kitchen.

Hannah shivered. She was wrong. The house wasn't the same as it'd been in her childhood. Mae had kept all fear, and all cause for fear, at bay.

"Found them," James said, joining her with a flame in his hand.

She opened the closet with trembling hands and pointed to a box overflowing with long white candles. "Take your pick."

James took a step back.

"What?" Hannah filled her hands with them and held their wicks up to the blaze.

"Those candles," he said, wincing as the first was lit.

"She got them in bulk. I think it was a discount. Don't worry, they burn fine. She used to leave them in the windows, and they'd burn for a whole day. I did it, too, for a while, but I guess I forgot."

James took the candles from her hands while she dug around for holders. "They're used for offerings in town, offerings to spirits. We've been fishing hoodoo bottles from the Vermilion for years, little stoppered things with scrawled spells and spices in them. Rootwork," he said, defensive before her pursed lips. James systematically inserted the candles into their holders, then distributed them around the living room, swearing as he bumped into furniture and tripped on clumps in the rug. "It's been a strange night, that's all. You woke me from a bad nightmare." He whirled around suddenly with wide eyes.

"What did you see?"

"Something's off here. Don't you feel it?"

Hannah tasted her own sour fear in the back of her throat, but shook her head.

"I grew up on stories about your mother. The kids at school used to dare each other to cross the woods, near the edge of the water, and stand behind this house. Rumor had it that there was a crossroads here, that some mornings there'd be blood in the water."

Hannah remembered James's cold eyes and bared teeth, his strong teenaged grip. Everyone had been wary of Hannah then, particularly the boys. She'd been too young to understand the murmurings, the challenge in the eyes of full-grown women as they stepped in front of their husbands, as if Hannah's stare alone could sap them of something vital. She'd never seen pools of blood, but she'd seen shapes that at first seemed to be bloated bodies. After a blink or two, they would clarify into logs, rocks, or the spindly back of an alligator.

"It's my home, James," she said.

"We've been watching her for years. I've been watching her." His shoulders were tight and squared. "I'd sound bat-shit crazy if I used old local tales to justify surveillance, but when the evidence shows up in hospitals and morgues, you start to wonder. I like cut-and-dry calls. I like shootings and drug busts, where handcuffs mean something. Even traiteurs are a dime a dozen, and most of them will give you a case of indigestion or land you in bed for a week. Mostly they like to fuck with tourists who have a fetish for voodoo."

His expression looked crazed in the candlelight as he headed down the hall toward the bathroom. "We don't know what goes on in that church of hers, in that barn on the other side of the swamp. They call that place a crossroads, too. But men wither before their wives' eyes, and young boys waste away in a matter of months. Every time we manage to get in, there's nothing to see. Just her and a handful of men who swear there's nothing wrong."

He tapped his heel hard against the floorboards and averted his eyes. "We've wanted to get under these floors for years." He peered at the worn wood so intensely that Hannah wondered what he was seeing in his mind's eye. Lost boys heaped in the dank dark.

"I give permission," Hannah said quickly. "It's my house."

James pressed his ear to the bathroom door and listened. "It's not your house," he murmured.

"She said—"

"I've looked into it. It's still hers. I'd bet anything that if we came in here, ready to dig, her and that crony Samuel would manifest quick as bunnies."

"Samuel isn't well," Hannah said, then wondered if he was even still alive. James's face told her he was thinking the same thing. "Why don't you stop her?" Somehow, she already knew what he would say.

"It's voluntary, you see?" The gentle tone of his voice undid Hannah, and she sunk onto the arm of the couch. "I still believe she forces them somehow, but they swear to their families, right into their deathbed, that it was their choice." James bit his fingernail. "And I literally mean deathbed. Most of them die in their sleep."

Hannah breathed in, surprised. "In their sleep? But how? What happens to them?"

As if in answer, another crack rang out, sounding like the house were made of bones, all snapped at once.

"They drain. Sure as a bucket taken by rust."

A few days before, she'd glimpsed Callum through the open bathroom door. When their eyes met in the mirror, he'd closed the door with a tight smile. He'd tried to clean the blood from the ceramic, but the surface retained a dark red smear. She'd felt frozen by a foreboding she couldn't place. Mae's scrawled medicine held a troubling treatment for nosebleeds—wadded cobwebs, tight into the nostril.

Something beat itself against the bathroom door and both Hannah and James jumped.

"That's one of the many perks of living on the swamp,"

James said. His forehead shone with sweat. "If your septic breaks down enough, little critters can find their way in."

The living room was luminous, each candle giving off its own halo. Painful nostalgia filled Hannah, for the candlelight beacons Mae would set in the windows, murmuring as she looked at her illuminated reflection in the glass. Some nights, Hannah would tiptoe downstairs for a midnight snack and find the kitchen bright as day, infused with the smell of burning wax. She'd felt safe then, the unexpected light making those moments feel like extensions of a dream.

Another knock sounded and Hannah stood and stepped forward. James put an arm across her chest. "You hang back. If there's a gator in there, you run."

Hannah gripped James's shoulder. "Don't go in," she pleaded. "We'll wait until morning." It had finally found her. Now it was toying with her. The bathroom door could be broken as easily as cardboard by the thing's heavy back. That anemic white, parched for red.

James shook off her hand and moved toward the bathroom, his face grim. She followed quietly, hugging herself.

All she could feel were the creature's fingers tapping against her belly, its cuticles stretched and bloody from trying to contain the gnarled claws. She wasn't sure where or when she'd felt them. A dream, maybe, as textured as memory. Suddenly, she felt humiliated. She wondered what James would think, seeing the nightmare creature made real against the tiles. The feeling was new, as if the creature was somehow her responsibility. Hers to explain, hers to hide.

James threw her one darting look before launching his body at the door. The smell of swollen oysters drifted out.

The white tiles were covered in black tendrils, corded and coiled, growing exponentially before her eyes. They writhed, wet and glistening from the pipes they'd crawled through, and moved hypnotically toward her. Hannah brought her bare feet down on them, without thinking about what she was doing. She slipped on their slick backs.

"Christ!" James cried and wrestled open the cupboard under the sink. "Snakes," he screamed. He pulled out a hammer and began to strike. The sound was hideous, and Hannah turned away, covering her ears. Behind her, something live and anatomical was being crushed. Then there was only James's heavy panting, echoing from the tiles.

James backed out of the bathroom and Hannah followed him as he sunk slowly to the hallway floor.

"It's just the flood," Hannah trailed off with a moan, realizing that her excuses were growing flimsier. Blood stained her heels. She closed her eyes and concentrated on slowing her rapid heartbeat.

"It's this house, isn't it?" He shook her arm urgently. "It's something to do with your mother?"

A briny odor filled the house, so thick it almost colored the air. "Are any of them poisonous?"

"No, they're Brahminys." James carefully pinched at a streak of blood on his pant leg. "You could eat their heart." To Hannah's shocked face, he explained, "Another story from my childhood. Eat the heart of a black snake for courage, or wear its skeleton to cure an ache." Something slid against the bathroom tiles and James reached over her to slam the door shut. "Am I still dreaming?"

"Maybe we both are." Hannah suddenly looked upstairs, toward the silence. She leaned forward and plucked a candle from a shelf on the bookcase. The white wax was already beginning to drip, and she relished each small instant of pain as it dried on the back of her hand. "Callum couldn't have slept through that."

"We were screaming bloody murder down here, and I haven't heard a peep from him. When did he get to have such a low tolerance?"

"His appetite's been bad." Hannah went to stand at the bottom of the stairs. Shadows wound ahead of her extended candle. "Callum," she called up softly, then climbed the stairs when there was no answer. Wax dripped onto her toes.

She paused in front of their bedroom and waited for James to catch up. The hammer swung weakly from his hands. He looked spent.

Callum lay on his back in bed. Hannah could make out a large crack that had appeared just under the window-sill, snaking toward the floor and disappearing below the rug. She gripped the gold candleholder with both hands to stop their shaking as she walked into the room.

Graydon stood on the dresser, tremors passing up and down his back. He stared unblinking at Callum's body and let loose low growls.

"Baby," Hannah whispered, as she rounded his side of the bed. When she saw him, the candle dropped from her hands as if it'd been slapped, and she scurried to catch it.

Callum's eyes were wide open, the whites of his eyes immense and reflecting the light of the moon. His hands were curled against his chest, fetal, and his legs paddled weakly beneath the covers. Hannah sat carefully on the edge of the bed and tried to hold down his feet. His mouth was curved into a manic smile, open and obscene, completely at odds with the terror she saw on his face. She had seen such an expression somewhere before. *Jacob*, she suddenly thought.

"Callum, snap out of it." Hannah shook him roughly.

A strangled sound came from his throat.

"What's happening?" James said from behind her.

"Something's wrong! He's not waking up."

James leaned over Callum and expertly found his pulse. "Come on, buddy. What did you take?" He mouthed out a count to thirty. "It's shallow," he said to Hannah, and took the candle from her hands. James waved the flame in front of his eyes, pushing back the eyelids with his fingers. "His eyes aren't following the light. Is he on anything? Has he been using again?"

Hannah shook her head. James rifled through the dresser drawers, tossing up Hannah's underwear. "What are you doing?"

"You can't always be sure." He knocked aside her hairbrush and a bottle of lavender oil as he searched.

"I told you, he's not on anything. Do something—"

Callum gargled from the bed again and his hand shot out, closing around Hannah's right wrist tight enough to close off her circulation.

"Okay, that's enough." James set down the candle and dove onto the bed. He tried to pull Callum's arm away, but his grip didn't loosen. James punched Callum's shoulder.

"Don't hurt him," Hannah yelped, even as Callum's nails dug so deep that they drew blood.

"Callum, stop!" James slapped his face, but the blanched, smiling mask didn't slip. Callum's other hand shot out blindly and struck James with incredible strength. The man crumpled, and fell off the bed.

"Jacob?" Hannah breathed, and in response, a burst of spittle left Callum's mouth, and a single fly, black and benign, fell from his lips.

"You are not yours," he howled. The veins of his face seemed to swell.

Then it was over. His grip loosened, but Hannah didn't move her hand despite the pain. His feet stilled and his mouth became slack. His eyes closed, and a few moments later, his breath evened.

Graydon hissed frantically from a corner of the room, but Hannah gave only a passing glance to her wrist. The duvet was dotted with blood. She didn't know how long she stayed like that, unwilling or unable to move. She turned his words over in her mind, trying to find meaning.

"What the hell just happened?" James asked as he struggled to sit up.

Hannah took a breath. "You had a bit too much to drink, James. You fell down. Do you feel concussed?" Her lie slipped out without effort.

James sat on the bed beside her, shaking his head. "Something was wrong with him. I think—he hit me." The words curled into a question. She saw recrimination in his eyes when they turned to her.

"No. Can you believe it?" she said, feeling herself smile. "He slept through the whole thing." She stood, sure-footed, and grabbed a sweater from the dresser. The sleeves came down to her knuckles. "Are you feeling nauseous at all? Dizzy?"

James felt the caked blood under his nose. "Did I fall on my face?"

Hannah nodded and pulled a clean towel from the top shelf of the closet. "Let's get you cleaned up, and then you should rest," she said, tossing him the towel. "It'll be light soon."

She hurried down the stairs, briefly distracted by the constellation of candlelight, and clicked the bathroom door behind her. The live snakes had retreated from where they'd come, but five dead bodies lay flattened. They seemed smaller now. Five snakes in a house could be explained, she hoped, but an army seemed the stuff of nightmares.

She lowered the toilet lid, pulled a towel from its rack, and sat down. Not realizing at first what she intended to do, she selected the largest of the crushed snakes and dropped it into the towel. She clutched a pair of cuticle scissors and carefully made an incision down its length. She felt far removed from herself, almost as if someone else was guiding her hands. No tremor disturbed her movements as she parted the flesh below its head, followed the skeleton to find its lungs, and touched the tip of the scissors to the sac that she intuited housed its heart.

She snipped the small shreds of tissue on either side and lifted it out whole. As she cradled it, her resolve wavered, replaced by revulsion. She stared with numb horror at the snake's body and, without thinking, slammed her foot down until the evidence of her cuts was lost. The cuticle scissors landed in the garbage can.

On her way out, she prodded another of the dead snakes with her foot and nodded to herself when it didn't budge. The heart she carried with her into the kitchen.

CHAPTER
TEN

Callum chewed half a piece of toast into mush, bleary eyed, while James ate a banana, massaging his nose. Neither of them noticed that Hannah sat straight-backed, only sipping a tea from Mae's collection. Dried lemon balm, to ease her nervousness.

The memory of what she'd eaten the night before, greasy under a crust of black pepper and chili peppers, would suffice for days. She'd cooked it quickly, reaching blindly for spices, and continuing to flavor the snake heart even after it was coated. She hadn't been able to finish it, but her body kept down what she consumed.

Then, she'd sunk to the floor and followed its passage through her body with a fingertip, the junctures at which her stomach resisted, the way it broke through. When it reached her belly, she patted it with warm hands, imagining that it would strengthen her baby. She had looked down and saw her wrist, raw as if with stigmata.

After their meager lunch, James left quickly, not giving Callum enough time to consider the delicate bruises under James's eyes, the elephantine swelling of his nose. "Something happened last night," James said on his way out.

"Snakes," she said wearily. "They came in through the drains. It seems like all the earth's plagues are coming down on us."

James patted the swollen tissue around his nose. "After that, I mean."

Hannah shrugged.

"You're not alone, Hannah, and it's not weakness to ask for help when you need it. There are things in this world that are out of our control."

Hannah could almost taste the relief of sharing her burden with someone, of accepting help, but she knew it would be short-lived. "I remember a boy who felt very differently. All those things you said last night? When did you get to be so knowledgeable about the other side?"

James's bloodshot eyes hardened. "To fight a thing, you have to understand it."

They stared at each other, locked in a contest to see who would yield first.

"You call me if you need anything at all," James said finally.

Hannah closed the door behind him, then walked slowly into the living room and let herself sag onto the couch. The baby was unusually slow but she could sense an undercurrent of strength since the previous night, some new measure of endurance. She felt it in herself as well.

The corner of the wedding magazine winked white from beneath the coffee table. She flipped the pages slowly. A pale redhead smiled shyly under her feathered head-piece, her shoulders covered with fine lace. She plucked a bouquet of dried lavender from a vase on the table and tapped Graydon on the head with it. "Couldn't I just walk this down my own backyard?" she asked. The cat snorted lightly, his tail swinging like a pendulum.

"I don't see why not," Callum said from the doorway. Hannah felt herself flush, and she quickly pushed the magazine behind her back.

"I was just bored."

He shook his head. "Don't make excuses. This makes me happy." He cleared a space on the coffee table and sat down in front of her. He reached behind her and pulled the magazine onto his knees. Upside down, the woman's face looked as if it were being swallowed whole by the frothy white. "Is this something you might want to talk about now?"

Nerves rose like a geyser into her throat. "Later," she managed to choke out.

"Later is fine, Hannah. Later is not never."

Hannah could only nod, as she touched a sprig of white hair at his temple.

"Well, I've cleaned out the snakes. Safe to say, we'll need a new mop. James really went to town on them."

"It was a shocking sight." When she thought of Callum finding out what she'd done, the barbaric violence of it, she felt ashamed. And yet, some small part of her felt brash, almost pleased by her action. It felt like resistance.

"Remind me of this next time I reach for the bottle, but I'm never drinking that much again. I had this terrible feeling," he smiled to dismiss his words, "that I couldn't move, like there was something holding me down. It looked like my father, and he was grinning."

Hannah ran her fingers over the nicked wood of the coffee table. She felt that she was standing at a precipice, and if she were to speak, she might topple. Instead, she thought the word: *cauchemar*. The spirits that were said to ride the living in their sleep, seated on their sternum. The pillow lines in the morning would be the indents of their lassos, tight and commanding.

Old Doug had once claimed that his daughter, Abigail, had visited him after her death. Her slender thighs had been like a vice around his body. When he'd tried to push her off, she'd lashed him with serrated nails and continued her slow rock atop his body, the creaking interminable. He'd told Mae this, his shirt unbuttoned around the gash in his chest. Hannah remembered his face, downturned and shamed.

"We all have nightmares," Hannah said. "Maybe, they're the mind's way of working through things."

Callum studied her for a long moment. "I have a show in town tonight. It was a last-minute cancellation, and frankly it's flattering that they even thought to ask, considering that every booker in town seems to have forgotten about me. Do you want to come?"

Hannah looked warily at the growing pile of dirty laundry in the hamper. It was close to toppling. She thought of the pressing bodies, the heavy smoke. The noise. "It's supposed to rain. Maybe I'll just sit this one out."

"You sure? Can it be that you finally trust me?" he asked.

"The jury's still out on that one," she replied evenly. "But go anyways."

Callum smiled sheepishly. "Can I get you anything before I go? Do you want me to whip up something for an early dinner?"

Hannah ran her thumb over the crease in his forehead. "Be good, that's all."

He shut his eyes for a moment. "Always."

"Out with you then."

"What are you going to do while I'm gone?" He was already up and animated, distracted by the set list Hannah knew he was shaping in his head, but every few steps, he'd stop his pacing and sway, as though stricken by vertigo.

"I have a busy night of domesticity planned," she said and scooped up Graydon. He nuzzled his wet snout against her neck and purred. He'd been neglected in recent months.

Callum zipped his guitar case and unplugged his amp. As he walked, he tugged off his shirt and Hannah felt a pang. His ribs were like frets. She could've fit her nails between them and plucked a melody from his groans. He pulled a black T-shirt from the hamper, sniffed it, then put it on.

"I'm going to pretend you said you have a busy night of lying on the couch and relaxing ahead of you," he admonished her.

"And you be careful on the water. I don't like you driving that boat in the rain."

He put down his gear and turned around, shaking his head. "What am I doing," he muttered to himself, then, louder, "I'm not going anywhere. I shouldn't leave you alone."

Hannah released the cat and held up her hands in a pantomime. "Four walls, see?"

"There were four walls before, too."

Hannah hesitated. She knew he was right, and it was tempting to claim him for herself, not to share him with the crowd's faceless fawning. But the temptation was tempered by the memory of his hand squeezing the muscles of her wrist to pulp. When he'd asked, she'd blamed the gashes on Graydon, and when he'd tried to bandage the wounds, she'd pulled away, searching his eyes for some covert presence.

"Stop it, I'm a grown woman. Go enjoy yourself."

After he left, scrawling the number of the club where he'd be playing on a notepad, Hannah turned on the radio and wrapped her sweater tightly around herself. She walked from room to room, turning on all the lights and wondering if the power would go out again. The music was old, before her time, and even though she didn't recognize it, she found she could hum along.

The thunder began outside and she turned the music up, beginning to sway lightly. "This is how you dance," she whispered to her stomach, her hips forming figure eights. "If you lead, it's important to consider your partner. And if you follow, and you're anything like your mom, it's important to actually let your partner lead. Even if your partner is your daddy, who's slow as molasses."

She thought of a toddler's small, swaddled feet padding along with hers, and realized she didn't know at what age her child would begin to walk. Callum had bought pregnancy and baby books for her in the early months, but she hadn't scanned their pages in a long time, preferring Mae's lined notebooks of recipes for teas, stews for pregnant mothers, and homemade baby food made from pureed prunes and honey. She'd thought she could manage on those alone.

Hannah tossed the clothes into the washer and the back of the house filled with the smell of detergent and the unsteady clanking of the ancient machine.

In the living room, the radio began to crackle. The music was interrupted by loud volleys of static. She fiddled with the dust-covered knobs, but everything was dissipating into static. A bright crack of lightning illuminated the trees outside and she clicked the radio off.

She poured herself a glass of orange juice and fell into Mae's old chair, covering herself with the afghan that had lain over it for years. The clock on the wall read nine, and she threaded her fingers together around the glass. Graydon was curled like a croissant on the couch, his tail flicking back and forth as lightning flashed outside.

The radio clicked back on by itself, flooding the room with a low crackle, and she only distantly understood that this was strange. She closed her eyes and tried to find a lulling rhythm in the sound. Her body felt heavy.

The static swelled like a deeply drawn breath. There were tones in the hissing, gathering and coalescing. Slowly, she stood and walked toward the radio. A loud boom sounded in the front of the house. She pressed herself against the living room wall. The sound shifted and Hannah flinched. The radio had spoken her name.

"Who are you?" she asked the empty room.

The radio repeated her name.

"I've done nothing wrong!" The absurdity of her voice echoing through the empty room made her fall silent, even as she heard thuds against the windows.

All she could see was a flurry of feathers, materializing out of the darkness, then briefly lit by the lamps inside. Dozens of birds breaking their skulls against her windows, leaving a smear of red in their wake.

"Stop," she whispered, and the lights began to flicker. Hannah could hear something rustling through the walls, worming through deep channels. "This is my house!"

A howl came from the radio. *Not yours*, the static gathered into words. The ceiling light above her began to shake. The bulb broke and rained down fine glass. As she watched, a large black fly stepped over the filament and settled on the edge of the lamp.

"What do you want?" She addressed the fly.

A black cord slipped out of the lamp's bottom. Then it separated and burst apart into a swarm of flies. Hannah gasped and dropped to the floor, covering her face with her hands. "No!" she cried, but they buzzed against her belly, tunneling into her ears. A fly flew into her mouth and she clamped her teeth shut on a wing. She felt its feet scuttling down her tongue.

One last word trickled through the radio, too heavy with static to understand, before fading into the flutters of fly wings.

Hannah pulled a fly from the corner of her eye with a moan and slapped it against the ground. Everything went silent. Hannah raised her head and saw the ceiling light bright and intact. She lifted her hand and her palm came away clean. Her tongue curved and explored her mouth.

A blast of thunder startled her, and she rose to her feet. The radio was playing a soft blues song. She pulled a small, veined wing from between her teeth. The filigree moldered between her slow-rubbing fingers.

The doorbell rang and Hannah jumped. She eyed the radio warily as she moved toward the front door. The porch light had burned out, and the keyhole showed only darkness.

"Who's there?" she called through the door, clasping an umbrella handle in one hand.

"Martha," came the muffled reply. "Do you have any motor oil?"

Hannah let out a long breath, and sagged against the door. She turned the doorknob.

Water-logged and huffing, Martha stepped into the foyer. Her hair was plastered to her face. "Jesus, it's a proper storm out there." A small puddle was forming at her feet. "I'm so sorry to disturb you, Hannah. My boat's been leeching motor oil into the water all day." The words came out of her in a torrent, and then she gasped. "Hi."

Hannah laughed. "Come in and dry yourself off. I'm sure Callum has some extra oil."

Martha took off her rain boots and stepped into the house. She looked around the living room. "This place feels so strange without Mae in it."

Hannah pulled off the woman's windbreaker and hung

it from a hook. "You get used to it. Or at least I hope I will, someday." Martha was shaking and Hannah rubbed her hands up and down the woman's arms. "Some tea to warm you up?"

Martha nodded. She rose on her tiptoes, a full head taller than Hannah, and squinted toward the stairs. "Is the young man home?"

"No, he's playing a show in town tonight. I'm all alone for a few more hours."

Martha's mouth tightened. "First he lets you go gallivanting through the woods, and now he's leaving you home alone and isolated? The two of you need to remember you're making a human being. It's important business."

Hannah moved into the kitchen and filled the kettle with water. Martha's stern, disapproving voice made the events of just minutes ago fade away. "Green or chamomile?"

Martha crossed her arms and clicked her tongue. "Chamomile, if you want me to sleep tonight."

"I'm not sure where Callum would keep the oil. I could take a look if you'd like."

The woman swept her hair back into a ponytail. "Never mind that. I'll sit with you awhile, at least until your man comes home."

Hannah opened her mouth to protest, then closed it. The woman's tall frame and perpetually wry expression still put her at ease, as it had when she was a child. She handed her a pack of stale cookies.

They took their steaming tea into the living room, and Hannah sat in Mae's chair, as far away from the radio as she could manage. Martha snapped her fingers and

Hannah wormed her feet into her lap. Her callused fingers scraped against the hard patches on Hannah's heels. "Jesus, girl, your feet are callused hard as rocks."

"It's hard to reach them. I can't even tie my own laces." Hannah covered her belly and squirmed in the chair. There was a permanent depression where Mae's weight had settled in over the years. It made her feel cradled by Mae's shape, and when the baby came, it would be doubly held, by two generations. Distantly, she wondered if Christobelle had sat there once, stroking her own swollen belly. "This would be so much easier with Mae around," she said, and her voice cracked.

Martha smiled fondly at the curve of Hannah's belly. "You're doing fine, girl. Look at you, you're big as houses. You know, I have yet to meet that man of yours in his official capacity as father. I've heard he's a bit of a drinker," Martha said, and Hannah pulled her feet away.

"We all are," Hannah muttered. She thirsted for a sip of wine, or a splash of amber rye crashing against an ice cube. "It's the regional pastime."

Martha's mouth broke into a grudging smile. "Sure, if you believe the stories. That and gator hunting. Last week, an old alligator practically climbed up into the boat with me. My boy nearly upchucked into his bowl when I told him what he was eating. He worries me, that one. He says he's vegetarian now."

Hannah looked reflexively toward the kitchen door, imagining how an alligator's spine would feel, then wondering how the creature's would be different. The phosphorescent presence that lay patient in the tall grass. She made a sound of assent.

"Do you know who else has been seen drinking around town?" Martha asked, her voice betraying her loneliness, her eagerness to gossip. "That girl, Sarah Anne."

Hannah tightened her grip around the mug of tea. "I've seen her."

"The two of you used to be thick as thieves. Doug mentioned that she even came to pay her respects to Mae. Sweet of her, don't you think?"

Hannah's hands began to tremble so hard she spilled tea on her shirt. She laughed to cover the tremor. "Yes. We only talked for a bit."

Hannah looked toward the ceiling light, convincing herself that it hadn't flickered again. A fog was lifting from her mind, and memory sliced her like a blade. How the fire had covered the swamp in ghost-white smoke and the singular smell of burning flesh.

Hannah had run through the woods away from the house, skinning her knees on sharp branches and gravel when she slipped, just beginning to taste the shame that would follow her always.

"I heard that her uncle rented out the old Wilson place. Funny thing is, no one's seen the uncle in months." Martha was saying. "Bit strange of them to rent that property in particular. They found Mr. Wilson in the basement. His heart just gave out at thirty-eight. Rumor was, he'd lost a third of his body weight in five months." Martha frowned at the ceiling and shivered. "He was hanging around that mother of yours."

"Mae was my mother." Hannah's voice came out bitter.

"Of course she was, love," Martha said quickly. "I didn't mean to imply—well, anyways. It's the town's dark little secret, how many of the men that take up with her end up dead, but I guess most towns have a few strange characters in their history."

Hannah thought of Christobelle's men, their disappearing bodies. She thought of Callum's ribs. "I'm tired," she sighed. "You can leave me, really. I think I'm about ready to pass out right here."

Martha inched closer to the chair and stroked Hannah's hair. "Poor love," she whispered. "Just rest your eyes."

Hannah twitched against sleep, but the woman's hand gave her a sense of safety she'd missed for many months. Her body sunk into the chair, and each time her eyes fluttered open, she saw Martha, stalwart and unmoving.

After the confrontation with Jacob in Sarah Anne's bedroom, Hannah didn't see her friend for weeks. She'd been struck by a fever that even Mae's broths and oil-infused steam baths couldn't shake. Hannah relived Jacob breaking through the bedroom door so often during that sweat-soaked stupor that it became unreal. When the fever finally broke, she was five pounds lighter and convinced that it had been a nightmare. After all, why would Sarah Anne's gentle brother try to harm her?

Mae slowly built Hannah's strength back up with blood-sausage stews and escargot set in flaky pies. Once Hannah was well enough, Mae started asking when she'd see Sarah Anne again. Hannah could only shrug.

Instead, she helped Mae in the kitchen. Hannah made her first bisque, a savory mix of yams and crabmeat, which came out watery and stale tasting, but Mae praised her. Oregano, dry sherry, and hard-boiled eggs became turtle soup in her eager hands, as she stirred in minced celery and a generous pound of turtle meat. The tough flesh turned tender before her eyes.

One morning as Hannah was eating breakfast, a furtive tapping sounded against the front door. When she peered through the peephole, Sarah Anne's curls were magnified on the porch.

Hannah opened the door enough to make a slit and regarded the girl. "You haven't been around. Not at Sunday school, or in town," Sarah Anne trailed off. She drew circles on the wooden boards with her feet. "Are you mad at me or something?"

Hannah shook her head and turned around, letting the door fall open behind her. She heard the girl follow, and the door close with a thud.

"Well, then, what? Are you mute?"

"After what happened in your room . . . with Jacob."

"He was just hungry, that's all. Just a little fit. You can't let it scare you."

"He hurt you," Hannah insisted. She wanted to search the girl's back for new bruises, but refrained from touching her.

"No," Sarah Anne said slowly.

Hannah stepped closer. "I thought—" Words failed her. "I don't know."

"Forget all that. I'm sorry, and I miss you," the girl said, lacing her fingers around Hannah's. "I think you should come over."

Hannah hesitated. She couldn't shake the feeling that

Sarah Anne was hiding something, but the girl's smile was friendly and sincere. Mae was visiting with Doug, and the house was uncommonly silent, all its groans suspended for a moment as it waited for her decision.

The girl's black eyelashes quivered like a Venus flytrap around her expectant eyes. "Well?"

Hannah nodded, her head bowing to the girl's gravity. She admitted to herself that there had never been a question.

Hannah scribbled a note for Mae while Sarah Anne packed a loaf of freshly baked andouille bread, the scallions and ripened cheddar still sizzling, in aluminum foil. "Mae left it for me as a snack," Hannah told her.

They ran along the edge of the swamp, Hannah's scuffed sneakers expertly mounting swollen tree roots.

Hannah was stopped at the outskirts of Sarah Anne's backyard by the pillared birds' nests, standing sentry in their verdant carpet. There were no chirps or whistles, and when she glanced inside, the nests were empty.

"The nests got overcrowded," Sarah Anne said. She scooped her finger into the piled hay and pulled out a blood-stained twig. "Apparently, birds are so aggressive, they'll attack nearby nests. That's why they're supposed to hide their nests and take care of their babies out of sight of other predators. This was a bloodbath." She gestured Hannah over to look into a nest, where three speckled eggs lay cracked, insides pooled and cooked by the sun.

Hannah swallowed her nausea and looked up at the house, the windows darkened by drawn curtains. "Is Jacob home?"

"Somewhere. He was hiding this morning," Sarah

Anne said, either not noticing or ignoring Hannah's wary tone. "Come on."

Sarah Anne's parents greeted Hannah cursorily, her mother putting a proprietary hand on her daughter's shoulder. Her bearded father sipped steadily from a glass of bourbon, and the whites of his eyes were marbled red.

Sarah Anne waited until both her parents retreated to their corners of the house before pouring her father's scotch into a water bottle and replacing it with apple juice. "He'll notice," she said, "but he'll think I'm being altruistic."

Hannah followed Sarah Anne to the basement, where they drank until they fell in a giggling heap.

They lay on a thick shag carpet, watching videos. Eventually, Sarah Anne began to explore the crannies of Hannah's body with a tiptoeing finger.

Hannah squirmed slightly, finding it difficult to play her part of the game. She remembered too clearly how it had felt to be dismissed by Sarah Anne after the last time, and although she knew that stillness was a requirement, jolts of heat were playing the nerves of her body like a xylophone.

Her hands made a blockade over her thighs when Sarah Anne's fingers ventured there, but a single stroke unlaced her fingers like cut vines. Sarah Anne's gaze didn't waver as she unzipped Hannah's pants and traversed the mound of pubic hair.

Hannah sighed when the girl's finger began to move inside her.

Suddenly, Sarah Anne paused. "Do it to me," she instructed, and guided Hannah's hand under her skirt.

Hannah hesitated, blushing, but Sarah Anne's finger found its place again and began moving rhythmically.

"Do you do this often?" Hannah asked, between small gasps.

Sarah Anne's doe eyes were remote. She drew a shuddering breath as Hannah's finger tried to replicate the motion inside her, then whispered, "Not like this."

Hannah tried to mirror Sarah Anne's movements, but when she focused on the sensations inside herself, her own hands went slack. Something was building—a rockfall, a collapse—and Sarah Anne was dogged, beckoning it still.

The heat of their bodies, clothed and writhing, was all-consuming. Hannah's senses were filled to capacity with Sarah Anne's coconut shampoo. The girl's body flowed and ebbed, squeezed and released against her finger like a throat.

Until there was smoke.

Hannah began to cough. Plumes of smoke were cascading down the stairs. Upstairs, there was a howl.

"Fire!" Hannah cried out instinctively, but Sarah Anne lay there for a moment, her eyes filmed and distant. She raised her head and studied the waves of smoke that were seeping under the door at the top of the stairs.

"We need to get out of here," Hannah yelled, pulling the girl up by her arms. "Where are your parents?"

Sarah Anne shook her head.

Hannah ran up the stairs and put her hand against the door. A branding, biblical heat lapped at her skin. "Windows?" she called back.

The girl pointed to two shrunken windows beside the fireplace, which was also beginning to spit up smoke.

Hannah pushed a plush recliner against the wall, climbed on it, then punched out the bug screen. She grunted as she heaved the window open, pushing aside clumps of dirt. "Climb on me, and then I'll hoist myself up."

Sarah Anne looked toward the door, the wood blackening like a bruise. Her head whipped around as if slapped. "Jacob!" she moaned, covering her mouth.

"He's probably outside already," Hannah said, coughing. Even on the tips of her toes, she could only see a slice of the early evening sky, funnels of black smoke obscuring the ruddy clouds. "We don't have time. We have to get out, and then we can look for him."

This seemed to convince Sarah Anne, who rushed over to the window. Hannah leaned against the wall and made a step with her clasped hands. Hannah nudged Sarah Anne's foot toward her netted hands, and with a single heave, the girl landed on the ledge and wiggled through the window.

Hannah balanced herself carefully on the back of the chair, braced her arms against the bottom of the windowsill, then groaned as she lifted. She swallowed a mouthful of smoke. It burned her throat like cayenne. Sarah Anne grasped her by the shoulders and pulled.

Hannah was almost out when she heard a crash behind her. *Fire*, she thought, and skinned her knees on the window ledge as she kicked herself out.

Smoke surged into the basement, and began to filter out through the window. Hannah peered into the din and saw a shape moving toward them, sometimes crawling, sometimes stumbling onto its feet.

"Sarah," it sobbed, and Hannah blanched.

"We need to go back in," Sarah Anne urged. Her curls were matted with soot, and she tripped as she stepped backward, sucking in fresh air. "Jacob's still in there. My parents might still be there. Why are we the only ones out here?" She twirled in the drifting smoke. "Jacob!"

Hannah lay on her stomach, looking in through the basement window. The smoke parted enough to show her Jacob. Half of his hair was gone, the remainder singed and smoking. The fire was a creature, hissing and spitting through the house. Hannah could hear it behind him, each crackle signaling another inch gained. It wailed and whistled like an indiscriminate banshee around them.

Jacob fixed one inconsolable eye on her. Its twin was roasted, swollen like a termite mound. Between lips charred to the gums, a pink tongue appeared. It stretched out and forked as Hannah watched. "You," he hissed.

"Is someone down there?" Sarah Anne's voice was filled with alarm. The shock was wearing off.

"Sarah," he wailed again, and Hannah began to close the window.

"What are you doing?" Sarah Anne screamed, lashing at Hannah's arms. She struck Hannah's head, beat at her back.

"It's not him," Hannah yelled.

"Jacob!" Sarah Anne threw herself over Hannah's body and reached her arms through the window. "Hold on to me!"

Hannah swore as she tried to fight the girl off, but her weight, bird-like minutes before, was suddenly immobilizing.

"That's right, little bear," Sarah Anne said, her voice

calmer. "Climb onto the chair and . . ." The girl trailed off with a quivering exhalation. "Oh God, Jacob. Okay, take my hand."

Hannah felt Sarah Anne's body jerk above her, hauled forward with incredible force. "Not so hard, Jacob." Her voice had changed, now tremulous with fear. Then she screamed.

Hannah squirmed out from under Sarah Anne's body just as it almost disappeared through the window. She caught Sarah Anne's feet and pulled, the tendons in her arms feeling as if they might snap.

Over Sarah Anne's blonde halo, she saw Jacob, scorched and grinning. Beyond that, orange flames were rushing like waves toward the open air. Hannah gritted her teeth and locked her elbows. Some part of her listened for sirens, for cries, but the swamp was silent as a padded room that absorbed all commotion.

Jacob cried out, and Hannah saw Sarah Anne lashing her nails over his ruined skin. He backed away but still held firmly to one of her arms. His features, what remained of them, were steeped in surprise. "Sarah," he whispered, just as the fire began to lick him.

Hannah pressed her mouth against her arm and tried to stifle her gasping breaths. Jacob was thrashing his body, dancing like a crazed marionette, to escape the fire. But then it crowned his head, spread over his face in an avalanche.

Hannah was paralyzed by the sight. It took Sarah Anne's piercing screams for her to realize that Jacob was still clutching the girl's arm. She watched the flames tiptoe across Sarah Anne's beautiful, porcelain arm as if it were a dream. Hannah heard Jacob beat his fist or head against something, and heard him roar as Sarah Anne shook free. She saw Sarah Anne's pleading look as she cradled her bubbling flesh, and the only urgency she felt flashed as a single word in her mind. *Run.*

So she did.

The baby's kicking woke Hannah, and she was surprised to find herself in bed. She vaguely remembered Callum leading her upstairs the night before. At first light, she'd walked the perimeter of the house, expecting shattered skulls from the birds' suicides the night before, but the grass held only the desiccated remnants of fallen cicadas. Their bodies would crunch underfoot for weeks to come.

"Martha gave me a talking-to," Callum admitted as he presented her with a tray of English muffins aglow with honey. "She said I'm being, and I quote, a proper jackass. That I'm not to leave your side until we hear that baby screaming."

Hannah finger-painted a child's sun with the runoff honey, searching herself for any hint of appetite. There was none. Still, she forced herself to take a bite, telling herself it was for the baby.

"To that end," Callum continued, "I've taken an official leave of absence from the boat. I plan to be at your beck and call for the next month."

"It'd be nice to focus on fixing the house for a while. If an alligator decided to set his sights on us, he could just wiggle through any old hole in the foundation." Hannah looked away as she thought of something else that could worm its way in, something white skinned and clawed. Maybe something was already inside.

"I was thinking we could put a moratorium on the repairs for now. It might be smart to start thinking about the move instead." His voice sounded casual, but Hannah knew the words were calculated.

"We'd need to fix it up before trying to sell it anyways, wouldn't we?"

Callum sighed at her question and Hannah patted his hand.

"Never mind. We'll talk about it later." She was afraid to leave. She was afraid to stay.

In the afternoons, when Callum's increasingly discordant notes sounded from upstairs, she sometimes sunk to the floor in the kitchen with a knife squeezed between her hands, watching the back door and the holes in the walls, her tired eyes almost tricking her into believing that something was about to burst in from the other side. She collected sun-dried rocks and pebbles and arranged them in a circle beneath their bed.

In the evenings, as they lay twisted together like pretzels on the couch, she watched Callum. Tracking his weight loss from day to day, and watching the shaking of his hands.

At night, she listened, creating an inventory of sounds. Itemizing rustles. Each unexplained sound was the shape of her fear climbing the stairs, its muscled, scaled tail strong enough to hold down a grown man. Its jaw big enough to close around her belly and squeeze as though popping a grape.

Eventually, the power of Martha's admonishments faded, and Callum took to the water again. At first, she studied the unfinished recipes, scrawls in books that she'd found in a slender wooden box behind the fridge. One word, one name, was repeated and invoked: *Elegba*. Hannah wondered if it was a spice, or the name of a dish, but Mae had jotted down what seemed like pleas in which she called it the owner of the crossroads. The remover of obstacles.

Beside the incantations that bore his name, Mae had sketched two lines crossing in an X. At first, Hannah mistook it for a cross, but then remembered James's words. "The house is a crossroads," she whispered to herself. Then, with a trembling hand, she lifted her dress and looked with horror at the lines that still remained on her belly. Could it be that her mother had meant to protect her? Then came a more troubling thought. Maybe she herself was the crossroads. Maybe she had been all along.

Hannah's practiced, blissful smile ushered Callum out the door. She waited until the sound of his motor faded before wrapping her sweater around her ever-growing body. Then, almost as an afterthought, she grabbed a knife. Hannah wondered if a prayer would be appropriate, but those she'd learned in Sunday school seemed to belong to a world that no longer applied to her. "Protect me," she said instead, with a conviction that seemed to rise from a part of her she didn't know existed. "Father of the crossroads."

She walked carefully up the hill, trying to stick to

known paths. When she arrived at the road, she sped up. She hoped that Callum wouldn't return early. She hoped that the feeling surging through her, whether courage or desperation, wouldn't fail her.

She heard a car up the street and she moved to the side of the road, trying not to step too far into the shadows of the trees. The car slowed and pulled up beside her. The door opened and a man's emotionless voice said, "Get in."

Hannah smiled tightly and clutched the cloth bag that housed the knife. "I'm alright, thank you." She risked a glance at the shadowed face behind the wheel.

"She sent me."

Hannah wasn't surprised. She searched the trees, weighing her options, then slid into the front seat.

The man gunned the engine and she reclined against the headrest, watching the road pass by in a blur, grateful for the stern silence of Christobelle's man.

Hannah was led past the barn to a squat, single-floor structure with small windows. The man stood to the side when they reached the front door and nodded his head. Inside, the house looked like little more than an oppressive single room. Dark red wallpaper seemed to peel before Hannah's eyes to show the cracked plaster underneath. Candles were lined up at the base of the wall and along the narrow shelves of polished-wood bookcases.

Christobelle sat on a cushion in the center, her legs crossed. Her arms were bare, her skirts hoisted high over her thighs. She gripped a fat red candle between her legs. The wax dripped and thickened on her arm, a growing sore.

"She comes again," Christobelle said.

Hannah lowered herself slowly into a rickety Queen Anne chair. "What is this place?"

"This is my home. Modest, I know, but more than enough. It's the living that matter, not the dead wood below their feet." Christobelle opened her eyes. "You're hurt," she said, her eyes lingering on Hannah's right wrist, then smiling slightly as she took in the bag that held the knife. "And perhaps you intend to cause hurt?"

"It's nothing. An accident," Hannah said, ignoring the question. The baby had started squirming as soon as she'd entered the room. It was paddling frantically now, sending out uncoordinated frog kicks. She breathed through the pain and tried to prepare her words. There was a block inside her, even now that she'd come. "I need your help."

Christobelle ran her thumb over the flickering candle. "Callum," she said simply.

"What's happening to him?" Hannah asked. Her voice was tinny, pleading.

The gaunt hollows of Christobelle's body shifted in the candlelight. "If he's ill, he should consult a doctor," Christobelle answered. "It would seem that you're immune to my brand of medicine."

"What did you give me that day?" Hannah asked, prompted by only the weakest curiosity. She no longer needed an answer.

"A solution, child. And also a test."

"You tried to abort my baby." It was the first time she'd

voiced her thoughts, and they startled her. "What kind of solution is that? What kind of test?"

Christobelle licked her finger and snuffed the flame. "Those are harsh words. Some would say that it is not a life yet. You are. There is a hierarchy of need that you, in your current state, are blind to. As for the test . . . mother and child are well, as I suspected." Hannah noticed a cherubic young man sitting in a crushed velvet armchair behind her, slack jawed. He seemed to be sleeping although his fingers flexed desperately over the chair's arms. "That's Timothy. He's new to our flock."

"I can tell." His body was taut with the youth that would leave him soon enough.

"You look tired, child. I can have someone cook something for you."

As Christobelle spoke, Hannah felt herself sway, her whole body growing heavier. There was a rhythm running through the room. "Don't trouble yourself. I know poison can't come cheaply."

Christobelle's mouth tightened.

"Something's wrong with him. With Callum. It's like he's fading a bit more each day. Mother," Hannah said, her voice breaking. The smoke from the candles was viscous in her lungs, coiling in a veil over her eyes. "Tell me."

"We make choices," Christobelle whispered. From his chair, Timothy gasped, rolled his head, and burped like a child. "There is always a price."

"What price? What choice? We're just living our lives."

Christobelle sighed, the sound whistling from her. "Everything costs, and life most of all." She rose like a praying mantis, unfolding her limbs. Timothy shuffled in his sleep as she stood over him, the shadow of her hand traversing his body. "They always misunderstood me. The business owners and apron wearers mistake this for a church." A crackling, throaty laugh. "They pray to their God for protection against me. It would surprise them to hear that I, too, pray, and our prayers are not that different. But God is just one element of what this world, and the next, contains, and I am little more than a vessel." Her mother was speaking in low prosodic tones. Hannah gripped the chair so hard her knuckles cracked.

"In truth, it's closer to meditation. We part the veil, and sometimes, if we're lucky, we're granted a peek beyond it. Or, more accurately, I am the one who parts it, and they are the ones who see. They speak to the ones they've lost."

Timothy's body seized slightly as she ran her finger over his closed eyelids. "But every parting costs them. It's why I prefer to deal with the sick. They have an easier time of it at first. In the end, however, they all see the same thing. A world unbearable with the crowing of the dead."

Hannah let out a choked sound. She thought of the wide-eyed woman in the woods, her knowing words: *See how she parts the veil.* What husband, brother, or father had followed Christobelle into the darkness and withered there?

Christobelle's eyes softened as she smoothed the boy's eyebrows. His mouth was wide open, his tongue lapping at air. "Don't look at me that way, child. I do not seek them out. But when they come to me," Christobelle paused, and leaned over his mouth. "Can you imagine a world where you can only breathe what others expel? Where your only strength is that which you strip from others? I am their channel, and it costs me most of all."

"You're still alive," Hannah whispered.

"Am I?" Christobelle said, sounding genuinely surprised. "The dead have turned me into an ant farm. I am burrowed through and through. How old do you think I am? Can you even guess? There can be no vanity among the dead, or the dying."

"Why be a channel at all, then?" Hannah asked.

Christobelle opened her mouth to say something, then seemed to change her mind. "That, too, is a price."

"For what?"

"You think I'm a monster." She offered a sickly smile. "Maybe I am, but do you think that the bringer of loss has not experienced it herself?" Christobelle asked. "I had you when I was twenty, the age that you are now. The universe appreciates symmetry, it seems. Now, age is no longer of consequence. I have been a conduit for drowned children and those who made it nearly to one hundred alike."

She turned her face away and stroked her cheek as if looking into a mirror. Hannah scanned the walls. There were no reflective surfaces anywhere in the room, and Hannah wondered if her mother feared whose faces would peer back at her.

"They've each lost someone close to them," she mused, looking back at Timothy. "The cost is small for them, compared to seeing their loved ones again."

"And what are they giving you in return?"

"Timothy lost his mother," Christobelle continued. "Pancreatic cancer. She was diagnosed eight months ago, and passed away a few weeks back. He looks like her," Christobelle breathed. Timothy was whimpering. "The same lips, the same curled hair. Their people are Greek, somewhere in the annals of that tree."

Hannah noticed a body half-hidden behind a curtain. She blinked against the smoke. "They're grieving and vulnerable, and you use them."

"We're all vulnerable. Months later or years later, it makes no difference. Grief is a scar that cannot heal. It is not corporeal. It carries over."

The body moved in and out of focus. It watched her with crinkled brown eyes. Hannah mouthed a single word. *Mae.*

Christobelle sighed deeply. "I hoped it wouldn't pass to you, but always knew it might. It's why I gave you to Mae, hoping to keep you safe. She buttressed you in that place, that house, and found a way to close the doors against you." Christobelle raised her head, studied the walls around her. "You see a house here, but it is not a house. It is a clearing. That's the thing about a crossroads. It is the safest place, and the most dangerous. The greatest hope and the greatest horrors coexist where all things are possible."

"Mae was a . . ." Hannah tripped over her words, "a channeler, as well?"

"Of a sort. She was pushed to grow very quickly under the circumstances."

Hannah cocked an eyebrow.

"Because of me. And you, child."

Hannah's breath caught. "Me?"

"Mae's gift was life. Though we dealt with similar

materials, she knew how to create. Mae could nurse depressives back to health with a spoonful of her gumbo. She'd cleared a child's pneumonia by flooding the mother's kitchen with spiced fumes."

The shape behind the curtain coalesced into a woman, smiling sadly.

"I'd heard about her even before she came to me, after her husband passed. He was her great love, and she was lucky to have had her time with him."

"Mae came to you?"

"She came to me, I came to her. This is how friendships are forged, how deals are struck. You could say we were brought together by forces bigger than either of us. The limits of the world extend further than anyone can possibly imagine. There is darkness so impenetrable, just as there is light. There are orishas, just as there are demons. And perhaps angels as well." Christobelle surveyed the room and lowered her voice. "The orishas value ability. Healers or simple channelers are sometimes granted small favors. But those of us who wield more power fascinate them. They linger near us, aiding and complicating."

Something nudged Hannah's memory. "Mae used to leave peeled oranges and cracked eggs on white plates. She'd light candles in the night. They were offerings?"

Christobelle nodded.

"For who?"

"For whoever was hungry. Elegba favored her most, and without him, nothing else would have been possible. He holds the keys to all doors, to all possible roads. A powerful being, but one with the heart of a trickster." Christobelle inclined her head. When she spoke again, her voice was grinding, like a scratched record caught and slowed down. "She called on Oshun, as well. Her domain is charity and fertility. Mae was an excellent cook. Her power was in her food, and Oshun recognized that. She's always dealt with the stomach." Christobelle's face turned wistful. "The day I gave birth, there was a terrible storm. Mae opened all the doors and all the windows, and water and wind battered the house, but we were granted favor by Elegba. The dead crowded around us, but they could only sniff the air. She'd already hidden you, and in giving birth to you, I had a moment of perfect peace. Their eyes passed over me as well." Christobelle looked pointedly at the area directly above Hannah's right shoulder. "It was a brief respite."

Hannah shook her head and lifted herself out of the chair. The smell of dying roses filled the air with a funereal stench, and peonies withered in their planters. Trinkets covered wooden ledges, white bone combs and faded coral necklaces.

Looking closer, Hannah saw that figures were carved into the wood. Slender, mean-faced men and wide-hipped women. "What are these figures?"

Christobelle waved her hand. "It's all the something behind the veil. It's been here long before I was born and will remain long after you're gone. The veil is thinner here, though, which is why the orishas' power is so clearly manifest. And, unfortunately, that of other malignant spirits. They linger when they should have passed." The last word was stressed and came out of her lips with a pop. She looked shrunken as she stroked her hands together, over and over as if washing them.

Hannah followed a deep crack in the wall, up to the ceiling. The ceiling was veined with cracks, its moulding sanded away by years. "Is it me?" she whispered to the whorl of plaster above her. "Am I making him sick?"

"If it helps," her mother began, gently, "it's not you. Not exactly. Your presence draws them, and they draw from him."

"Why?"

"It's the price you pay for what grows inside you. It's the price I paid, and the price I pay still." Christobelle's eyes shone. "There are so many spirits in this swamp, souls of the dead, lingering out of vengeance or love. Some of them are older, sprung from the fabric of the other world. Sometimes it's the will of the spirit that possesses, or else the living invite them in, without knowing they do so. The child is a flame, and they're all just moths to it."

"My father," Hannah said simply, and her mother's eyes dropped. A tear snaked down her face. Would her tears be salty and clear like her own, disappearing as they dried on pillowcases? Or would they be different—aromatic as turmeric, fading to brown?

"His name was Dylan, child, and he was a good man. You have his eyes, that same moss green. Then, after a while, they turned gray." Christobelle leaned over and ran a finger along Hannah's brow. "He's here. Right in this haughty ridge." She tapped Hannah's chin. "He lives on through you. That's what a child is: permanence."

Hannah slapped her mother's hand away. "Did he know? Did he understand what was happening to him?"

"Even I didn't know. It began with terrible nightmares. His nose bled, his eyes sank into his skull. He wasted away. We took him to specialists who couldn't find any-thing wrong, until suddenly everything was wrong and he was beyond the reach of medicine." Her voice broke. "He wanted so much to meet you, to know you. He kept me up with his plans for you."

Hannah shuddered at how similar this was to her life with Callum. She'd never imagined that her mother had once known such simple pleasures. "Was there nothing you could do?" Her voice rose. "So many people following you and this is all the power you have?"

"We all have certain gifts, but mine is not life." Christobelle shook her head. "Your father was fascinated by physics. I remember one thing he told me: energy can neither be created nor destroyed." She squinted into the candlelight. "The swamp is like flypaper. Nothing ever flies away." She touched her temple. Her eyebrows were sprinkled with white. "It's teeming in here."

Hannah became still. She urged the blood in her ears to hush. They were coming up on the heart of the matter. Hannah could see it looming in her mother's face, even as it began to dawn on her. "The men. The men you've used. They stay, don't they?"

"All souls do. It's what seduces the living, at first. But the men are different. They give permission, but it's always, somehow, a surprise. Death always is. They pass and then feel cheated. Their rage is very nearly a phys-ical thing. It occurs to them too late that they might have healed, that the true purpose of death is to remind the living of their fortune."

"How do they die?" Hannah asked quietly.

Timothy yelped in his sleep, and Christobelle cooed

quietly down at his sleeping form. "How do any of us die?" Christobelle shrugged. "The machinery slows, then stops. Organs cease their functions. Consciousness wilts. One night, the heartbeat stops and the silence is absolute. They visit death, come too close to it, and then topple over its edge."

"Callum never volunteered," she cried. Her fists struck her mother and hit hard bone. Each contact sounded a knell in her right wrist.

Christobelle caught Hannah's hands and restrained them with surprising strength. No sign of effort showed on her face. "He volunteered himself. Love is tacit. Love is the ultimate surrender." She held Hannah's injured wrist. "They're growing stronger with each passing day. They did this to you, through him." Sensing Hannah tense, Christobelle raised her voice. "They were in him. I can feel their touch. I can recognize it. They go to break the right hand, always, as if a person's power rests there."

Hannah fell slack. The room seemed to drain of color, of sound. Her mother's mouth moved soundlessly. "It's my fault," Hannah said. The words were perverse, unnatural. She looked down at her scuffed shoes, her swollen feet bulging out of them, but couldn't feel the matted carpet beneath her anymore. Everything was suspended.

She saw Callum's face, his eyes dry, his lips stale. The awful clicking of the inner workings of his jaw sheathed in the thinnest layer of skin. This was death. This was the slow decomposition that began it.

Christobelle's shoulders were wider than Hannah had thought, her frame large and imposing. "They managed once before to get close to you, but I contained it." When

Hannah frowned, Christobelle went on. "A young girl, long ago. You loved her, too, in your way."

Hannah's breath stopped, heat taking her like kindling.

"Her brother's mind was spoiled. Whatever locks we have against them were broken. They would've killed you if I hadn't acted."

"Help me now, then," Hannah whispered, and tasted salt on her lips.

Christobelle's eyes, always possessed, always elsewhere, were wet and present. She was remembering, Hannah realized. A muscle hammered in her cheek. "They're patient, unfortunately, and bitter with me. Bitter, in some small part, with all who live. The dead are never satisfied."

Christobelle picked up an alligator head from a shelf, shellacked and preserved. So small, its black eyes were plain, its teeth smaller than a house cat's. "This is just a baby. If you look here," she tapped it between the eyes, "there's no bullet, no knife mark. The man stunned it with a blow, held its body, and carved right through the living, writhing neck. Most wouldn't be so stupid, but they'd killed the mother that morning. This small creature was anyone's for the taking."

Hannah flinched at her mother's words. "Why can't we leave?" she asked in a small voice.

"They won't let you. Not while it's inside you. To the dead, a gestating birth is the purest light. It is—sublime."

The woman turned to Timothy's sleeping form a second before he jolted awake. The boy looked like a drowning man breaking the surface. He raised his arms as if to defend himself, panting audibly.

"You have a choice. Ask yourself what it's worth."

Christobelle peered into the alligator's mouth. There were no more answers. Christobelle threw Timothy his shirt. "You'll take her home." The boy nodded and turned away to dress himself.

Hannah picked up the bag that held the knife and wondered what she'd hoped to accomplish by coming here. "Who do you see?" Hannah asked her mother as Timothy held the door open for her. "Who's your loved one?"

"My punisher," Christobelle answered and turned her back.

CHAPTER
ELEVEN

Time began to toy with Hannah. The clock ticked errat-
ically, the minute hand stood still for hours as Hannah
watched. Her face should've been full and flushed, but
instead, all she saw were jaundiced cheekbones in the
mirror. She'd never seen her clavicles so clearly.

She and Callum slept well past noon, sometimes waking
and lying silent side by side, as if speaking and rising were
beyond them. Alone with her thoughts, she repeated a
mantra to the baby: *Live*. In private, she searched Mae's
scribbles for more answers, but there were only prayers
that granted Hannah nothing, no matter how feverishly
she spoke them.

The plumber came, a bald man whose pate bore an old
scar. He took a single look at the damaged house, shook

his head, and ordered a clean-up crew. For two days, the house was filled with the sound of drilling and cutting.

Callum called a carpenter and pulled out his own tools, insisting that he help, but soon resigned himself to watching from a chair. The carpenter's crude jokes were met with hollow chuckles.

Hannah massaged her stomach as she watched them work. If she pressed the skin, she could make out the crossed lines on her belly, etched where she couldn't erase them. The baby had been still for the last few days, hibernating, and she woke sweat-drenched from nightmares of birthing a stone, gray and dry. She worried that there had been something in the scent of Christobelle's house, some destructive fume burning from the candles. Christobelle's feelings toward the child clearly hadn't changed.

"What happened here?" the carpenter asked her, nodding his head in thanks as she handed him sweet tea one afternoon.

"Really, we were hoping you could answer that."

He grimaced as he sipped. "Could I add some sugar to this?" Hannah gestured to the ceramic sugar bowl on the counter. "I'm not sure, ma'am. It's unlike anything I've ever seen." The man gave it serious thought for a moment, then shook his head. "It's like something broke the house from the inside. Sometimes with the newer subdivisions, you'll get a really weak foundation that'll collapse in on itself. People just don't have the same workmanship that they used to, but this place, old as it is, is built to last. Well, was."

"We don't have a lot of money," Hannah trailed off, but the man held up a hand.

"And you'll be keeping most of it. I've put some

band-aids over the worst, some cosmetic touches, but the foundation work is too big for me. It's real unfortunate, this happening to such a beautiful old place."

Hannah looked away.

The morning after the men left, she ran her hand up the frame of the kitchen door. The nicks in the wood that marked her growth over the years were distinct, a corresponding age jotted down in Mae's rough script. Thirteen had been her spurt. First breasts, then long limbs as if someone had stretched her out overnight. She'd imagined that her own child would stand obediently, heel to wall, then marvel at how he sprouted.

Callum sat at the kitchen table and stared dreamily out the window. His spoon dripped cold milk over his bowl. She'd taken to serving him cereal throughout the day, encouraged by the litany of nutrients listed on the side, but Callum downed water and nothing else.

"Baby, you need to eat," Hannah urged him, pouring herself a cup of tea at the kitchen counter.

He pulled up another spoonful of soggy cereal and it hovered below his chin. "What do you think of John?"

Hannah fingered the handle of her mug and considered the toast she'd buttered for herself earlier. Even though her stomach felt hollowed out, the bread looked like corrugated cardboard. "Who?"

"No, for our baby. We should name him John."

Hannah fidgeted. "You should eat," she reminded him and watched him stir his cereal again, his movements erratic.

"Do you see him?" he asked softly. "He's crawling in the grass."

"Who?" Hannah asked. She followed the line of his staring eyes out the window but saw only lighted trees.

"My father." Milk sloshed onto the table. It was laced with red.

"Callum," she whispered, and her hand fisted shut around a napkin.

He put a knuckle against his nosebleed. "I'm sorry. I've had a migraine all morning." The blood streamed in rivulets down his hand.

She collected the bowl and tilted his head back as she passed him, pausing to stroke his hair. The gray was becoming endemic, shooting through his golden strands like a sickness.

"Maybe you should go back to sleep," she said, leaning on the counter. She willed herself to spoon out some orange marmalade, but her tongue only tasted spoiled rinds. Graydon was lapping the milk from the bowl, his eyes frenzied. She lifted a hand to wave him away, then let it fall. Everything seemed immutable.

"I don't want to sleep anymore," he said, fear plain to hear in his voice. "I want to help you." He blotted the wet table with his bloody napkin. "You're so pregnant and you're taking care of me. It's not right."

"I'm beginning to think that's a stupid idea," she said, and hated the bitterness in her voice. "Rightness, I mean."

He looked chastised. His expressions were unguarded now. Pretensions were an extra effort. She searched him for a sign of the old bravado, the chest-pounding self-confidence of a musician onstage, but all she saw was dripping sweat, an ashen face. Deep lines were being etched on either side of his mouth, trenches manifesting along his forehead by the minute.

He reached for her and nuzzled into the taut skin of her belly, stretched like a gourd's. "I want you to stay right here."

Hannah stared blankly over his head. She was beginning to understand true loneliness. The solitude that came from being alone was incidental, par for the course. But the loneliness that surfaced in the presence of a loved one pierced much deeper.

"I'll finish the porch," he insisted. A fresh red squeezed through the drying blood and trickled into his beard, untrimmed for days. He looked almost feral.

Hannah moved to stand behind him and massaged his shoulders. She could feel his shoulders click, the bones sliding like a paper doll hinged with tacks. "Don't worry so much about the porch."

It mocked her. It was long enough for a single chair, a single miniature wicker table to hold a single glass of lemonade. He'd put down the frame for it, wooden spikes lining the sides of the house like a medieval moat. The planks that had been set down wavered whenever weight was put on them, and Hannah only sat there when Callum was outside, when she could be seen to enjoy the fresh air on the porch.

She'd look up and Callum would be smiling at her, leaning on the handle of his spade. Every moment between them was strained, choreographed poorly.

That night, Callum pulled a book for expecting mothers from her hands and lifted her from the couch.

"I want to show you something," he said, smiling like his old self. He buried her in a sweater and scarves and led her outside.

Frogs croaked and she could hear the distant singing of grasshoppers. The sound was beautiful, lulling. She closed her eyes and loosened a scarf. "It's too hot," she said, when he gave her an admonishing look.

He spread a towel on the grass and waited for her to sit before he lowered himself behind her. "See that?" he said, pointing. The full moon sat above the trees, streaming a clear white runway through the water. "That's *gumusservi*."

"Gummy what?"

"*Gumusservi*. It's Turkish for moonlight shining on water."

"How could you possibly know that?"

Callum wrapped his arms around her chest and pulled her closer. His wet breath tickled her ear. "I'm a very worldly man," he said, putting on a vague accent. He chuckled. "Actually, it's embarrassing. When I first started boating, one of the perks of the job was taking out girls after hours. I memorized all these obscure sayings in different languages, and pretended I'd visited all these places. Indonesia, Japan, Turkey. I made the whole business of gutting fish on the boat sound very glamorous. I didn't last long in that job, though. They don't have a wealth of expression, but fish eyes are eyes all the same, and they fix on you as you're slicing them open."

So closely attuned was she to him that she felt him grow serious behind her. "Hannah, I don't feel well," he said, and her heart broke at hearing the apology in his voice.

"I know," she said, and covered his hands with hers.

Neither of them had said a word about the sour smell of the sheets when they woke or the smell of elemental iron coming off his clothes, as if blood were evaporating from his pores.

Hannah looked out over the water, where a traipsing heron was scribbling a black line through the white moon. She remembered her mother's words, and felt the night's chill grip her feet. "I want you to see a doctor. Tonight. This has gone on long enough."

"You too," Callum said, and Hannah looked up at the stars. She wondered how high up their prison went. She pitied butterflies, their wings providing no promise of escape, tearing against the glass.

Dr. Merrick palpated her belly, a slow revolution with her belly button as the sun. "You're just about due. What's your birth plan?"

"We'll come here, I think," Callum said, "I've spoken to the obstetrician."

Dr. Merrick nodded, then frowned at Hannah. "You're much improved since the last time I saw you, but the heartbeat is on the quick side. Do you want to know the sex?"

Hannah peered at the ultrasound screen, trying to see a Cupid's bow mouth. The curled creature inside her betrayed nothing.

"We've been discussing that," Callum began.

"And we've decided against it," Hannah finished. Her instincts told her to wait. It wasn't hers yet, not until it was in her hands, squealing with eyes unfocused. "The knowing will dull the surprise. This way, it'll truly be a gift when it's born."

"It's a gift either way," Callum grumbled.

Dr. Merrick closed his chart and his brow furrowed. "Alright then. It's you that worry me. The two of you."

Callum stepped forward and squeezed Hannah's ankle. "I had some tests done last week," he explained, averting his eyes.

"What do they say?" Hannah asked, sitting up. The frozen image of her sonogram distracted her, her belly like a cave coated in ice sheets, the frozen child inside huddled for warmth.

Dr. Merrick held his pen up to Callum and addressed Hannah. "You're extremely anemic, for starters. It's common during pregnancy as the amount of blood in your body can double, but . . ." he hesitated, and tapped the chart, "it's unusual to experience such a drastic decrease in hemoglobin. Has your diet changed?"

"My appetite hasn't been very good."

The man nodded to himself as his eyes moved clinically over her body. "I'd like to weigh you before you go. Have you been experiencing fatigue or weakness?"

She met Callum's eyes. "We both have," he answered quietly.

"Stress and nausea can affect a woman's appetite, but you need to eat properly for your baby's health, as well as your own. You're also running a low-grade fever and your white blood-cell count is rather high. I'd like to see you again next week to monitor it."

Hannah peered beyond the men to the posters of

pregnant bellies, warning about the effects of alcohol. There were brightly colored cross-sections, the baby swaddled in layers of flesh like a bean in a pod.

"And you, Callum, are also severely anemic." Suspicion entered the old man's voice as he scanned Callum from head to toe. "I asked the nurse to weigh you twice. I thought for sure the first number was off. One hundred and twenty-three pounds, Callum."

Hannah gulped hard.

"Expecting fathers can lose weight from sheer stress, or gain it," the doctor continued. "It's rarely more than five pounds in either direction. You were a slender build to begin with, so I'd like you to tell me what's been happening."

The off-green walls highlighted Callum's pallor, and the hospital light was interrogative, picking up fading bruises on his arms and the faint outline of ribs under his T-shirt. Hannah could see him clearly for what he'd become: an old man. A sick man.

"We can talk alone, if you prefer," Dr Merrick said, and gave his watch a passing glance.

"No, whatever you have to say, say it here. My appetite's been shit. It's been stressful. We've had some," Callum gave Hannah a pained look, "extenuating circumstances. Really, I came here to find out what was wrong."

"Your liver's failing," the doctor said bluntly, then let it sink in. Slippered feet shuffled in the hallway, accompanied by the ever-present undertone of soft, reassuring beeps that signaled life. "The liver's a very forgiving organ. It works quietly to filter out all the harmful things you might put in your body—alcohol, drugs, prescription and otherwise, and other everyday toxins—until it can't anymore. It's also one of the few organs that reaches a point of no return. You've heard of cirrhosis?"

Callum nodded, scratching a raw patch of skin on his arm. Hannah put a soothing hand over his.

"From the looks of it, you've had cirrhosis for several years. Except you haven't. We have your liver function tests from a few years back, and they were, if not pristine, perfectly in line with a male in your age range."

Callum released a laugh and immediately covered his mouth. "Are those words supposed to mean something to me?"

"You're in liver failure. The only explanation for such accelerated symptoms would be hepatitis, but you've tested negative, as has Hannah. I'd like to admit you to hospital, except, Callum, I have to say that your levels are so low there's not much we can do except put you on a transplant list. Before I can do that, though, I need to know what you did to induce this. The transplant committee has rules when faced with suicidal motives, indirect or otherwise."

Callum lurched forward and for a panicked moment, Hannah thought he meant to throttle the doctor, but instead, he clasped his hands together in a posture of prayer. "I have a child almost ready to push its way out into this world. How could I possibly want to leave it? No, no, I promise," Callum said. "I just started getting sick, really sick. I came here half-expecting that you'd say we had a gas leak somewhere in the house."

Dizziness struck Hannah as she saw the thoroughly yellow tinge of his skin, the jaundice in his eyes. She'd never known yellow could become so morbid when imprinted on human skin. Tears trickled, hot and salty, into her mouth.

"I'll leave you to get dressed, Hannah. There are paper towels on the cart. Callum and I are going to have a chat outside." Dr. Merrick flicked off the screen.

Callum attempted a quivering smile. He was trying to be strong, but there was only so much strength to be summoned when the odds were stacked so high that they eclipsed all else. "We'll just be a moment," he said as he followed the doctor out of the room.

After the door closed, sounding like an indrawn breath, Hannah swung her legs around and wiped the gel from her stomach. As she dressed herself, she cooed and shushed, whispering, "It's going to be okay." The words were meant as much for her as for the baby.

She waddled into the waiting room and perched on the edge of a seat. She watched Callum at the end of the hall. He gestured frantically at the doctor, whose face was implacable. At a distance, Hannah could see his weariness, his fear, and she turned her eyes to the smears of mud on the emergency room floor and gum pasted to the candy-red plush chairs.

When Callum came toward her, he was reduced. He'd fooled them both with his buoyant spirit. His hope had inflated him, made him appear larger. Now she saw him whittled. He knelt before her and laid his head against her belly.

"What did he say?" Hannah said, hugging him tightly. Passing nurses looked at them knowingly, then gave them privacy. ·

"I don't believe it. Any of it. I'm too young for this. He

asked that I stay for a few days while they do more tests. I just don't understand." He sat up and looked carefully at her. "You believe me, right? You know I'm not using drugs?"

Hannah searched his face, hating herself for a moment of doubt. Then, she nodded, although she was no longer listening. Beyond him, the seated men were garish under the light. Their faces drooped over their bones. Some clutched their chests, acknowledging angina and arrhythmia. Others lay slumped in their chairs. Only their panicked eyes, roving back and forth, betrayed their racing thoughts. How many were dying? How many were afflicted by Christobelle? In this town, was there any difference?

"Hannah?" Callum came back into focus.

"Let's rest here tonight," she said. Callum began shaking his head, but Hannah steadied it between two firm hands. "What if we go back only to have the baby come? The best thing we can do is find out what's going on with you. I need you strong." Her voice faltered.

"You'll stay?"

"Of course." Hannah wanted to end the conversation, to get him hooked up to machines that promised to subdue the sulfurous hue of his skin. "Where else would I go?"

He sighed as though he was laying down the whole world onto the scuffed linoleum, and for a moment, Hannah thought he might lay down his body as well.

She walked him to the line of stretchers by the wall. His eyes stayed glued to hers as he put his head down on the pillow. Dr. Merrick caught her eye from further down the hall and nodded.

Hannah could only grip Callum's sweaty hand in hers as an orderly began to wheel him into a hospital room.

CHAPTER
TWELVE

When Hannah first awoke, she thought it was morning. Bright lights buzzed above and machines beeped around her, announcing life. Callum's hand was still in hers and his ragged breath came in spurts. She sought the numbers and wavy lines that blinked on the monitors around Callum's bed for some answer, but didn't know their language.

Hannah felt her belly. A reassuring kick answered her roving hand.

"Your baby's fine, for the moment," came a voice from behind Hannah. A woman sat in a chair in the corner. She pointed a knitting needle. "Strong and healthy, in spite of everything against it."

Hannah looked carefully at the woman's stained teeth, doubting. "Who are—" she began, but the woman pointed to the other bed in the room, hidden by the curtain.

"Name's Laura. That one's mine."

Hannah studied the woman's face. Was there some semblance of Mae hovering in her features?

"Well, aren't you the very picture of gloom. Keep faith, child. Hope comes free."

Hannah turned back to Callum and brushed back his damp hair. Each labored rise and fall of his chest made her want to pray, although she wasn't even sure what she'd pray to.

"I think I did this to him," Hannah whispered. The ache was double-edged: seeing the father of her child sick and struggling for life, and the spoiling guilt inside her at having put him in danger despite the many warnings. "I've been so selfish." Hannah suddenly looked toward the drawn curtain beside Callum's bed. "Is he—was he with Christobelle?"

"No, although there's not a corner of this swamp that the woman hasn't touched with her ugly magic."

"She should be cast out," Hannah said, not realizing what she was saying at first.

Laura cocked her head. "She is unnatural, yes, but her aims are not evil. Once you see clearly, this world and the next, it can be difficult to stay permanently in either."

Hannah shuffled uncomfortably.

The woman bared her ground-down crooked teeth. Her gums were spotted like a lizard's back. "The living are born with sparks inside them, and spirits of all sorts flutter around them like moths. Some get sick and fall into the in-between place. Others knock on the door and can't be surprised at what answers. And some are just plain suited to it, whether they like it or not."

Hannah flinched.

Laura's kind brown eyes squinted. "You're frightened." She set down the knitting and nodded to herself. "And you should be. Relations between the two worlds are seldom peaceable." Laura hoisted her girth forward onto the edge of the seat. Her hair was white and rigid, almost as if it could be crumbled in a fist. "Us horses ridden by the orishas have felt this tension growing for a long time, but we can't see the outcome. Something must change, but who would go willingly into the demon's den? There's brave and stupid, and you've got to know which you are."

"I don't know what to do. I wasn't raised with this," Hannah said, then considered Mae's gifts, the rejuvenation she experienced when rising from the breakfast table, the sleepy satiety after dinnertime. She had a vague recollection of an arts camp in town, children speckled with chickenpox, the affliction taking everyone but her. "I think my mother was trying to keep me from it." She didn't know whether she meant Christobelle or Mae.

"Pity," Laura said. An expression of pure longing filled her face. "You have what others spend a lifetime striving for. The orishas are with you right now."

Hannah jumped up. A scatter of light faded where she'd been sitting, dissipating like startled fireflies.

The woman frowned at her and clucked her tongue. "There's no malice. Just curiosity. Nothing charms the other side like a new birth."

"I just want to have my child, and have my life. I want a normal life."

"That's an awful lot of want," Laura chastised.

Hannah stroked Callum's arm, warming the goosebumps. "This is the father. What life will my child have without him? Will these spirits, these orishas, even let it live? They're breaking down my house and tearing the swamp apart to find me." She looked nervously around for flickers in the light, lines that wavered. "They want my baby."

The woman's eyes narrowed. "No," she said slowly, "you don't understand." She waved a hand. "The orishas are not malevolent. Elegba's tendency for tricks can sometimes be misunderstood by us, but the orishas rarely intervene of their own accord into human affairs. Except to steer things onto their proper path." Her eyes ran a slow circle around Hannah's head. "It's something else that haunts you." The woman puckered her mouth. "It's a crown." She sighed as she looked at Hannah with an expression of immeasurable sorrow. "One not meant for you." Laura fingered her gums, running her nails up and down the translucent enamel of her teeth.

"What do I do?" The words slipped out unbidden.

The woman shook her head and muttered something inaudible as she went to sit back in her chair. The knitting needles began moving again in her deft hands. In the silence, Hannah watched the woman's brows move as if they were conducting an argument. A shape was taking form out of the soft blue yarn in the woman's lap.

Hannah had no choice but to sit, even though her body was flooded with nerves. Her knees chattered together and her fingers performed elegant concertos up and down her thighs. Deep inside herself, she could feel her child, feeding and growing and very nearly ready to breathe the air.

"Mae was very special," the woman said. "She was never properly ordained into the faith, but the orishas granted her favors, because she never asked for herself. She was able to protect you." Hannah shut her eyes. All she saw were Mae's hands, cleaning frog legs, crushing peppercorns. Smoothing frowns from Hannah's mouth with a swipe of her thumb. "The orishas asked for a promise of balance in return. Your mother made it, but didn't keep it. Maybe they overestimated her humanity. Or underestimated it."

"What do you mean?"

"Who can say what she sees in the darkness? Is it someone she loved? Or is it herself, gorged on suffering? Maybe it's the most unbearable thing of all: just darkness. And now," Laura looked up at Hannah, "a new generation must be protected."

Hannah looked down at her stomach, bulging with her child, nearly ready to scream its way into the bright world. "I'll do anything," she said.

A deep sigh came from behind the hospital curtain and Laura regarded it with a half-smile. "Tell me, child. Have you seen a white alligator?"

Hannah's head snapped up. She braced herself against the bed frame, ready to run.

"They're extremely rare, and extremely lucky. A normal alligator can camouflage itself, but the albino alligator, especially when just a baby, is like a beacon for predators. They almost never make it past their first year. But somehow, one has survived. One that's been seen wherever something bad happens. Some claim it's an omen, forecasting the place of a tragedy, of a death."

"It's evil," Hannah whispered, but Laura shook her head.

"Some might think so, but I think differently. After all, Elegba has many faces, and what crossroads is more significant than the moment between life and death. Or, when new life begins." Laura's voice faltered. "I told you the orishas don't interfere; that's true. But sometimes, they correct as they see fit. In everything, there must be balance. The scales have been tipped toward death for too long."

Hannah massaged her belly. What would happen when her child was exposed to the madness of the outside world? Would she have the strength to send it away, as her mother had done to her? Would it survive?

"I wish I could help you," the woman said. "But you must face them. They won't be ignored, they're almost strong enough now. They're weaving into her very flesh, into the bones of her body. They won't be expelled."

"Whose body?"

The fluorescent lights above cast Laura's face in a nimbus of light. Her gold-flecked eyes were shrewd. "Death's." She snapped the yarn with her teeth and smoothed the garment in her lap.

Hannah covered her belly. "I won't give the baby—"

"Then give the man."

Hannah shut her eyes tightly and gritted her teeth. "I can't." She shook her head vehemently, then felt something soft set down over her belly. A baby's hat, sized for a newborn.

"Your options are few, child, and prayer is chief among them. Tie copper around your wrists, your ankles. Tie nine knots in it. Nine knots can be a protection, if you will it so. Ward them off." Laura cocked her head toward Callum. "What will you do about him?"

As spasms passed through Callum's body, Hannah tried to conjure up the first night. It was perfect for having been new, for having been the first. She remembered the red scarf. His smell, raw beneath shampoo and soap. What she'd seen crawling from the corner of her eye. Maybe it had been a warning from the very beginning, but pure emotion had overridden it.

"Will he forgive me?" she asked, pointlessly.

Laura bundled her yarn, and her knitting needles disappeared into a bag. "Who can say?" She stood and smiled down at the bed behind the curtain. "Nothing is easy."

"Hannah," Callum whispered and Hannah turned to see his eyes flutter open. "Where are we?"

"The hospital. We're getting you some help," she said.

"I just need to sleep for a bit," he said, and his head sunk heavily into the pillows.

She tried to imagine the open road rushing past them, the rain-stained buildings of a city. They would be happy for a time, encased in concrete. The echo of high heels on pavement would replace the clicking of crickets, and Hannah would bundle herself through the winters. Snow would startle her. But how long until they were found?

She nuzzled against the bristles on the side of his face to hide the tears in her eyes. "I love you, you know that?"

His face softened as he looked at her. He noticed her tears and tenderness filled his eyes. "I love you, too." He craned his head back further. "You're so beautiful."

Hannah felt a forceful kick in her belly.

"He's almost here," Callum murmured, his voice choking off.

"Yes," she said simply, and covered his mouth. Wet breath moved through the grate of her hand. "I'm leaving."

"Don't." A whole conversation flared to life across his

face. His hands fluttered up, then fell gracefully, like butter-flies dying mid-flight. "You're safer here. The baby is coming any day now." Whatever cocktail of drugs was seeping into his arm held him down better than she ever could.

She tried to bolster her words with the memory of Callum and Leah, together against red brick. She tried to convince herself that she'd forgiven too much. But then, she saw the raw fear in his eyes, and thought of Mae. Maybe all faces were alike in the loneliness and helpless-ness of death. Hannah suddenly knew that someone had been in their living room, standing blank-faced above her adopted mother's choking mouth. Coaxing another feather, another wingtip between her lips.

Then she thought of Christobelle. How many men had she reduced to husks of their former selves? Surely she'd stood over some of them, watching their faces wrestle through the same dumb motions of fear and hope. Had she felt as Hannah did now?

The thought that she was the source of that look in his eyes made her sick, but she bore it; she let herself be filled with the certainty that she had to let him go.

"I have to." The baby kicked again. "I'm making you sick."

He would never forgive her, she realized. The child was equally theirs, but the choice to take this risk was hers alone. How would she bear her life, without his breath beside her in sleep, without his exploring fingers guided against knots in her back as if by magnets? All the possible versions of their child that they'd imagined were rushing away from her.

"I can't explain it," she went on as if she were talking

herself into something. "I'm still not sure I believe it, but I have to try."

"Things will get better," he insisted.

"Yes, they will." Her voice cracked as if her very body disbelieved the words. She pulled away, and the simple motion was the hardest of her life. The small blue hat fell from her lap and she turned quickly, remembering the woman, but Laura had left silently during their exchange. Hannah leaned down to pick it up, then, seeing her hands shaking, left it there, half-hidden under the hospital bed.

Callum mumbled weakly, his eyelids struggling against sleep, as Hannah peered behind the curtain separating the room in half. The other bed was empty and recently made. Atop the sheets, there was a long, thin imprint. A reptilian body, the scales pressed into the sheets through its weight. She touched her hand to the bed and could almost feel it, like the echo of a pulse. It had been here, she realized, but for the first time, she hadn't been aware of it. Hadn't been afraid of it.

She walked briskly past Callum's bed. She glimpsed his eyes still half-open, no longer fully understanding where he was or what was happening. As she paused in the doorway, she remembered an old myth of a man sent into the bowels of hell to retrieve his wife, who then lost her with a simple but forbidden backward glance. The opposite was true. If she turned, her face disproving her words even as she spoke them, she would be frozen in her tracks. He would never let her leave. And seeing him, the kinks of his curls, the curve of his mouth, she would allow it.

She walked out.

CHAPTER
THIRTEEN

The tears, heaving out of her, finally left her empty. Graydon mewled as he followed her around the house, pawing at her ankles. She unlocked all the doors, opened all the drapes, and lay down on the couch. She lit a white candle and placed it, tentatively, in the kitchen window. It illuminated only her own wavering reflection in the darkened window.

Her last thoughts before she slept were of Callum, and with her eyes swollen shut and her tongue parched, she said goodbye to him. The trees outside were lit by the full moon, and she waited for whatever would come.

But nothing did and she slept deeply.

When she woke, all the doors and windows were wide open, a loose scatter of leaves the only sign of trespass.

She rubbed the sleep from her eyes, and understood. The house was no shelter. Something was teasing her.

Phantom cracks appeared and dissolved across the walls like roots pulsing from inside the plaster. For once, Hannah didn't care. She moved to the tall grass by the shed and sat down. The morning chill seeped through her dress and sweater. She was waiting, although she didn't know what for. The baby was wrestling inside her, chasing helplessly after its father like a hamster in a wheel. She rubbed her hand over her belly in circles, singing snippets of lullabies, and rocking back and forth over a growing soreness in her pelvis.

It was then that she saw the crows, crowding on the branches around the house. Their squawks were a harsh laugh, echoing from every corner of the swamp. A light mist drifted off the water, and through the fog, hulking trees rose like fireworks frozen mid-burst. Hannah hugged her sweater around her, and tried to shake the sense that even if Martha's boat were to float by, Hannah would be invisible to her.

Every few minutes, her breath caught and sent her into gasping sobs. Even the tears that made her vision swim were caught, unwilling to fall. Mae had smacked her gently on the head many times during her childhood, chastising her for second-guessing herself.

"I've never understood faulting a child her misery over spilt milk. It's a sad thing. But to sit there and mope over a choice you yourself made, without any strong-arming, is just plain stupid," she'd said, and Hannah's generous pout would suck back in between her lips. "What's done is done, and you can rest easy knowing it was done by you alone."

A whistle, clumsy and high-pitched, sounded in the swamp. Hannah squinted through the fog. A pale figure was rising out of the water. Hannah gasped when she recognized the girl.

Sarah Anne stood in the water. Her curls were wet, the dip of her waist elegant as a cello scroll. The skin on her arm was unbroken, as if the fire had never happened. Hannah stood slowly, using the wall of the shed to support herself, and shook her head pointlessly. Fear paddled desperately in her heart, urging for flight. "Not her," she pleaded.

As Sarah Anne came closer, Hannah saw that her face looked as it did when they'd first met.

"Who are you?" Hannah asked.

"Your playmate," the girl said. "You sent him away. The man of the house." Her voice was mocking.

"He had nothing to do with this." Hannah hid her face in her sleeve. She tried to focus on the sensation of the wool scratching her lips, anything that might ground her in the rules of the real world. She understood that Sarah Anne couldn't possibly be twelve again. But the girl's pungent breath, like meat gone off, smelled as real as the must in her sweater's sleeve.

The girl's face shifted, became more mature, as she watched Hannah. The changes were incremental, as if her features were an aerial map, storm clouds moving. Had she always looked so much like Jacob? He was hidden in the strong line of her jaw, her hooded eyes. Hannah couldn't remember.

"What do you want?"

Sarah Anne's nostrils flared. She turned her head and scanned the placid waters. "Retribution."

"I was a child," Hannah countered. "I was terrified. I've done nothing to you." She inched backward.

The woman's lips thinned, her hair momentarily darkening. Tricks of light were dappling the woman's face, despite the uniform gray of the day. "You have, as she has. You're the same, the cells and the light beneath it. Yours is so warm, so mild. So mild, with child." Sarah Anne giggled and reached out her hand toward Hannah's belly.

Hannah balked. "She who? Christobelle?"

"Don't speak her name. It offends us," the woman hissed. She seemed taller than she'd been a moment ago, her shoulders squared and wide, her breasts smaller. A burst of rich chestnut brown was spreading like an ink stain over her right iris. Hannah felt a pang inside her, as if a vice had tightened in her belly.

"Jacob lived for a few hours, then died that night. I saw him part the flames, crawl out on all fours like an animal. I heard him scream as if he wanted to split open the skies. He was blamed for the fire, but he would never have harmed me."

Sarah Anne drew a breath.

"That night, in the hospital bed, he writhed and moaned. His legs shot out, his neck bulged with the effort of sitting up. But he couldn't. There was something sitting on his belly. I saw it then, saw it in its multitude. All the hollow men that died by your mother's hand. I touched him, and for a moment, his eyes cleared. He looked me in the face, my poor sweet Jacob, and screamed. When his lips closed, he was dead." The woman let the words sink in. The fog released itself in small droplets down her skin. She stroked a finger through the air as if writing on a blackboard.

"I'm sorry." Hannah tried to repeat the words to herself, tried to etch them into her mind, into some tissue that would always remember and always feel the shame. For a moment, she leaned forward, exposing her neck like an animal surrendering. But then the child kicked inside her, reminding her of what she had to lose. Of what she refused to surrender.

"I'd heard them whisper before, calling out in the darkness. I'd heard your name in the cries of birds. They visited me sometimes in the night. Sometimes, they looked like my brother, or another man taken by your mother's hand. Sometimes as a presence I couldn't touch. Some nights, they'd sit there on my stomach, many-legged and many-handed, and watch me with their many blinking eyes. I couldn't move."

The pressure in her stomach grew and Hannah took an uneven step backward, trying to mask the pain. She cradled the bottom of her belly like a basket.

The woman continued in Sarah Anne's languid, playful voice. "But the night that my family died, the night that Jacob died, they spoke, and for every night after. And they were right. You are just like your mother, sacrificing others for your own gain." Sarah Anne closed her eyes and sniffed the air. "Every time I smell smoke, I'm reminded of that night. She set the fire, your mother."

Hannah reeled. "She wouldn't."

"You're her child. She thought she was protecting you."

Veins crept up Sarah Anne's arm, twisting like snakes and turning the skin to a coarse, blistered red. Sarah Anne gripped her swaying wet hair in a fist and pulled it off. Hannah's knees nearly gave out at the sight of the woman's smooth scalp. The wig fell into the grass. Hannah stifled a scream.

"My uncle put me in therapy; I took fistfuls of pills. One day, their whispers turned to yells. Constant, unyielding, and so loud I felt flayed." Sarah Anne paused. "I resisted at first. I tried to convince them that you were different from your mother, but they helped me see that you are the same. They promised me vengeance. They promised that you would ache, and I surrendered. I gave myself to them." She ran her hands down the sides of her waist, then up to circle her neck like a choker. "They coiled inside me, feeding on me, and we are stronger for it."

"I'm so sorry," Hannah said, panting with the effort of remaining upright. There was tightness in her chest, a pounding pulse like war drums in her ears. The pain in her stomach came in waves. "You never deserved any of this."

Sarah Anne smiled sympathetically and gripped Hannah's chin. The cold from her fingers shot through Hannah's body. "Sorry is not enough. We're so hungry."

Sarah Anne's sudden punch pushed Hannah backward against the shed with a force that cracked the wall. Hannah's gasp echoed in the swamp's silence, then bubbled as blood welled in her throat. "Why?" she whimpered. Hannah slid down the shed's wall and lay down on her side. She braced her hand against Sarah Anne's bare leg, trying to hold her back.

"We died because of her. We went willingly, like

livestock over a cliff. We've tried to harm her, but she's powerful beyond reason. But we can harm you now. We can take this. We want this." The woman knelt beside her and gently touched her stomach. Then she slapped Hannah, and pushed her face down against the dew-wet grass until mud seeped into her mouth.

Hannah coughed and felt her thighs flood with liquid. An ant, teeter-tottering on a blade of grass, tickled her eye. She was grateful for the release of pressure in her abdomen and reached down to feel between her legs. She sighed with relief when her hands came away simply wet, not viscous with the stick of blood.

"That old woman, the black one, protected you for so long. She was strong for so long. She nourished you. The whole house pulsed with life."

Hannah could feel the woman changing again. The sudden stretch of skin, the movement of bones, was sonorous. When she spoke, her voice was low. "We were here at your birth. It was our time. Your mother should not have lived, but that woman intervened. Her, and her orishas. They judged us and found our case unworthy." The sentences were clipped now, a garbled accent coming through.

The woman, if it was that, grabbed her right hand from between her legs. Hannah looked up into a face like a patchwork quilt, features roughly sewn together, the edges blurred as if in a dream. An eye gazed at her with tenderness, as a mouth, breathing heavily, sneered.

"We cannot harm her. She cannot harm us." A tongue coated in white darted out between the thing's chipped teeth. It pushed back Hannah's index finger. Hannah seized in its grip, then the world went white and deafening with static as the bone snapped.

"We make our own justice," it said. With one hand, it held the slender bones of her forearm. With the other, it pushed back her right wrist until the nest of bones there snapped. Hannah only groaned. She tried to turn her body away, but it grabbed her waist and whirled her around as if she were a rag doll.

"Please," Hannah mumbled, and felt tears spill down her face. She stared blandly at her limp wrist. Her instructions to move it trickled down her arm. The ache in her belly had returned, and she recognized the rhythm from the birthing books. She was contracting.

"No," she groaned, and tried to shimmy away. She looked toward the house, wondering if she could make it to the back door. "It's too soon." The baby couldn't come yet. Something moved behind the kitchen window and disappeared into the hallway. Hannah glimpsed a crushed crimson dress, a candle flickering, before her vision whited out again.

The creature had her pinned by her knee, its foot nestled in the joint. "Soon," it echoed, then pressed down. "There is no soon. There is no time. There can be no regret."

It turned her over by the shoulder and straddled her. It was no longer Sarah Anne, no longer recognizably female. With one finger, it circled her belly button. Hannah hit at it with her good hand, but the creature didn't even blink. It placed the tip of its thin, cracking nail in her belly button and pressed down. Hannah remembered the crow's beak, the beading blood.

Hannah's neck felt impossibly weary as she let her head fall back against the grass. Above her, the treetops formed a circle, framing a patch of perfect white sky. The fog was absolute.

"That's enough."

Hannah didn't look. The voice was familiar enough, the rasp that came from treading the fine line between worlds. She couldn't differentiate between the white of the sky and the white unconscious. Only the jolts in her belly stirred her.

"No," the creature said, but it loosened its grip. A note of uncertainty entered its voice. "You have no command."

"Step away from her," Christobelle continued calmly.

A contraction reddened her vision, and she cried out. Above her, the creature had morphed. Its legs were jointed like a mantis, its scalp a history of injuries.

"This is our due."

"You're owed nothing," Christobelle said, and the creature hissed and rose off its haunches. "Our bargain was fulfilled. You all saw what you needed to see; I delivered my promise. Nothing comes without a price."

"This is our price," the creature howled and threw back its head. Tendons were knotted like tree roots. It screamed at the sky and dug a knee into Hannah's belly.

The wetness between her legs was becoming thick. She could almost feel red seeping from her body, and in her mind, it was the dark crimson of poppies. To her right, her mother held up her hands. "Stop. There are two lives."

"We are innumerable. We are legion, for we are many." It chuckled dryly. "What are two, compared to that?"

"She didn't enter into this bargain. Her child," Christobelle's voice quivered, "is blameless."

"It is not our concern." The creature's kneecap felt like a gavel against Hannah's womb. For a terrible second, she saw its faces, countless torments whirling like negatives across a white screen. Its hand closed around her neck.

"Take me!" Christobelle shouted.

The creature stepped back and raised its head, considering. "How?"

"However you wish," Christobelle said quickly, and sunk to her knees. She showed it her palms in a gesture of surrender. "Please." She looked around. "I know you are here. If you can hear me, I do not know which of you can grant this, but please. Let me make this right. Let it end with me."

The creature licked its lips. "You would do this?"

The woman nodded and her shoulders slumped.

It cocked its head, listening to the voices that Hannah could almost make out, then it looked at Hannah, who panted through the agony. Her insides felt scraped, growing more raw by the second.

Christobelle held up her hands and shuffled toward Hannah on her knees. A low, throaty growl sounded from the creature, but it allowed the woman to come forward. Her skirt was sodden with mud.

Beyond her, Hannah saw bodies. The hazy shapes of men and women, tall and wavering as trees, standing around them. She could almost hear the low hum of conversation. "Who are they?"

Christobelle looked at Hannah with an expression of wonder. "You can see them?" she whispered.

Hannah squinted through the haze of tears. "I can almost see them."

"I'm so sorry." Christobelle smoothed Hannah's hair. Hannah could tell from her shaking hands, her rough motions, that she was unsure how to soothe but sincerely wished to. Hannah didn't flinch. Instead, she closed her eyes and whined through another contraction. Christobelle's touch moved to Hannah's injured hand, her cold fingers barely registering on the swollen tissue.

"I never meant for this." Christobelle was speaking quickly, and when Hannah opened her eyes, she saw her mother's face sagging with regret and knew it was a mirror of her own. Hannah clenched her teeth, but a scream tore out of her. "You have to push now," Christobelle said, her voice taking on an edge. "Push hard. Take ten quick breaths, then push."

"I can't. It hurts too much," Hannah stuttered. "It's too soon." She jammed the hem of her dress up between her thighs and squeezed, pulling rather than pushing. It felt as if a razor blade was couched in the muscles of her womb.

"You don't have a choice, sweetheart." Mother and daughter looked at each other. The word hung between them like a tightrope walker. Christobelle broke eye contact first. She ran her hand along the circumference of Hannah's belly. The intimacy felt natural, and Hannah could almost imagine Mae in the gentleness of the touch. She blinked up at her mother.

"I have failed terribly, in all things," Christobelle murmured, more to herself than to Hannah. "I couldn't protect you. I couldn't protect your father, and after I lost him, I spent every moment longing for one more glimpse of him—" Christobelle's voice caught. "I lived my whole life with the dead, and in the end, failed to live at all." She squeezed Hannah's good hand as another contraction seized her body like an electrical jolt. "Push," she reminded Hannah.

Above them, the sky darkened, and Hannah had no sense of how much time was passing. She could've been in labor for days, or seconds. The pain overwhelmed all things.

The creature watched them from several steps away, its rasping breath the only sound in the swamp. In the numbing relief between contractions, Hannah saw that it wasn't as monstrous as she'd first thought. Faces moved across its head, unassuming men with kind eyes and pensive mouths. Hannah gasped as Timothy's beautiful, cherubic face flashed, followed by Samuel's.

"It's the men," she murmured.

"It's the price of things," Christobelle said, blotting the sweat from Hannah's forehead with her sleeve. Christobelle took a deep breath and looked in the direction of the creature. Her eyes widened. "This is the face you choose? After all this time, now you let me see him?"

The creature had shrunk to the approximate size and shape of a man. The face was settling as well, a light red dusting of stubble on a sharp chin. The man's light brown hair was trimmed into a military cut above a pleasant, scholarly face. Hannah's eyes, the same color and shape and framed in the same thick curtain of lashes, shone back at her. Hannah recognized her father, despite having never seen him.

The creature smiled and stretched out a hand. "A mercy."

Christobelle drew a shuddering breath as Hannah began to weep. "I have loved you," she said to Hannah and bent down. She kissed Hannah's forehead just as she crested a contraction. Then Christobelle stood.

Hannah swatted at her mother's waist, her knees, her ankles, then pulled on the edge of her skirt like an ignored child. All the while, a soft whimper whistled out of her. *Don't go,* she wanted to yell, but there wasn't enough breath in her lungs. She watched her mother stop and stagger, her hands covering her mouth. Then she shook out her shoulders and walked toward the man. Hannah's father listened as Christobelle spoke quietly, then looked over her shoulder to where Hannah writhed on the grass. He nodded, and extended a gallant arm toward the house.

"No, no, no," Hannah chanted in the rhythm of her breaths, the tenth yelled out as she tried to push. Nothing was budging, the baby having glimpsed the horror of the world and chosen to remain in its place. Her mother and the creature with her father's face disappeared into the house. Hannah heard water pipes creak to life inside the house. Graydon mewled frantically in the kitchen, five pulsing, throaty meows, then trickled off into a low growl.

"Kitten," Hannah whispered. Her breaths blossomed into moans no matter how she tried to quiet them. Suddenly, there was only a thud, as innocuous as Mae's broken glass a seeming lifetime ago, and then silence.

She waited in the tall grass for what seemed like an eternity, her mouth opening and closing like a dying guppy's. When she managed to hoist herself up enough to see her feet, she saw her blood glistening on the grass. Whole blades were tinged in red as if her blood had seeped into the roots, already siphoned into the chlorophyll.

Through the kitchen door, the house was dark.

"Mother," she said softly. She'd meant to call it out, but the pain in her wrist cautioned her to keep quiet. Instead, Hannah lifted and parted her knees, then cautiously explored between her legs. She was dilating.

She searched the trees for the figures she'd seen before, but they, too, had left her. Above her, the sky was shading toward gray, and she found herself wishing for a downpour to wet her chapped lips. She felt the baby move, her body jostling it out. She'd heard that some babies slipped out, as if the uterus were a slide, but the pain building inside told her to expect otherwise.

She pushed through the next contraction and rolled her head toward the water, willing Callum to manifest in the fog. The memory of their goodbye, his confused, wounded eyes, gave her vertigo despite her supine state.

Hannah passed out in the chill, half-dreaming of a motor slicing through weeds, her pushes like involuntary seizures. Her dreams were kind, filled with piano riffs and the comfort of having her head cradled against the splintered wood of a boat. The rocking current lulled her, and the waving of cypress garlands sounded like harps plucked by the wind.

And Callum, always above her in a heady, outdated fiction. Callum, who might survive in the real world but never forgive her if she lost the baby, if she lost herself. He would love her less with each passing day, until she would exist only in these fine-spun fragments.

Her body felt cold and filled, bombarded with memories. She fixated on simple ones. How she'd cracked the browned crust of Mae's sour cherry pies like a surgeon and spooned out the steaming cherries with her fingers. The red hid under her nail beds for days like an angry wound.

Push, a voice said.

She winced against the intrusion, and the tickling sensation on her chest was momentarily not Callum's head resting there. *Pull*, she replied, and clutched him closer. Callum's blue eyes were empyrean, the whole of the sky. Lips moved mutely against her neck, and her pulse answered, chant-like, *Yes*.

"Push!" A rousing yell knocked her into consciousness.

The clicking came from the water. No adrenaline coursed through her body. Her stores were sapped. She veiled her face with her hair and waited.

The grass betrayed its movement, swishing as it slid toward her. It leeched the scent of bones and soot. Hannah waited a few seconds before turning, finally, to face it.

It was marbled white, from claws to tail and the stretch between, and chalky. Filmed orange eyes regarded her. The alligator looked fossilized, ancient crisscrossed scales like shattered bones sewn together. Worn teeth hung from its maw, the edges dull like limestone pulled from the wreckage of the world's first temples.

It was beautiful, its hypnotic sway allowing teasing glances at its ribbed tail, the peaks like plumage. She saw how its translucent white would make it vulnerable, how so many would die as babies, and yet this one had surely seen the birth of mankind.

It crawled up to her, then lowered its head near her

shoulder. Thyme and blue cohosh rode on its warm breath. She didn't flinch from its open mouth, or the sandpaper tongue that ran up her arm. It left goosebumps in its wake.

Hannah's eyes rolled back into her head and she felt an immense pressure well up between her legs. "Oh, God."

She felt the creature's girth swing around. Its head came to rest by hers, and the tail formed a semicircle around her feet. Their breaths merged. Hannah laid her hand over its scaled back as sound pumped back into the swamp. She could almost hear it purring. Chirping crickets swelled, crows cried overhead, and all around and beneath her— burrowing into her ears and armpits—ants. Nature held her, and she was not afraid.

Hannah opened her eyes to blue irises framed in dark lashes. A dream then, and she sighed happily.

"She's up," Callum said to someone standing behind him, and Hannah tried to raise her hand to trace his lips. It ached, sleep prickling it like nettles. There was dried blood on her fingers. She could almost remember where it came from. Hollowness, unfamiliar and painful, pierced her stomach. It felt excavated, as if she'd vomited for days. Something screamed, a car alarm in the parking lot, or a heron accosted by a toothed fish.

"How do you feel?" he asked, stroking her face.

"Happy," she breathed. She tried to lie as still as possible. She didn't want to wake herself. Faces were difficult to render in dreams, and Callum's was perfect, unwavering even as her thoughts raced.

"You've lost a lot of blood." Her thighs were sticky, and the hairs bristled as if coated in honey.

"It's all been a dream." The words were hard to form and her breath was shallow, but she pushed through. "We're back where we started." Everything smelled of damp earth. "God, your sheets," she whispered.

"Hannah, you're outside. You're going to be alright," Callum said shakily as she dropped her head back onto the grass. The water was dark green with weeds. Dried moss trailed in the water like sunlit hair. "The baby is alright."

Two men in blue uniforms covered her mouth with a plastic cone, and she thought of blanched eyes standing guard. They wound a band around her right arm and she cried out.

"What happened here?" one of them muttered to Callum. "Her wrist looks like it's broken."

"Jesus," someone exclaimed from inside the house. The voice was familiar. "We have a body!" Both men lifted their heads, but Callum's eyes didn't move from her face.

Hannah wailed softly into her mask. So many bodies circling her. How many more were hiding in the shadowed corners of the room that suddenly felt vast. The ceiling above her was drab, a single bezel light screwed into its center. Or was that the sky? What had Callum said about a baby?

"Callum," James said, peering into Hannah's field of vision. He paused to squeeze Hannah's shoulder, then whispered into Callum's ear, indicating behind him.

Hannah was surprised to see the back of the house. She was still in the swamp then, ants bustling along exposed skin.

The blackened doorway was threatening, and the longer Hannah looked, the more she felt a potent gravitation pulling her backward, down dim corridors of recollection. A stranger who was not a stranger. Her mother led inside, someone's punishing hand like the final blow that bends the iron nail.

"Mother," Hannah muttered, fogging the mask.

Callum's jaw tightened above her. "Don't think about that now. Just rest."

"Why," she began, and coughed convulsively. "How?"

He smoothed her eyebrows, and she felt a raindrop strike the tip of her nose. "I woke up in the hospital and my mind felt clear for the first time in months. My heartbeat was stronger, even. The doctors crowded around me with their clipboards trying to figure it out." His voice quavered. "I was angry at you, at first. I wondered why you'd come back here and put yourself at risk. They tried to keep me in bed, but I insisted that I had to come find you." He cleared his throat. "When I went out to the boat, I saw something. Maybe it was a dream, I don't know, but I saw a white gator curled up under the bench."

Hannah stretched her fingers and could almost feel the Braille of the scales that had hunkered beside her. She gasped, but the sound was swallowed by the domed mask over her mouth.

"It had your eyes, Hannah, if that doesn't sound too crazy. It looked long and hard at me, and then slunk back into the water. I knew I had to come find you, and thank God I did. Our baby was in your arms. He was barely breathing, but he's going to be alright. They're taking him to an incubator."

"Him." Hannah closed her eyes. "Don't go," she begged.

Callum lowered his face and his curls rippled against her nose. He lay beside her, filling a space that had been recently vacated, still indented with its shape. "Never," he said, his voice cracking as if it were swimming upstream, pounding against pebbles. Trickling over her closing eyes.

CHAPTER
FOURTEEN

Hannah stood up straight and studied Callum's body, lying on the blanket. Since their child's birth, it had grown, fueled by a ravenous appetite. The whites of his eyes were pristine. In the full Texas sunlight, he was ignited as a meteor toppled.

Here, desert and greenery mixed together. Cacti pierced the wavering mirages on either side of their new house like alien barbs, and in the distance, ruddy mountain ranges loomed. Texas was a single state over, but a world apart from the swamps she'd spent her life in. The heat was dry, the earth arid, and the bones of horses and occasional stag horns were out in the open, bleached and harmless as rocks.

When they sold the house by the swamp to a wealthy middle-aged couple from Georgia, they'd disclosed as much of the house's dark past as they thought could be believed, and focused on the damaged foundation, but the woman, face ruddy with makeup, put her palms together and declared it a "colorful history." The man bobbed back and forth on his heels, and sheepishly admitted that they were more interested in the land and planned to demolish the house.

The couple's offer had easily paid for a three-bedroom Texan ranch. It had a pond set in the middle of a plant-filled backyard, as if some small part of Louisiana had been uprooted with them.

Hannah looked around at it now, appreciating the sight of so much vast sky, then sighed, prompting Callum to look up at her.

"What's wrong?" he asked.

She shook her head. "Just admiring you, that's all."

Callum patted his belly. "I could be a bit more . . . let's say aerodynamic."

Hannah smiled slyly. "Blimps are aerodynamic." He dove for her and caught her around the waist.

Callum's health had improved, and he wasn't alone. Within days of Christobelle's death, more and more men experienced the same thing. Advanced illnesses faded away. Callum didn't ask Hannah what had happened, and she knew he'd compile theories. Somehow, it was better than the truth.

He kissed her neck while Gavin cooed in his stroller. His head was covered in fine white-blonde hair that curled like his father's. Wide eyes considered the world seriously, one hazel and one green.

"Look at those eyes," Callum whispered in her ear,

hugging her from behind. "Do you think he sees the world differently?"

Callum pulled her down onto Mae's afghan and ran his hand over her stomach, now empty. She was still surprised by how much she missed the sensation of having something growing inside her. It was a new loneliness. Now Gavin was outside her body, a free agent subject to all dangers.

Hannah moved to kneel by Gavin's stroller. She put her lips against one pudgy leg and whistled a sweet note. Gavin's eyes widened, then he burst into convulsive laughter. His pleasure was endless and intoxicating. "Our little chimera. You know Dr. Merrick said his eyes are fine. Just a kink somewhere in our genes."

"What about chimerism?" Hannah had asked Dr. Merrick at their first check-up, having stayed up late to read all the possible causes. "Isn't it true that two different blood groups could come together within one body?"

"Gavin's healthy. We'll monitor him, of course, and if anything develops, we'll deal with it then. You sustained a significant amount of damage during birth," he'd paused, allowing Hannah the opportunity to explain the contusions on her belly, her broken arm, her mild concussion. Hannah remained silent.

Hannah tugged the squirming boy from the stroller and laid him down between them. They watched him silently as he rolled himself over. A cricket paused its noisy hand-rubbing and Gavin giggled again, blowing spit. He waved his hand over the insect until it hopped away, then smiled up at her.

"Are you grinning at your mama? Can you say 'mama'?" Callum asked, tickling him.

Hannah felt her own smile freeze as she thought of Christobelle. It was still difficult to think of herself as an orphan. Days after Gavin's birth, she'd begun to poke and prod for details of what had happened. Hannah's memory of the birth was hazy, although she remembered Christobelle's voice and a presence that had sheltered her against the chill. Her mother's body had been found collapsed in the kitchen, the faucet overflowing. "She drowned herself," Callum said, his eyes haunted.

Hannah thought she'd misheard. "Drowned herself?"

Callum nodded. "There was nothing under her fingernails, no bruises on her neck. The only sign of struggle was Mae's broken urn. Christobelle's were the only footprints in the ashes. Even the way she, well, breathed the water seemed to be peaceful. It's as if she put her head down and went to sleep."

"What about Sarah Anne?" She tried to remember Sarah Anne as the honeyed girl she'd once been, not the hateful creature she'd become. She knew, instinctively, that the girl wasn't entirely to blame, that other forces had shaped her.

"Sarah Anne?" Callum repeated, cocking his head. "James said they found her uncle's body in the house, and the girl's missing, but—" He studied her face. "That has nothing to do with what happened to you, does it?"

Hannah knew that Sarah Anne would never be found. Somehow, although matter could neither be created nor destroyed, hers had softened and dissolved into the peat and moss.

After the policemen ruled out foul play, Hannah had knelt carefully by the mound of gray ash and sifted through it. She found a few specks of black. *Raven feathers*, James's voice echoed in her mind, and she pressed her forehead against the cool counter to calm herself. Then she began gathering the ash into an empty spice container.

Hannah had found Graydon's limp body on their bed as they finished packing up the house. From afar, he seemed to be sleeping, his small, pink tongue hanging from his mouth. Tears hurried into her eyes but didn't drop. As she stroked the cat's cold fur, sapped of its sheen, she knew he belonged to the house.

"Should we go in? It's almost dinnertime," Callum asked, picking up Gavin and cradling the child's head against his shoulder. He hesitated, closely watching her face.

"Sure. Are you cooking?" she asked, slapping his arm lightly.

Hannah's return to the kitchen had been hesitant. She was cautious in improvising recipes, knowing now how magic could be couched in the simplest of ingredients, but couldn't resist the scents of cooking and their familiar effects. She followed blind instinct, and discovered she was talented.

The container of ash she kept in the very back of the pantry, labeled "Mae." Although the woman's wish had been to have her ashes scattered, the Texan night winds were strong, and Hannah couldn't bear the thought of her Mae spread so thin over an unfamiliar land. Occasionally, she would tap out a few specks across their front doorway as a shield, and sometimes she'd light a slender white candle and set it in the kitchen window.

The nightmares persisted for months, but the memories began to fade. The bruises on Hannah's belly faded as well, although she found she still sometimes woke in the night, scratching out an X across her belly button. The startling brightness of the Texas sun and how it heated the pond's rock enclosure made the dankness of the swamp seem surreal, the open space erasing the enclosed feeling of cypress trees packed together.

It was too hot for fish, but she'd found lizards with bold, iridescent scales sunning themselves, one leg languishing in the warm water. Gavin liked to be set a small distance away from them. He'd dip his finger in the water and wait with infinite patience, statue-still, until their webbed feet tapped over his hand. The eyes, set like gems in scaled faces, made Hannah's hairs stand on end. Some unremembered dream teased the edges of her mind.

Each morning, Hannah made their bed with sheets the color of granite. When Callum entered her, one hand pasted over her mouth, the mattress didn't sag with the imprinted memory of former bodies. She arced her back happily, with abandon. The birth had caused tearing, and when she was well enough to have sex, they moved slowly. She felt each thrust like a war drum.

They were synchronized, passing coffee and orange juice back and forth. Synchronized, too, in their mutual refusal to discuss that day. Sometimes she caught Callum watching her, the trauma of so much unexplained brutality obvious in the unconscious way he chewed the inside of his cheek. The day she dropped on one knee and slipped a simple silver ring onto his left hand, saying only,

"You mean everything to me," his arms closed around her back like a second skin. Like a turtle's hard shell.

One night, in the dry June haze, Hannah slept fitfully. She dreamt that she pulled on a terrycloth robe and stepped into the Texas night, the moon gleaming over the sand like a lesser, arctic sun. She had the sense that something was calling her, on a frequency too low to hear.

The garden looked frost-tipped in the cold light, and she touched the violet blooms of the purple sage bush as she passed. She unlatched the back gate and stepped into the expanse. Small eddies of dust rose like temporary towers.

She didn't see it at first, so camouflaged against the desert. The spiny ridges down its back shone like ivory. Its body was pointed away from her, its head turned over its shoulder. Hannah looked down at her bare feet and saw the telltale smear of sand leading up through the open gate and toward the house. When she turned back, it was gone.

She awoke standing at the entrance to Gavin's room. His mobile drew shapes in colored lights on the walls and released lilting xylophone notes. Beneath the glow, he was standing, gripping the bars of his crib.

"Sweetheart, you did it," she said. She moved quietly, trying not to startle him. "I'm so proud," she said. Her hands covered his own impossibly small ones.

His mismatched eyes met hers, then drifted over her shoulder.

"Gavin?" she asked, leaning closer.

He peered intently at the empty space behind her and burst into a chiming laugh.

ACKNOWLEDGMENTS

Thank you to my parents and my family, without whose love, patience, and trust none of it would have been possible. I am so lucky. Thank you for never letting me stop striving, hoping, hammering through.

Sincere thanks to the countless educators and mentors who have helped me along the way, with special mention to David Baird, Mr. Pearce, A.F. Moritz, and Myna Wallin.

Thank you to the University of Toronto and Rosemary Sullivan for spearheading a tremendous M.A. program, which introduced me to the indispensable mentorship of Jeff Parker and Camilla Gibb, and a solid group of fine people—Andrew MacDonald, Laura Clarke, Spencer Gordon, Catriona Wright, E. Martin Nolan, Matt Loney, and Jon Simpson.

Special thanks to my agent Sam Hiyate (and the Rights

Factory), who stood strong by this book during its many tweaks and turns.

Many thanks to the whole wonderful team at ECW Press, in particular Jen Knoch and Crissy Calhoun—your humor, kindness, and keen eyes turned the editorial process into a true pleasure.

Finally and importantly, more love and thanks than I can express to my husband, Mark. Your belief in this, support for this, and influence on this can't be measured, and neither can my gratitude. Thank you for teaching me how to write a love story.

*Alexandra Grigorescu has a Master's degree
in creative writing from the University of Toronto.
She lives in Toronto. This is her debut novel.*

Copyright © Alexandra Grigorescu, 2015

All rights reserved. No part of this publication may be reproduced, stored in a retrieval system, or transmitted in any form by any process — electronic, mechanical, photocopying, recording, or otherwise — without the prior written permission of the copyright owners and ECW Press. The scanning, uploading, and distribution of this book via the Internet or via any other means without the permission of the publisher is illegal and punishable by law. Please purchase only authorized electronic editions, and do not participate in or encourage electronic piracy of copyrighted materials. Your support of the author's rights is appreciated.

This is a work of fiction. Names, characters, places, and incidents either are the product of the author's imagination or are used fictitiously, and any resemblance to actual persons, living or dead, business establishments, events, or locales is entirely coincidental.

Printing: Friesens 5 4 3 2 1

Published by ECW Press
2120 Queen Street East, Suite 200
Toronto, Ontario, Canada M4E 1E2
416-694-3348 / info@ecwpress.com

LIBRARY AND ARCHIVES CANADA
CATALOGUING IN PUBLICATION

Grigorescu, Alexandra, author
Cauchemar / Alexandra Grigorescu.

Issued in print and electronic formats.
ISBN 978-1-77041-234-7 (pbk)
978-1-77090-718-8 (pdf)
978-1-77090-719-5 (epub)

I. Title.

PS8613.R584C39 2015   C813'.6
C2014-907602-9   C2014-907603-7

Editors for the press: Jennifer Knoch and Crissy Calhoun
Cover design: Natalie Olsen/Kisscut design
Cover images: house on water
© michaelmuecke/Photocase, mosquitoes
© gernot1610/Photocase
Author photo: Maja Hajduk

The publication of *Cauchemar* has been generously supported by the Canada Council for the Arts which last year invested $157 million to bring the arts to Canadians throughout the country, and by the Ontario Arts Council (OAC), an agency of the Government of Ontario, which last year funded 1,793 individual artists and 1,076 organizations in 232 communities across Ontario, for a total of $52.1 million. We also acknowledge the financial support of the Government of Canada through the Canada Book Fund for our publishing activities, and the contribution of the Government of Ontario through the Ontario Media Development Corporation.

PRINTED AND BOUND IN CANADA